THE ESCAPEE

Layton's senses had been enhanced as an unintended side effect of the molecular transformation process. Any living thing within range of the madman's ability to smell, see, or hear would satisfy his crazed desire to kill something. Layton seemed to achieve the same bloodthirsty high from ripping rose bushes out by the roots as he did from strangling cows.

Layton had the advantage. The fugitive's ability to shift bone and muscle into an elastic rubbery state made him nearly impossible to track. He could stretch or swing from tree to tree without touching down.

A chorus of animal squeals shattered the twilight stillness.

Withdrawn
Hillsborough Community College
Plant City Campus Library

making the bus to meet my curious criteria. Dark.

OTHER BOOKS IN THE SERIES

ATTENTION: CORPORATIONS AND ORGANIZATIONS:
Most WARNER books are available at quantity discounts
with bulk purchase for educational, business, or sales
promotional use. For information, please call or write:

Special Markets Department, Warner Books, Inc.,
135 W. 50th Street, New York, NY. 10020-1393
Telephone: 1-800-222-6747 Fax: 1-800-477-5925

SMALLVILLE

SHADOWS

by Diana G. Gallagher

Superman created by
Jerry Siegel and Joe Shuster

Hillsborough Community
College LRC

ASPECT®

WARNER BOOKS

An AOL Time Warner Company

SMALLVILLE and all related characters, names, and indicia are trademarks of DC Comics © 2003. All rights reserved. DC Comics. A division of Warner Bros.—An AOL Time Warner Company. The characters, names, and incidents mentioned in this publication are entirely fictional.

If you purchase this book without a cover you should be aware that this book may have been stolen property and reported as "unsold and destroyed" to the publisher. In such case neither the author nor the publisher has received any payment for this "stripped book."

WARNER BOOKS EDITION

Copyright © 2003 by DC Comics
All rights reserved under International Copyright conventions. No part of this book may be reproduced in any form or by any electronic or mechanical means, including information storage and retrieval systems, without permission in writing from DC Comics, except by a reviewer who may quote brief passages in a review. Inquiries should be addressed to DC Comics, 1700 Broadway, New York, New York 10019.

Cover design by Don Puckey
Book design by L&G McRee

Warner Books, Inc.
1271 Avenue of the Americas
New York, NY 10020

Visit our Web site at www.twbookmark.com.

Visit DC Comics on-line at keyword DCComics on America Online or at http://www.dccomics.com.

 An AOL Time Warner Company

Printed in the United States of America

First Printing: September 2003

10 9 8 7 6 5 4 3 2 1

For Kyle William Streb,
super grandson #4,
with all my love.

Prologue

October 1989

Master Sergeant Adam Reisler replaced the last panel on the environmental control console, but his mind was not on missile support systems. His son, a junior at Middleton, was playing defense in today's big homecoming game against Smallville High. Steve Bacic, one of the Crows' best offensive players, wouldn't be easy to cover, but Joe was confident and determined.

Just like his dad, Adam thought, smiling. He had worked hard to rise through the enlisted ranks, and he never shirked his duty or questioned the responsibilities associated with his job. Every maintenance detail was as vital to national security as the two-man teams in charge of the launch protocols for the Minuteman II missiles deployed throughout the Midwest.

But today I'd much rather be in the bleachers cheering on my kid than running another routine inspection of R-141. Adam glanced toward the Power Control Center on the far side of the huge steel-reinforced concrete structure known as the Launch Facility Equipment Building or LFEB.

Staff Sergeant Jonah Wallace ducked out of the cramped room that housed the diesel engine. Fueled from a fourteen-thousand-gallon tank buried in concrete beside the LFEB, the generator powered the installation when commercial energy sources failed.

Wallace gave Adam a thumbs-up, flipped off the light, and secured the engine room door. The loud mechanical noise that overwhelmed the equipment complex made talking a useless exercise. They both wore protective covers over their ears to lessen the deafening effects.

Rising, Adam waved Wallace to follow him back to the massive entry door. The distance from the back wall of the LFEB to the far side of the Launch Control Center located across the tunnel junction was 120 feet. Another access tunnel forming the stem of a T behind the elevator shaft ran outward 100 feet and connected the operations complex to the silo. The missile shaft extended 80 feet below the level of the main facility, which was 60 feet underground.

Adam was not just anxious to find out who had won the big game between archrivals Middleton and Smallville. The missile had been taken off-line, so it couldn't be launched while his men were working in the silo. The sooner they were done so that the bird was free to fly again, the better. Although the Russians had left Afghanistan in defeat last February, and several Eastern European countries had broken their ties to the Soviet Union, the USA couldn't let down its guard.

Adam paused by the chemical, biological, and radiological filter he had inspected when he first arrived. The equipment had checked out, but as usual, he hoped the device would never be tested under fire. Washington insiders believed the Cold War was winding down, but until one of the superpowers blinked or surrendered, the termination of the mutual annihilation threat was nothing but academic wishful thinking.

When Wallace caught up, Adam stepped onto the hinged drawbridge that spanned the space between the lime green concrete walls and the steel floor.

Provided an enemy bomb didn't score a direct hit, the Launch Facility was safe, designed to withstand the shock of a near miss. The floors in the Equipment Building and the Launch Control Center were suspended from the ceiling and rested on hydraulic shock isolators measuring a foot across and twenty feet tall. Everything, including the twenty-ton air conditioner, was bolted to the steel platform. Under attack, the floor would shake and bang into the walls, but damage would be minimal.

Theoretically, Adam thought, shouldering his tool bag to push open the thirteen-ton LFEB door. It was balanced so one man could open it from the inside, but since the air pressure was lower in the tunnel junction, the combined weight of two men was needed to push it closed.

Adam led the way into the access tunnel, and Wallace turned off the lights as he passed through. After the door was pushed back in place, Adam spun the wheel to lock it and stowed his earmuffs.

"Think the game is over, yet?" Wallace's son was still in grade school, but he followed the local high school teams.

Adam glanced at his watch. "Probably, but we'll have to wait until we get topside to find out the score."

"Yeah, but we might not have to wait for the KTOW radio report." Wallace chuckled as Adam lifted a headset off a holder in the curved wall. "If the Crows won, they'll post the final score on the water tower as soon as they can get someone up there with a bucket of paint and a brush."

Nodding, Adam fitted the headset over his ears and pressed the call button. Although the sound of machinery rumbled through the tubular corridor, it was quiet compared to the din in the LFEB.

"B Team," Technical Sergeant Ron Jackson answered from the silo. "We just finished over here, Sergeant. We can hand this baby back to Control anytime."

"Pull the SCS and get back here, then" Adam said. The Safety Control Switch in the Launcher Equipment Room was used to safe the missile manually. Once work in the silo was completed, the switch was thrown back to return command of the bird to Launch Control. "As soon as LCC confirms they've got the power, we'll get out of here."

Adam replaced the headset and reached for the phone. Every silo was hardwired to the commander's console at the Launch Control Center. Fifteen Launch Control Facilities in the Missouri-Kansas region were responsible for 150 missiles. R-141 was mated with Romeo Eight.

Romeo Fourteen, the installation Adam's environmental systems team had just finished inspecting, had been built as a Launch Control Facility for ten additional missiles in the central Midwest. Budget cuts had prevented it from becoming operational. Although the underground complex had been completed, the remote silos and on-site support structures for the LCF had not progressed past the blueprint stage.

The installation was located on land the government leased from the Creamed Corn Factory, a local business that was owned and operated by the Ross family. Surrounded by fallow fields, the one-hundred-ton concrete silo lid, entry hatch into the operations complex, ventilation shafts, and a locked chain-link and barbed-wire security fence were the only evidence of technology in the rustic landscape. Since the environmental, security, communication, and monitoring systems were functional, Romeo Fourteen was maintained as an emergency backup site, but the commander and deputy's safes in the Launch Control Center had never contained Sealed Authenticators or launch keys.

When Adam picked up the handset, the Maintenance Control Network was activated and a light flashed on the commander's console in Romeo Eight many miles away.

"Capsule," Captain Timothy answered. "How's it going out there?"

"Jackson is throwing the SCS now, sir," Adam said. "Your board should be lighting up."

"Got it," Timothy said over the sound of a routine alarm. The alarm went silent when he hit the reset button. "The printout confirms. R-141 is ours."

"We'll radio back in when we're packed up and outside the perimeter, sir." Adam glanced back as Jackson, John Harris, and their security escort, Everett Corey, emerged from the connecting tunnel hatch.

After signing off, Adam joined the other four men in the elevator. A staircase spiraled up around the elevator shaft, but no one climbed seven stories to the surface unless an emergency threatened to take out the power.

"I hope Joe stopped the Smallville offense cold today," Corey said.

"Me too." Adam pulled the outer wire cage doors closed. The interior elevator doors closed when he punched the UP button. An athletic scholarship was Joe's best chance to get into a good university, an essential step to being signed by the pros. If Joe's higher education depended on Adam's military pay, the boy would be commuting to East Hennessey Community College in Metropolis, where his dreams of goalpost glory would die.

"Yeah." Jackson shifted his tool bag. "The Crows' winning streak is getting really old."

"Unless you're from Smallville," Harris said. His poker face dissolved into a boyish grin.

"I forgot you were from around here." Jackson arched an eyebrow. "Do the Smallville jocks really turn some poor sap into a human scarecrow for luck in the Homecoming game?"

Harris shrugged. "If they do, they don't talk about it."

The elevator lurched to a stop. Since there wasn't a ranch house—an aboveground equipment and supply building that housed security personnel, maintenance teams en route between LFs, and others who supported the launch teams—the lift opened onto a platform eight feet below ground.

Wallace headed up the ladder first and opened the hatch. He climbed out and paused to take in the crisp October air.

"Man, what a perfect day."

Adam nodded in agreement as he stepped outside. White cumulous clouds dotted the azure sky, and the woods between the Stoner farm and the factory's expansive cornfields were vibrant with crimson and gold leaves. The top of the water tower was visible on the horizon, but they were too far away to read anything written on the tank.

"Do you think Howard is watching us?" Corey asked as he gave Harris a hand up.

"Wouldn't surprise me," Adam said.

Howard Stoner owned the neighboring farm, and the government paid him not to plant the fields near the Launch Facility. A Vietnam vet in his midforties, Stoner kept watch over the sensitive missile site. Although the installation was secure, the farmer considered it his patriotic duty to make sure no unauthorized personnel tried to break through the fence or into the silo.

"What the hell is that?" Wallace frowned.

Adam followed his gaze, tracking a glowing orb that trailed plumes of black smoke across the sky. "Get back down that ladder! Now!"

A split second after Adam spoke, the unidentified object struck a nearby cornfield. The impact set off the Preliminary Alert System sirens in Romeo Fourteen, which triggered the PAS in the distant, Romeo Eight Launch Control Facility. Smoke and debris spewed skyward as the unidentified burning object carved a scorched path through the corn.

Corey and Harris had joined Jackson on the elevator platform when the second orb hit the town.

"I thought the Soviet Union was on the brink of falling apart!" Wallace yelled as he threw his tool bag through the hatch and dropped. "Why would they want to start World War III now? In Kansas?"

"Let's not jump to conclusions," Adam advised as he moved down the ladder. Judging from the explosions, he didn't think the incoming objects were nuclear warheads.

"Who else but the Russians?" Jackson demanded as he started down the spiral staircase.

"We'll find out when I call Command," Adam muttered to himself, wincing when the water tower exploded. Steam, twisted metal, and splintered wood fell from a billowing fireball as he closed and sealed the hatch.

"This doesn't feel like a nuclear attack." Corey called out as he raced downward behind Jackson and Harris.

"No, but whatever it is"—Adam raised his voice to be heard over the blare of the PAS siren—"the safest place for us is sixty feet down in the LCC."

"I won't argue with that." Wallace hit the bottom of the shaft within a second of the three men ahead of him.

Turning left toward the Launch Control Center, they waited for Adam outside a curved yellow line painted on the floor. The line marked the swing arc of the six-ton door into the LCC. In an operational Launch Control Facility, the door could only be opened from the inside. They would also need to coordinate their entry with Romeo Eight because only one LCC door in the entire network was allowed to be open at any one time. However, since Romeo Fourteen was nothing but an expensive missile silo, the NCO in charge of the maintenance detail had the lock codes to access the restricted area, and he didn't need permission.

No one said a word as Adam checked his crew log for the second time that day and punched the lock code into an electronic panel. He and Wallace had inspected the LCC before they had gone into the Equipment Building. At least, they knew all the environmental systems were working.

Adam glanced at the red-stenciled warning on the massive door as it swung open.

NO LONE ZONE. SAC TWO-MAN POLICY MANDATORY.

If Romeo Fourteen had been utilized for its original purpose, no solitary individual would ever have access to the Sealed Authenticators and launch keys stored inside. But there were no launch protocols in this LCC, so the rule did not apply.

The entry through the thick wall was a narrow tunnel. The men followed Adam single file, stooping slightly to avoid the low ceiling. Wallace, the last man in, triggered the door to close, spun the wheel to lock it, and slipped the dead bolt into place.

The steel drawbridge between the walls and the floor of the outer room clanked as Adam jogged across. The rush of temperature-controlled air that protected the electronics added to the noise levels. Earplugs were usually worn in this section, but he couldn't spare the time to find them.

Adam tried not to assume the worst as he kept moving past a galley kitchen on the left and a latrine and storage locker on the right. Still, his wife and son were on his mind as he ducked through a doorway into the acoustical enclosure of the Launch Control Center proper, where rubbery floors and walls absorbed excessive noise.

Adam tried to force the thoughts of his family to the back of his mind as he dropped his tool bag and slid into the commander's chair. He silenced the PAS alarm, picked up the handset, and punched the call button for the LCC commander at Romeo Eight.

"Capsule. Identify yourself, please."

"This is Master Sergeant Adam Reisler on routine maintenance duty at R-141." Adam checked his crew log again and gave Timothy the team's assigned Maintenance Control Number.

"Roger, Sergeant," the captain said. "That checks."

Even though Captain Timothy sounded cool and collected, Adam didn't dare breathe easy. Every man and woman assigned to the Strategic Air Command missile defense system had nerves of steel. They didn't crack under pressure.

"Guess you're wondering what's going on out there." The tone of Timothy's voice remained matter-of-fact.

"Yes, sir," Adam responded evenly, sensing the tension in the men standing behind him. "We're a little curious. The Smallville water tower just blew up, and—"

The floor under Adam's feet shuddered, a sure sign that one of the objects falling from the sky had landed way too close for comfort.

"It's a meteor shower," the captain explained. "Sorry we didn't warn you, but nothing registered with the Twenty-fifth SW until they entered the atmosphere and started heating up. NORAD was notified immediately, and they've confirmed. It's meteors."

Adam nodded, letting out a long sigh. The Twenty-fifth Space Wing was a global network of missile warning sensors that also tracked every man-made object in space. A swarm of cold boulders the size of trucks or smaller wouldn't be easy to spot if no one was looking for them.

"Thanks, Captain," Adam said. "Give us a heads up when it's over, okay?"

"Will do." The line went dead.

"Rocks?" Jackson exclaimed with an incredulous lilt.

"From outer space." Harris wiggled his fingers in the gesture people often used to indicate something bizarre and creepy.

"What's that supposed to mean?" Jackson frowned.

"Well," Corey drawled, "if this was a science fiction movie, it might mean an alien invasion."

"Yeah, right." Jackson laughed.

"Except this isn't a movie. This is real life—" Wallace cringed when the floor underneath them shook again, and the power went out.

When the diesel kicked in a second later and the lights sputtered back on, Adam's pulse was racing. "Real life with a megaton punch."

CHAPTER 1

Present Day

Heading home from school, Clark followed a route through the woods and fields that he didn't use very often. It passed too close to a neighboring farm and skirted the far side of the LexCorp Fertilizer Plant property. He just didn't want to risk running into the surveyor he had spotted along his regular path yesterday. Sometimes he was late and missed the bus. Today he wasn't riding it because he had stopped by the Talon to unwind over a cappuccino with Pete Ross, his best friend since first grade.

As luck would have it, one of the waitresses had called in sick, and Lana Lang, the manager and unrequited love of his life, had been too busy to talk. He wanted to be more than friends, but the secrets he couldn't discuss always stood between them, a barrier to the total honesty Lana needed, but he still enjoyed her company.

Clark continued home, staying well out of sight of the two-lane state highway that intercepted Hickory Lane, the country road that ran past the Kent farm. Route 19 was too heavily traveled to be safe. Though a casual observer probably wouldn't realize that blur speeding through the corn at Mach 2 was a teenager, he had learned it was best not to take any chances.

Curiosity once aroused was impossible to suppress, an aspect of human nature Chloe Sullivan, aspiring investigative reporter, editor of the *Torch*, and another of his closest friends, demonstrated with maddening regularity. Chloe's insatiable desire to know had given him more than a few uncomfortable moments over the past couple years, since moving out of adolescence toward adulthood had caused his latent powers to emerge.

This afternoon was no exception. Knowing Lana was short-handed, Chloe had volunteered to dump the Talon trash. She had come through the back door just as a car screamed out of the alley, a moment after Clark saved a cat from being flattened under the tires. The startled animal had dulled its claws digging into his arm before it sprang free and ran away. Although Clark was adept at inventing lame explanations for the inexplicable, Chloe's inquiring mind never took anything at face value.

Chloe was probably in the Smallville High classroom that served as the *Torch* office right now. Clark envisioned her sitting at her desk, absently twirling a lock of blond hair as she mulled over the improbable facts: that the car had seemed to pause with wheels spinning a foot off the pavement an instant before Clark appeared holding a yellow tabby cat. Hopefully, she'd conclude that the glint of afternoon sun off polished metal had created an illusion.

If I'm lucky. Frustrated by the constant need to be on guard, Clark whacked a dangling limb off a maple tree. The branch disintegrated into splinters and sawdust with the force of the blow.

Other teenagers' raging hormones give them acne or fits of moody rebellion, Clark thought, peeling a strip of loose bark off a dead tree as he zoomed by. He had suffered a personality meltdown into dangerous delinquency because of red meteor-rocks, which a jewelry company had substituted for rubies in the Smallville class rings. *On top of X-ray vision and a heat ray that almost burned down the school and the Talon.*

Clark had learned to control his fiery gaze, but being able to cook an egg at thirty paces just by looking at it was not the most useful of his incredible gifts. The bus left without him more often than not, so his ability to navigate the dense woods at high speed without running into anything came in handy almost daily.

Clark made a sharp right to avoid a dense thicket and jumped a tree lying across the path. His reflexes were instantaneous, too fast to clock by any conventional means. *Not that anyone will ever get the chance to time me*, Clark thought, smiling as he ducked under a low-hanging branch. A flurry of dislodged leaves swirled in his wake.

Pete was the only person besides his adoptive parents, Jonathan and Martha Kent, who knew about his extraordinary abilities. Clark hated lying to Lana and Chloe, but he had no choice. As his father had drummed into him over the years, the truth was too dangerous and the responsibility too great.

Pete had almost died learning that some people would stop at nothing to find out Clark's secret. Pete was threatened by a doctor who planned to inject him with a lethal meteor-rock formula in order to find out who the ship belonged to. Imminent death had not broken Pete's silence, but there were too many vicious people like that doctor in the world.

When Sam Fallon had tried to blackmail Clark into stealing an incriminating police file, Clark had double-crossed him. In retaliation, the dirty Metropolis cop had framed his father for murder. Jonathan wouldn't be intimidated by Fallon's threat to reveal the family secret, either. That was the only time Clark had been so angry he wanted to kill. He had outsmarted Fallon instead, but the memory of his destructive rage still gave him nightmares.

Clark deliberately avoided speculation about how Lex Luthor would react if he knew. Deep down, he suspected that the son of Lionel Luthor, a corporate tycoon whose wealth had been accumulated with unwavering ruthless resolve, wouldn't be able to resist exploiting the boy he called friend.

That was a test of character Lex would never have to pass. There was no way Clark would ever tell him or Lana or anyone else he cared about that he had arrived on Earth in the midst of the 1989 meteor shower.

I wouldn't have told Pete, either, except that keeping the secret wasn't worth losing his friendship. Besides, the truth had been the only way to explain why the Kents had a legitimate claim on the spaceship Pete had found in a cornfield after the Spring Formal twister.

Clark came to an abrupt halt in the trees lining the old government access road behind Howard Stoner's farm. The stench of fertilizer chemicals and the damp musk of forest decay drifted on a light breeze. Irritated by the combined odors, he wrinkled his nose as he scanned the large field that bordered the LexCorp plant property.

In keeping with the Arms Reduction Treaty George H. W. Bush and Mikhail Gorbachev had signed in 1991, the military had stripped and vacated the local Minuteman II missile silo in 1994. When the government left and the lease on the land expired, ownership had reverted to LuthorCorp. Mr. Stoner had maintained surveillance when the Launch Facility was active and, even though LexCorp owned the site now, he still felt duty-bound to protect the empty installation from vandals.

Most people had either never known or had forgotten that Smallville was once on the front lines of the country's missile defense system. Clark had researched the Launch Facility after he stumbled across it a few years back, when Mr. Stoner had tried to chase him away. On the rare occasions when he came this way, he always slowed to a normal pace in case the farmer was playing sentry.

Spotting Mr. Stoner heading toward his barn, Clark kept walking. The weeds that had overgrown the rutted dirt track from lack of use had been flattened. Someone had driven this way recently, probably by mistake since the road dead-ended. He hoped so. If people started using it, he'd have to find another alternate route.

Clark had no reason to hurry and didn't mind the leisurely pace. Except for a biology paper that was due the end of next week, he had finished his homework in study hall, and no practices had been scheduled for track or the swim team.

Like I need to practice, Clark scoffed with a disgruntled sigh. His remarkable memory and high IQ were much easier to hide—or explain when he slipped—than his exceptional speed, strength, and coordination. However, the physical attributes that made training unnecessary also gave him an unfair advantage in competition. After his father convinced him that football was too dangerous for everyone else if he played, he had begun participating in individual sports. He always performed at a level he thought he could have achieved with normal abilities. Only Pete knew he was holding back.

The farm chores his father gave him as a matter of principle, since he could do them without breaking a sweat, wouldn't take more than a few minutes. And he had no casual or pressing social engagements to round out his pathetically boring schedule.

Clark sighed again, recalling the conversation he had just had with Pete at the Talon. *Maybe it is time I started dating.*

Now that Lana was living at Chloe's house, having a romantic relationship with either one had gotten way too complicated. Clark, Lana, and Chloe had decided to just be friends after Ian Randall and his instant clone had almost killed both girls. It wasn't an ideal situation, but neither was constant emotional turmoil. He had warned Chloe and Lana that Ian was using them to secure the Luthor Foundation College Scholarship. They had both misread his intentions and dismissed his concern to side with Ian, a boy they hardly knew. He had finally come to terms with some undeniable truths. Lana couldn't deal with his secretive nature, and Chloe couldn't deal with being second to Lana. He was just tired of worrying about everyone else's feelings while his own were being shredded by misunderstanding, circumstance, and bad timing. Letting go had been sad, but liberating, too.

Deciding to date is one thing, Clark thought with a glance back at Mr. Stoner. *Going out on one requires a hot prospect I don't happen to have.*

Clark tensed as the farmer turned toward him, but Mr. Stoner wasn't going to run him off. The man clutched his throat as though he was choking.

"Mr. Stoner?" Clark called out.

The farmer sank to his knees and fell over, unaware of the boy streaking toward him. He wasn't breathing when Clark reached him.

"Hang on, Mr. Stoner." Clark dropped his books and tilted the man's head back to begin mouth-to-mouth. As he leaned over, he was stricken with a wave of familiar nausea.

Meteor sickness!

The effects diminished when Clark sat back on his heels, which meant the offensive alien material was near or on the man's body.

Bracing himself, Clark shoved his hand into the overall bib pocket on the man's chest. He bore the pain of muscle and tendon being twisted off bone and gritted his teeth while he patted down the man's sides. All the pockets were empty.

Did Mr. Stoner eat meteor particles? Clark wondered as he moved back out of range. Since he couldn't resuscitate the man without passing out, his ability to help was severely limited.

Unwilling to do nothing, Clark scrambled to his feet and sped to Stoner's small farmhouse. When he returned from Vietnam, the farmer had become a recluse, never marrying and living alone. Clark leaped over four steps onto the porch and pulled the screen door off its hinges in his frantic haste. Flinging the door aside, he burst into the small kitchen and dialed 911 on the wall phone.

"I was just walking by on my way home from school," Clark told the dispatcher after he identified himself and gave the address. "He looked like he was choking, but I suppose it could have been a heart attack."

"The rescue units are on the way, Mr. Kent." The woman's voice was void of emotion. "You will stay there, won't you? The police will want to get a statement."

"Yeah, I'll be here." Hanging up, Clark took a deep breath and glanced out the open doorway. He didn't want to leave Mr. Stoner lying in the field alone, but he had a bad feeling.

"Maybe because I've got a thicker police file than most of the petty crooks in Smallville," Clark muttered, dialing his home number.

His mother was working as Lionel Luthor's executive assistant at the Luthor mansion, and his father was setting fence posts. Except for the back pasture, they had replaced the fence the tornado had torn out the previous summer. Clark hoped to catch Jonathan on a break, but the answering machine picked up. He left a message.

"Dad, I'm at the Stoner farm waiting for the police so I'll probably be late. Mr. Stoner just collapsed in his field. He's—he's dead."

Clark replaced the receiver. His heart was heavy. This wasn't the first time he hadn't been able to save someone, but that didn't make the failure easier to bear. He would never get over losing Ryan James. He had been the young mind reader's Warrior Angel, the boy's comic book hero come to life, except that all his powers couldn't cure a brain tumor.

Clark raced back to the farmer's body, unable to shake a persistent sense of dread. What if the next person he couldn't save was someone else he loved?

◆◆◆

Clark glanced over his shoulder as a silver Porsche turned into Howard Stoner's driveway and stopped by the sheriff's patrol car. The roadster was the classic silver with black interior Lex Luthor seemed to prefer. The red Ferrari Clark had once borrowed was a holdover from the young entrepreneur's earlier life as a wild playboy in Metropolis.

"Nice car," Clark said, as Lex Luthor eased out.

"The GT2," Lex explained. "I'm test driving it for a few days." Impeccably dressed in a camel blazer, white shirt open at the neck, and dark brown slacks, Lex closed the door without a glance at the dust clinging to the perfect paint. "I like the Lamborghini Diablo VT better."

"Tough choice," Clark quipped.

"I don't have to choose, Clark," Lex said evenly. "Just decide whether I want to buy."

"Right." Clark shook his head with a sardonic grin. The combined price of both cars was probably close to $450,000, more than most people in Smallville made in ten years.

The heir to the Luthor fortune was not as indifferent as his father to the financial hardships borne by the working class. Blindness and a limp, the result of injuries incurred during a recent tornado, had not softened Lionel's heart or changed his perspective. Lex, on the other hand, often opened doors that might otherwise be closed to those who were willing to work and take risks.

The managers who mortgaged their homes to help buy the fertilizer plant from LuthorCorp had not just demonstrated faith in Lex, but also in themselves. Lex expected them to produce, but he also appreciated their courage and ambition. When anyone impressed him, as Lana had with her plan to turn the old Talon movie theater into a chic bookstore coffeehouse instead of a parking lot, Lex was generous with his praise and support.

The only exceptions to the Lex Luthor rule of personal engagement seemed to be Clark and his dad.

Clark knew that Lex's relationship with Lionel was more a war of wills than a bond of affection. For whatever reason, the young Luthor missed no opportunity to try to win Jonathan Kent's respect and approval. All his efforts had been futile, and that was before they found out Lex had hired the *Inquisitor* reporter, Roger Nixon, to investigate the car accident that had brought Clark and Lex together. Even though Lex had shot and killed Nixon to save Jonathan's life, he had little hope of getting into the elder Kent's good graces. Some burned bridges simply couldn't be re-built.

But it can't hurt to try. Clark wasn't thrilled with Lex's compulsive curiosity, either, but unlike his dad, he sensed there was a decent man beneath the hard exterior. For one thing, Lex had promised him the accident case was closed.

Lex's bald head gleamed in the late-afternoon sun. Lex had lost his hair in the meteor shower when he was nine, and growing up bald had been as influential in his development as his demanding father. The entire Luthor fortune could not have bought the inner strength and self-control the poised young man possessed.

As they strode into the field, Lex gestured toward the sheriff's deputies and paramedics gathered around Howard Stoner's still form. "I heard you were a witness to this."

"Where'd you hear that?" Clark asked, but only to

tease his unlikely friend. Nothing happened in Smallville or Metropolis that Lex didn't know about. If by chance he didn't know, he had the resources to find out.

"Your use of barbed nuance is improving, Clark." Lex rarely smiled, but his inflection betrayed amused approval. He moved on without addressing the question. "What happened?"

Exhaling, Clark shoved his hands in his pockets and related the basic details. There wasn't much to tell, but his remorse was evident when he finished.

"It wasn't your fault." Lex fixed Clark with his steady gaze. "It sounds like Mr. Stoner died of cardiac arrest or respiratory failure. In either case, there wasn't anything anyone could have done to prevent the inevitable."

"On one level I know that, but on another . . ." Clark let his voice trail off as the paramedics picked up the stretcher with the farmer's body.

The men moved past Lex at a discreet distance. Out of fear or respect, Clark couldn't tell. In one way or another everyone in town depended on LexCorp and the fertilizer plant.

"What are you doing here, Lex?" Clark asked.

"I came to see if I could help a fallen neighbor—" The end of Lex's sentence was lost in the whupping sound of a helicopter flying in from the east.

Clark shielded his eyes with his hand as he looked up. "Your Dad?"

"Not a chance," Lex said. "My father doesn't pay his respects to anyone unless it represents a profit. Besides, he's getting ready for a business trip to New York."

"New York?" Clark's gaze snapped back to Lex. "Is my mother going with him?"

"No. Starting tomorrow, Mrs. Kent will have a week off with pay." Lex shook his head slightly, a rare demonstration of amazement. "My father is obviously pleased with her work."

"I know she likes her job, but it'll be nice having her home for a few days." Clark waited until the chopper was close enough for people with normal vision to read the printed words on the door. "It's from the Center for Environmental Protection. Who called in the CEP?"

"Your father, perhaps." Lex yelled to be heard over the sound of the descending helicopter.

Clark looked toward the drive as his father stepped out of the used red pickup they had bought after Roger Nixon blew up the old blue Chevy. The insurance money had been just enough to cover the purchase price, taxes, and licensing fees.

Jonathan stuffed a pair of leather work gloves into the back pocket of his worn jeans and slammed the door. His total disregard for appearances—scuffed boots, a denim shirt with frayed cuffs, and the shadow of a beard on his lean, weathered face—spoke of his confident, independent nature.

The air churned up by the chopper setting down several yards away whipped through Clark's dark hair. A dozen questions swirled through his head as his father drew closer. Had he come to offer support, or did he have another motive? Lex seemed to think the latter, but except for being causally acquainted neighbors and members of the Grange, the Kents had no connection to Howard Stoner or his farm.

A young man wearing a navy blue CEP jacket and cap got out of the chopper before the rotor blade stopped turning and jogged across the field. He and Jonathan reached Lex and Clark at the same time.

"Mr. Kent?" The CEP agent's glance flicked from Lex to Clark's father.

"That's me." Jonathan extended his hand, his expression grim. He put his other hand on Clark's shoulder. "This is my son, Clark. He saw Howard collapse."

"Gary Mundy," the young man said. "The field agent assigned to the case."

Guess that answers that. Clark's jaw tightened with the realization that his dad had called in the local environmental watchdog organization. Since Jonathan hadn't even given Lex a nod of acknowledgment, it wasn't hard to figure out why.

"Isn't it premature for the Center of Environmental Protection to be involved?" Lex asked. He handled Jonathan's snub with quiet diplomacy, by not recognizing that the slight had occurred.

Jonathan anticipated Mundy's next question. "Lex Luthor, CEO and controlling owner of the Smallville Fertilizer Plant."

"Mr. Luthor." Mundy nodded curtly, but he didn't offer his hand. "My field tests may take several days."

"What exactly are you testing for?" Lex pressed.

Clark grew increasingly dismayed as he followed the exchange. The CEP and the Luthors' corporate interests were almost always opposed, but Lionel and Lex usually prevailed. No one could prove that the preferential treatment and legislative cover their business enterprises enjoyed were secured with political contributions or intimidating practices.

"Chemical contamination from your plant, Lex," Jonathan said.

Clark sagged. "Dad—"

Jonathan silenced him with a sharp look. "If Howard didn't die of natural causes, the town has to know what did kill him."

Lex was unperturbed. "Wouldn't it be easier and less costly to wait for the medical examiner's autopsy report tomorrow?"

"Maybe, but the data from my initial tests won't go to waste." Mundy shrugged as he surveyed the unplanted field. "I'll just add the results to the database we keep on this whole area."

"I see." Lex's calm tone and demeanor didn't fluctuate as he continued. "It would be wise, Mr. Mundy, to be absolutely certain you have irrefutable evidence that my company is responsible for Mr. Stoner's death before CEP or anyone else files an official complaint."

"Is that a threat?" Jonathan's blue eyes narrowed.

Clark winced. His dad blamed himself for bringing the fertilizer plant with its smokestacks and toxins to Smallville. Lionel had formed Metropolis United Charities for the sole purpose of arranging Clark's no-questions-asked adoption. Jonathan had not known the process was a sham until after the fact. In return for Lionel's silence, he had reluctantly agreed to convince the Ross family to sell the Creamed Corn Factory to LuthorCorp. He had done it to protect Clark and his mother, but Jonathan had never forgiven himself for giving in to Lionel's extortion. His guilt fueled the belief that Lex was as unprincipled as his father.

"It's good business, Mr. Kent," Lex said calmly. "I really don't want to see you in court."

And Lex was always giving Jonathan reasons to think he was right.

CHAPTER 2

Pete hustled to keep pace with Clark's long stride as he marched into the *Torch* office. Chloe was seated at her desk, surrounded by files and notes, staring intently at her green computer.

"Why weren't you on the bus, Chloe?" Clark asked.

"What?" Chloe blinked with surprise as she looked up from the screen at Clark. "You were?"

"Clark was *waiting* at the end of his driveway," Pete said with a grin. "That's got to rate a couple inches on the front page of the next edition."

Ordinarily, Clark was immune to the teasing about his proclivity for being tardy, but he resented it today. Mr. Stoner's death was weighing on his mind, but his unease was lost on his friends. Pete knew he didn't have to rely on ordinary modes of transportation and was needling him in fun. Although Chloe was intrigued by how often Clark beat the bus, she was enjoying the friendly banter at his expense too much to mention it. Rather than make them uncomfortable, Clark let the humor run its course.

"Below the fold, maybe." Chloe squinted, pretending to consider the suggestion. "If it's a slow news cycle."

"Around here 'slow news cycle' stretches the bounds of the probable, doesn't it?" Pete walked past her and dropped into a straight-backed chair at another desk under the windows. "This is Smallville after all."

"Good point, Pete!" Chloe's smile faded into a feigned look of regret. "You're going to have to do better than making the bus to meet my editorial criteria, Clark."

"Doesn't seeing somebody die qualify?" Pete asked, pained expression flashing across his face the moment after the words were spoken. "Sorry, Clark. I didn't mean to sound so—"

"Insensitive?" Clark perched on the corner of the desk that stood back-to-back with Chloe's in the center of the room. He held Pete's dark gaze for a moment before letting him off the hook. "Not a problem, Pete. You were just stating the facts. I did see Howard Stoner die."

"At the risk of sounding even more insensitive," Chloe said, "people die in Smallville all the time. What's the hook with Mr. Stoner?"

"You mean a startling and/or strange angle?" Pete shrugged. "There isn't one, is there, Clark?"

"I don't know about 'strange,'" Clark said, "but it's pretty startling to watch someone drop dead."

"On a scale of what to what?" Pete asked, clasping his hands on his knees. "I mean compared to killer posies, girls that suction body fat, and tormented teenage poets who turn into sunlight monsters and toss people through windshields?"

Pete's yardstick for measuring the bizarre was based on numerous odd and ghastly experiences that were routine by Smallville standards. The country's most prestigious academic, scientific, and government institutions gave no credence, at least publicly, to the idea that meteor-rocks caused molecular changes in some individuals under undetermined, and perhaps myriad, conditions. Chloe had independently arrived at that theory after she moved to the farming area from Metropolis in the eighth grade. Although the evidence, by chance or design, never survived long enough to prove or refute the meteor hypothesis,

Clark, Lana, Pete, and Clark's parents all had reasons to believe it.

"On a scale of one to ten?" Clark hesitated.

"Mr. Stoner gets a spooky factor of zero," Chloe answered. "His death isn't relevant to life at Smallville High, either. Sad, yes, but not exciting enough to risk testing Mr. Reynolds's idea of acceptable topic parameters."

Clark understood Chloe's concern. She had been fired as *Torch* editor once for writing inappropriate articles based on conjecture. Now, rather than tempt the wrath of authority, she censored her more outrageous inclinations before the school newspaper went to press.

The new principal was more willing to give Chloe creative latitude than the old one, who had been crushed between his car and the back wall of his garage. Although Chloe knew more about that incident than the professionals reporting in the *Smallville Ledger*, she had curbed her investigative instincts to write a noncontroversial, tasteful obituary for the deceased principal.

If Chloe had to go to the mat for a story, the story would have to be worth putting everything on the line. Clark, however, wasn't interested in a headline.

"This isn't about a story, Chloe," Clark said. "I had another reason for wanting to talk to you on the bus."

"Which brings us back to Clark's original question," Pete said. "Why weren't you on the bus, Chloe?"

"Lana wanted to do some research in the library before class, so I rode in with her and Dad." Chloe sat back with a sigh. "This paper doesn't write or publish itself, you know. I've already drafted a scathing critique of the cafeteria's most recent assault on student stomachs—"

"You mean that ground beef in white gravy stuff they served on burned toast last Wednesday?" Pete asked.

"That tasted like paste?" Clark grimaced.

"Exactly," Chloe said. "And I've exchanged two e-mails with Chad."

"Who's Chad?" Pete asked.

The answer popped up from the reams of trivia stored in Clark's memory. "Isn't Chad your Goth friend at the Medical Examiner's Office?"

"The dark and brooding one and only." Chloe laughed. "Do you know how many shades of gray there are?"

"I don't care." Pete held up a hand to end further discussion.

"Can you find out Mr. Stoner's cause of death?" Clark asked.

"Asphyxiation." Chloe tapped a command on her keyboard, starting the printer. "Like I said before, unless something unusual turns up in the lab work, Mr. Stoner's demise is strictly obit material."

Clark took the e-mail Chloe pulled from the printer tray. Chad's memo style was short and to the point. The one word answer, "asphyxiation," was apparently in response to a question Chloe had e-mailed him about the farmer's death. *So she was curious*, Clark realized. *Until Goth Guy's message killed her hopes for a scoop she could peddle to the* Ledger.

"He choked to death?" Clark asked.

"Not necessarily," Chloe said. "A lot of things could have made him stop breathing."

"I saw him grab his throat before he collapsed." Clark stared at the floor, frowning as he replayed the events of the previous afternoon in his mind. Whatever had stricken the farmer had been sudden. "Will Chad give you the lab results?"

"Sure." Chloe nodded. "Do you think something funny might turn up?"

"No, just curious." Smiling to mask his distress, Clark handed the e-mail back. Something in his tone or manner had registered on Chloe's reporter radar, but there was no hot story to pursue. He just wanted to know, beyond any doubt, that there was nothing he could have done to save the dying man.

Max Cutler glanced over the unoccupied round stools at the lunch counter in the Uptown Diner. All the red vinyl seats were torn and patched with gray duct tape. He chose the stool with the fewest repairs to prevent snagging his trousers.

Dressed in a blue suit and red tie, Max stood out like a solitary red barn on the vast prairie among the truckers and farmers. However, his current circumstances didn't require a cover that blended in. He had spent the morning posing as a real estate developer from Metropolis looking to buy large tracts of land. Economically depressed people who were anxious to sell large tracts of land were always eager to talk to a prospective buyer.

So far, he hadn't learned much, but it was too early to say if that was good or bad.

"Coffee?" A heavyset, middle-aged woman wearing a pale green-and-white waitress uniform asked without smiling.

"Please. And a Danish." Max set the overturned cup on

his saucer upright and glanced at the name tag pinned to her apron. CARLA SUE.

"Heated with butter?" Carla's dour expression didn't change as she finished pouring. She reached into a tub of ice under the counter and set a chilled dish of creamer packets in front of him. "Apple or cheese?"

"Apple, heated, no butter." Max answered with a strained smile. Standing just under six feet tall, with a muscular physique, he had a classic chiseled profile and straight teeth. Lacking the patience to fuss with his un-ruly, thick brown hair, he kept it clipped short. He was not Hollywood handsome, but most women found him attractive and charming. Carla Sue obviously did not.

Annoyed, Max unfolded the local newspaper he had purchased from a coin box outside. Making idle conver-sation with the brusque waitress might not be necessary. The Smallville *Ledger* was a journalistic joke compared to Metropolis's *Daily Planet*, but it might have the an-swers he was looking for. He took a careful sip of black coffee and scanned the front page.

The elderly man sitting two stools down leaned closer. "You that fella looking to buy some land for a housing project?"

"Yes, sir, I am." Max set down his cup to shake the old man's hand. "Max Cutler."

"Hank Sidney." Hank dropped a spoon on his saucer and picked up his cup. "You can probably get the Stoner farm pretty cheap if Lionel Luthor wants to sell."

"Stoner farm?" Max adopted a studied look of puzzled ignorance.

"Top of page two," Hank said. "Poor Howard just

keeled over dead yesterday. Didn't leave any family that I know of."

"Really?" Max lifted the paper out of the way as Carla Sue returned with the Danish. "Just up and died, huh? For no reason?"

"Nothing weird, if that's what you're getting at." Hank sighed and rubbed the stubble on his chin. "Of course, there's probably a bunch of legal stuff to be cleared up. Before the land can go on the market, I mean."

"Probably, but thanks for the tip." With a curt nod, Max turned his attention back to his breakfast and the news story about Howard Stoner's death on page two. The only information of any interest in the short article was the undisclosed identity of the teenager who had found the body.

Ten seconds after Hank drained his coffee cup and left, Carla Sue was back. "Believe me, mister, you don't want to build houses on the Stoner property."

Max swallowed a bite of his warm pastry. "Because that guy died?"

"Maybe," Carla Sue answered cautiously.

"Hard thing for a kid to see," Max said, fishing for a name. "I hope the experience doesn't traumatize him."

"It won't." Carla Sue sounded certain. "Clark Kent was raised on a family farm. Got loving parents. He's one of the most down-to-earth kids in town."

Max pressed on without a hint that he had learned something he needed to know. "So why wouldn't I want to build houses on the Stoner farm?"

Still holding a coffeepot, Carla Sue cast a wary glance at the door. "Because it's right next to the LexCorp fertilizer plant."

After he retired as a CIA field agent to seek more lu-
crative employment, Max had put many of his acquired
intelligence-gathering techniques to use in the private
sector. All his professional methods were effective, but
none had proved as informative dollar for dollar as the
waitresses in the coffee shops throughout America.

"Hmmm." Max arched an eyebrow. "A fertilizer plant
could present some difficulties. The plant must really
stink up the neighborhood."

"Much worse than that, pal." Carla Sue lowered her
voice. "People around here suffer from all kinds of odd
sicknesses. A lot of them die suddenly, just like Howard
Stoner, and there's only one explanation that makes any
sense at all."

Max blinked. "Which is—"

Carla Sue rolled her eyes and hissed. "They've been
exposed to some kind of poison runoff from that plant!
Not that anyone will say so—except me, of course."

Max didn't have to ask for clarification. In a town the
size of Smallville, at a time when small family farms
were increasingly unable to compete with more efficient
agribusiness corporations, an enterprise such as the fertilizer plant would be the main support of the community.

"Don't the police get suspicious?" Max asked softly.

"Ever hear the saying, 'You can't fight City Hall'?"
The large woman shook her head, sadly. "Around here
nobody tangles with Lionel or Lex Luthor. Nobody. Not
even the sheriff, if he can help it."

"I will keep all that in mind, Carla Sue. Thank you."
Max pulled a ten from his wallet to pay for his three-
dollar meal. "Keep the change."

"Come back anytime." Carla Sue's expression re-

mained stony as she put the money in her apron pocket.
"But if anybody asks, you didn't hear nothin' about
nothin' from me."

"About what?" Max asked.

He drank another leisurely cup of coffee and finished
browsing through the paper to dispel any speculation
about his conversations with Hank and the waitress. He
left the diner without another word to anyone, stopped by
the drugstore to buy two paperback spy novels, then
drove his rental car out of town at exactly two miles over
the limit. The speed was calculated to reflect the driving
habits of most people. As expected, the cop in the patrol
car he passed paid no attention to him.

Max didn't reach into his inside jacket pocket for the
cell phone until he hit Route 19.

The phone wasn't there.

"What the hell?" Slamming on the brakes, Max
swerved onto the shoulder and threw the gearshift into
park. His throat went dry, and he tightened his grip on the
steering wheel to stop his hands from shaking. He filled
his lungs with air and exhaled slowly, forcing himself to
calm down.

As part of his cover, Max had stayed at a motel the
night before. He remembered using the cell phone to call
Dr. Farley that morning from the car after he had checked
out.

Remembering that cleared Max's muddled mind. He
had been annoyed last night when he realized he hadn't
packed the cell phone charger. This morning, to boost the
drained battery, he had plugged the phone into the cigarette lighter adapter, which he *had* remembered to bring.

Max glanced at the ashtray in the console below the

radio. The cell phone was lying inside the plastic insert where he had left it. Taking another deep breath, he picked up the phone and speed-dialed.

"Yes?" Dr. Lawrence Farley answered abruptly. Caller ID had informed the scientist that his operative was checking in.

"Nothing," Max said, and disconnected.

Considering Dr. Farley's less-than-stellar scientific reputation, it wasn't likely anyone would go to the expense or trouble to listen in. Even so, maintaining meticulous security was a habit Max's covert ops training would not allow him to break.

Dr. Farley was just one of many oddball researchers funded by Continental Sciences, a consortium of banks and businesses headquartered in France. Since the geneticist had been dismissed from the university after losing a government grant, his project proposal had been met with little enthusiasm. However, the men on the consortium's board had accrued great wealth by gambling that an unorthodox or seemingly preposterous area of study would eventually pay off.

Dr. Farley had sold Max on the financial potential of his idea with a single key point. Development of a technology often occurred before all the possible applications were understood. The unique and specific technological requirements of the space environment and program had resulted in thousands of product spinoffs, particularly in the fields of medicine, miniaturization, and computers. While the government was mandated by law to make any discoveries freely available, he and Dr. Farley were motivated by the promise of profit.

There's no such thing as being too careful, Max

thought as he drove back onto the highway. Scientific and industrial espionage was as cutthroat and dangerous as the political game, especially when billions of dollars were at stake. He would brief his partner in person, which would take all of five minutes.

Max couldn't believe their accidental luck. Isolation wasn't the only benefit of setting up shop in Smallville. Not a single person he had contacted suspected that Howard Stoner had been murdered. Even better, since everyone assumed the fertilizer plant was responsible for any unexplained deaths in the area, the Sheriff's Office probably wouldn't open an investigation. It made sense that nobody, including the authorities, would want to rock the boat that paid the bills.

It was also imperative to confirm that his assumptions were correct and no loose ends remained to trouble them later.

Dr. Farley would be greatly relieved by his report, which would settle Max's jangled nerves. When the scientist worried too much, he had trouble concentrating on his work, and the work was vital to his future.

Max sighed as he put the cell phone back in the ashtray. He could no longer delude himself that his memory lapses were temporary aberrations. The mental blanks and spasmodic shakes were symptoms of something much more serious.

"Mrs. Kent to the rescue!" Lana rushed forward to greet Clark and his mother, but her gushing gratitude was aimed directly at Martha. "You're a lifesaver."

"You're lucky Lionel went to New York, and I had today off." Martha held the Talon door open for Clark.

"Thanks." Clark exchanged a knowing glance with his mom. The tray laden with freshly baked pies wasn't heavy for an alien with super-human strength. He could have easily balanced it on one hand to open the door, but he was supposed to be human. His mother had been acting out the charade of the Kent kid's normalcy for so long her responses were automatic.

"I know." Lana's bright smile lit up the entryway. "I couldn't believe the bakery shorted my order! I was in a panic this morning until Clark told me you were home."

"Where do you want these, Lana?" Clark asked.

"On the back counter by the pie case." Lana waved toward the far side of the room, then inhaled, closing her eyes to savor the scents rising off the warm pies. "These smell heavenly."

"Tell me about it," Clark said. The aroma of apples and custard spiced with cinnamon and nutmeg had driven him crazy since they had left the farm. "Tortured by tantalizing temptation all the way into town, and no way to sneak a taste."

"Not if you want to keep your fingers." Martha smiled. "I set aside two pies for you and your father."

"Two pies each?" Clark asked, sagging when his mom shook her head.

Lana laughed at the affectionate repartee.

Clark's heart seemed to swell as he looked into Lana's gentle brown eyes. Everything outside the frame of her flawless face and long, dark hair lost focus. The effect she had on him was as disconcerting now as it had been the first time he had noticed she was a *girl*, back in middle school. *Just friends*, he reminded himself, ignoring the warm flush that crept up his neck as he edged past her.

Lana walked behind Clark with Martha. "I really can't thank you enough, Mrs. Kent. I was dreading having to spend all night explaining why we didn't have any pie. Now we've got the best pie in Kansas."

"I was happy to do it." Martha's blue eyes sparkled above a beaming smile as she handed Lana the bill.

"I'll vouch for that." Clark set down the tray. "To watch her in the kitchen, you'd think she gets up at five every morning to bake muffins for fun."

His mother had started a home baking business to earn extra money before Lionel Luthor had hired her. Except for the occasional special order, such as the wedding cake for Lex's disastrous wedding to Desiree Atkins and Lana's emergency pies, she sold muffins to convenience stores, the retirement center cafeteria, Denehey's Pitstop, the Talon, and the Uptown Diner. She worked too hard, but she wouldn't give up either endeavor. Being perpetually broke was not the only reason. She loved the challenge of dealing with the headstrong corporate mogul and the personal sense of accomplishment represented by the long list of muffin clients. His dad complained now and then, but didn't interfere.

"You mean she doesn't slave over a hot oven for fun?" Lana pretended to be shocked as she opened the cash register and handed an envelope to Martha.

"Actually, she does," Clark admitted.

"How about a mocha cream cappuccino?" Lana shoved the cash drawer closed. "My treat for service above and beyond, Mrs. Kent. You, too, Clark."

"I'd love one, Lana, but I've got a date with a pair of

scissors at Charlene's. I am weeks overdue for a trim," Martha replied, patting her shoulder-length, auburn hair as she slipped the envelope into her purse. "But Clark doesn't have any plans."

"No, I'm free." Nodding, Clark folded his arms and looked at Lana. "If the offer's still open, and you can sit down for a few minutes."

The hesitation before Lana accepted the invitation was almost imperceptible. "We're kind of busy, but—since everyone showed up for work today, a cappuccino break sounds great."

Martha called back over her shoulder as she walked away. "I'll be done in an hour if you want a ride home, Clark."

"I'll be here." Clark's eyes filled with admiration as he followed his mom out the door. He was certain that no one but Martha Kent could have coped with raising a willful child who used hay bales as building blocks and won tug-of-wars with stubborn cows. He was also positive that no one could have taken better care or loved him more.

"You might as well sit down and relax while I make these, Clark." Lana pulled two large cups off a shelf.

As Clark scanned the crowded room, he caught Sharon Farley watching him. She sat by herself near one of the supporting pillars decorated with Egyptian graphics. Pretty, with gray-green eyes, short blond hair, and freckles, she nervously averted her gaze. The girl hadn't been very sociable since transferring to Smallville High three months before. Some kids thought she was conceited, others assumed she was shy.

Maybe nobody's tried to make her feel welcome.

Although it wasn't deliberate, Clark felt badly for making her feel self-conscious. There was a free table next to Sharon, which gave him an ideal opening. He ambled over and spoke as he sat down.

"Hey, Sharon. How's it going?"

Sharon sat with her back to the pillar and her feet propped on the opposite chair. She looked up from a paperback book with a start. "Uh, fine."

"Clark Kent." Clark folded his arms on the small, round tabletop and smiled. "We're in the same biology lab, but I don't think we've actually met."

"Yes, I know. I mean, no, we haven't—" Sharon winced. A stressed smile emphasized an expression of aghast disbelief, as though she had just committed the social gaffe of the year.

"Until now," Clark added, to put her at ease.

"Until now." Sharon sighed with an apologetic shrug. "So—have you picked a subject for your biology paper, yet?"

"No, but I've got a couple ideas." Clark had the distinct impression Sharon was surprised and pleased that he knew her from class and had made the effort to engage her in conversation. "To be honest, the 'lifestyles of primordial single-celled organisms' isn't particularly inspiring or exciting."

"Maybe not"—an impish twinkle brightened Sharon's eyes—"unless you're the first single-cell to get the bright idea of combining with another single-cell to reproduce, thus changing the pace and character of evolution forever."

Was that a serious attempt at conversation, or is she flirting? Either way, Clark was momentarily speechless.

He recovered quickly. "I don't think conscious thought was a factor."

"For what?" Lana set down two cups of cappuccino laced with chocolate and topped with whipped cream.

"Topics for our biology papers." Clark nodded at Sharon. "We're in the same class."

"Hi. I'm Lana." Lana smiled and slipped into the chair opposite Clark. "And you're Sharon, right? Am I interrupting?"

"No, not at all. I've got a lot of homework anyway." Sharon held up the paperback.

"Are you sure?" Lana twisted to look behind her.

"Thanks, Lana, but I can't today." Sharon pulled a small notebook out of her backpack and began to write, leaving no doubt that the conversation was over.

"Okay." Lana turned back to Clark with a confused frown.

She shrugged, sighed, and picked up her cup.

"Busy place," Clark said. Although sitting so close to Lana incited his hormones to riot, he was determined to make the "just friends" pact work for real and not merely as a pretense. "Almost every table is taken."

"Yeah." Lana gave the crowd a sweeping glance. "Thank goodness. I think Lex will be pleased with this month's financial report."

"I'm sure he will." Clark lifted his cappuccino cup and sipped, pretending to be afraid he'd burn his mouth.

"So you had quite a day yesterday," Lana said. "It must have been terrible, seeing Mr. Stoner die like that."

Clark nodded. "Not my idea of a fun afternoon. He was walking across his field one minute and then—wham. His air is cut off, and that's it."

"He choked on something?" Lana frowned. "The newspaper didn't say anything about that."

"I'm just guessing, based on what I saw." Clark sighed. Behind Lana, Sharon was still scribbling in her notebook.

"Well, the *Ledger* got the time wrong, too." Lana shook her head. "You left here at four-twenty-five, so you couldn't possibly have called 911 from Mr. Stoner's house at four-forty."

Clark swallowed hard. He hated being in a position where a lie was his only option. For someone who could run faster than a jet could fly, it was entirely possible to have made a phone call from the Stoner farm fifteen minutes after leaving the Talon. He wished he could tell Lana everything, but he couldn't ask her to bear the burden of knowing. Pete was still constantly stressed out by the fear that he might let Clark's secret slip. Clark regretted that, but he couldn't take the truth back after it was known. So he felt it was best to keep Lana from knowing.

"It's the Smallville *Ledger*, Lana," Clark said. "Not the *Daily Planet*."

Lana shrugged. "Yes, but they usually don't make such sloppy mistakes."

Clark decided to let the subject drop.

At the next table, Sharon shoved the notebook and pen into her backpack and zipped it up.

Preoccupied with the disturbing necessity of deceiving Lana, Clark didn't register that Sharon's fleeting glance and smile had been meant for him until the girl was gone.

Lie to one girl and brush off another. Way to go, Clark, he berated himself. For a supersmart guy, sometimes he was really dense.

CHAPTER 3

Clark paused at the top of the stairs. Judging from the intense discussion going on in the kitchen, his parents weren't expecting him to come down early. Even he was a little surprised that the new morning routine was working so well.

His mom had suggested putting his new alarm clock on the chest across the room so he had to get up to turn it off. Before, crushing clocks had been an unavoidable consequence of hitting the snooze alarm when he was awakened suddenly from a sound sleep.

"But Lex wasn't responsible for poisoning the herd, Jonathan," Martha said evenly. "A man pretending to be that girl's dead fiancé did."

"You're missing the point, Martha." Jonathan sounded annoyed. "If someone doesn't take a stand soon, the Luthors will just keep poisoning this county until nothing can live here."

"I know, but that's not *my* point," Martha countered.

Clark felt uncomfortable eavesdropping. His parents often disagreed, but they rarely had a heated argument. He wasn't sure what to do. He just knew that he didn't want to walk into the middle of verbal parental combat.

"You're not defending *them*, are you?" The edge of irritation in Jonathan's tone sharpened.

Sighing, Clark focused his X-ray vision on the floor. Wood and air ducts vanished to reveal the solid objects in the kitchen. His father's skeletal form was seated at the table. His mother bent over to pull a muffin tin out of the oven.

"No, but some hotshot attorney will, and *that's* my point." She kicked the oven door closed with her foot. "You can't sue LexCorp for illegal polluting without proof."

Dad wants to sue Lex? Stunned, Clark blinked. His vision flickered back to normal for a second before he readjusted.

"If the CEP tests prove that chemical seepage from the plant caused Howard Stoner's death, I'll have all the proof I need." Jonathan drained his coffee mug and set it down.

"Maybe." Martha gingerly transferred the hot muffins to delivery boxes. "Here's something to think about, though. The main reason my father's law practice was so successful is that he never took a case he wasn't sure of winning."

"Let's leave your father out of this, okay?" Jonathan snapped. "There's a principle involved, Martha," he continued, softening his tone. "This has nothing to do with money."

"It has everything to do with money, Jonathan." Martha untied her apron and draped it over a chair as she sat down. If she felt stung by her husband's remarks, she didn't let it show.

"Maybe you're right," Jonathan said. "Since money is all the Luthors care about, losing a few million will hit them where it really hurts—in their bank accounts. It's their Achilles' heel."

"If we win, yes," Martha agreed. "But there are some hard facts about how the judicial system works we can't afford to ignore. All the new laws tend to favor big business over us little people."

Jonathan nodded, but he wasn't deterred. "I was thinking about a class action lawsuit. The united-we-stand approach would give us a fighting chance."

"Don't get me wrong, Jonathan." Martha placed her hand over his. "I'll be right there fighting with you, if you decide this is something you have to do. I just want to be sure you understand that if we lose in court, we'll have to sell the farm to pay for it."

"Some fights are worth the risk." Jonathan clasped Martha's smaller hand in both of his.

Taking that as an all clear, Clark zipped down the stairs.

"What's the rush, son?" Jonathan glanced at the clock on the stove. "The bus won't be here for another half hour."

"Breakfast." Clark dropped into a chair beside his dad. "I was hoping Mom made an extra tin of muffins."

"Blueberry or bran?" Grinning, Martha pushed a basket across the table.

"Both." Before his mother finished removing the cloth napkin that had kept the muffins warm, Clark jumped up, pulled a glass from the cabinet, opened the refrigerator, poured himself some OJ, grabbed the butter dish, and returned to his chair. "Do we have any more of Martha's Wild Strawberry Jubilee?"

"I'll get it." Jonathan stood up to refill his coffee mug and brought a jar of homemade jam back to the table.

Clark unscrewed the lid and pried the paraffin seal out with the tip of his knife. Every batch of his mom's jams and jellies was dubbed with a fanciful Martha name. His favorite was still Martha's Moose Morsels, a blackberry and red currant concoction she had created and he had named when he was eight.

Rising, Martha set the empty muffin tins in the sink. "I've got to change and make my deliveries. There're so many things I need to catch up on around here, I don't want to waste a minute of my week off."

After his mother went upstairs, Clark bit into a blueberry muffin. He chewed slowly, enjoying the taste of tart berries and warm, buttery bread while he put off asking his dad about the lawsuit for a few more seconds.

"It might be a good idea to take the bus or ride into town with your mother today." Jonathan blew on the hot coffee to cool it. "We wouldn't want Mr. Mundy to catch a glance of you whizzing by while he's collecting soil samples from Howard's field."

"No, that wouldn't be good." Clark brushed the crumbs off his jeans. The CEP agent had seemed pretty sharp, and probably wouldn't miss a disturbance that cut through the woods like a horizontal twister. "I probably shouldn't say this, Dad, but—"

"But what?" Jonathan lowered his cup.

"You don't have to sue Lex." Clark took a breath and plunged ahead. "Anytime there's damage linked to the fertilizer plant, Lex pays for it—even when it's not his fault, like when we lost the herd."

"That's the problem, though, Clark." Jonathan didn't raise his voice or get defensive. "LuthorCorp leaves environmental destruction, death, and ruined lives in their wake with impunity."

"LuthorCorp maybe, but Lex always tries to make things right," Clark argued. "What about Earl Jenkins?

Lex wasn't even in charge of the plant when that explosion happened. He didn't even know there *was* a level three, but he's paying for Earl's treatment's anyway."

"Ask yourself why, Clark," Jonathan suggested. "What's the real reason Lionel is paying to find a cure for Byron's problem with sunlight?"

The teenager Clark and Lana had befriended suffered from side effects as a result of being in a Metron Pharmaceuticals' medical study when he was eight. Clark wasn't surprised when Chloe found out that Metron was a subsidiary of LuthorCorp.

Clark sighed, but he didn't interrupt his father.

"Because he feels remorse and responsibility for his actions? No." Sitting back, Jonathan rubbed his chin and looked past Clark at the wall.

"Okay," Clark said. "Then why?"

"Because your mother convinced him that a generous and genuine attempt to help was more cost-effective than trying to recover from a drop in the LuthorCorp stock price."

"At least, he's doing something." Clark had a habit of looking for the best in people, even those with few redeeming qualities. His father usually admired that particular character trait, except when Clark applied it to anyone surnamed Luthor.

"You and your mother both have a blind spot when it comes to Lex and his father." Jonathan was more perplexed than angry, and he couldn't hide his frustration.

"Maybe your *prejudice* is what's off. Not our *judgment*." Clark felt frustrated, too.

Jonathan stood to get another cup of coffee. The pot was empty, and he set it down harder than he had intended to. "Someone has to stop them from buying people off to avoid embarrassing court appearances and bad press. The Luthors use their money to make sure that no costly precedents are set."

"But if you push this lawsuit, and we don't win—" Clark looked away.

The thought of losing the farm was something the Kents lived with every day. Defaulting on their loan because they couldn't make a financial go of it was one thing. Clark just couldn't accept selling to pay for losing a misguided lawsuit they shouldn't have filed in the first place.

"I haven't made a decision, Clark. Consider me an exploratory committee of one." Jonathan smiled to reassure him. "I'm just looking into the possibilities, getting some advice. That's all."

Clark nodded and reached for another muffin. There was no point in pressing the argument. Once his father set his mind on something, he had to follow through. With luck, the medical examiner's lab report would show, beyond doubt, that contamination from the fertilizer plant was not a factor in Howard Stoner's death.

Nothing less than absolute proof of Lex's innocence would convince Jonathan Kent to back down.

CHAPTER 4

Pete leaned against the wall, watching Clark shove books into his locker. Carrying the extra weight wouldn't bother his powerful friend, but nobody hauled afternoon work to morning classes.

"Did Chloe hear back from Chad, yet?" Clark asked.

"She didn't say anything on the bus, so I guess not." Pete shrugged. Clark had ridden into town with his mother. He didn't know Chloe had adopted a wait-and-see attitude regarding Howard Stoner's sudden death. "Our intrepid *Torch* editor doesn't seem to think anything weird is going on."

"Or maybe she's just keeping a lid on because she doesn't want to give Reynolds any ammunition." Clark slammed his locker closed. "Why buy trouble for nothing?"

"Excellent point," Pete said. Chloe's investigative instincts often overrode her better judgment. However, she had no problem subverting her inner reporter if the survival of the school newspaper and her job as editor were threatened.

"Believe me," Clark continued, "if something even a little unusual turns up in Mr. Stoner's lab report, Chloe will be all over this story for the *Torch*."

"Or the *Smallville Ledger*," Pete added. He turned, surprised by a muffled gasp behind him. He didn't know how long Sharon Farley had been standing there. A stricken look faded from her face.

Upset because we ignored her or embarrassed because we caught her eavesdropping? Pete wondered.

"Hi, Sharon." Clark smoothed over the awkward moment with a friendly smile. "Do you know Pete Ross?"

"From English class." Sharon nodded, her mouth pressed in a tight smile. She clutched a notebook to her chest as though it was the only thing keeping her afloat in a stormy sea.

"Going through *A Tale of Two Cities* line by line," Pete joked. "Kind of takes the fun out of reading the story, though, doesn't it?"

"Uh-huh." Sharon cleared her throat and handed Clark paper-clipped pages that had been torn from magazines. "I, uh—thought these might give you some ideas, Clark—for your biology paper."

So she was working up her courage to interrupt, Pete realized. He couldn't imagine being so shy that just talking to someone was traumatic. It seemed especially sad for a girl as pretty as Sharon Farley. Apparently, Clark had breached the introduction barrier in the not-too-distant past and just hadn't thought it was worth mentioning.

" 'The Absence of a Fossil Record' and 'Single to Multicellular Organisms: The Missing Leap.' " Clark read the titles and scanned the top pages of both articles. "An interesting concept."

"I thought so. Maybe it will help." Sharon's hesitant manner eased as she began to relax.

That wholesome Clark Kent appeal is certainly working like a charm. Considering Sharon's obvious infatuation, Pete had to wonder if all females were born with some instinctive mechanism that sensed a superior male, the primal prerequisite for the perpetuation of the species.

*For all the good it will do her. Clark doesn't have a clue
that she's interested in him!*

"It might." Clark glanced at the torn edges of the
pages. "Where did you find the magazines?"

"My dad never throws away anything related to science." An unexpected smile brightened Sharon's face.
"But he keeps all of it hoping that I *will* get interested
enough to rip out the articles."

"Is your father a scientist?" Pete asked.

"He was. He worked for a university back East."
Sharon sighed. "But he lost his research grant and decided on a midlife career change."

That explained the magazines, Pete realized, but his
question had also struck a nerve. He hated having to explain why his father and uncle had sold the Creamed
Corn Factory to Lionel Luthor shortly after the 1989 meteor shower. He didn't put Sharon on the spot by asking
what her dad was doing now.

She volunteered the information with a sheepish grin.
"My dad has a wild imagination so maybe he'll make a
great science fiction writer."

Pete started. "He's writing a book?"

Sharon nodded. "A novel. We moved to Smallville so
he could work without distractions. Nobody knows us so
nobody bothers him."

"Isn't that a little hard on you?" Clark asked.

"A little, but it's getting better." Sharon blushed.

"Well, thanks for these." Clark slid the magazine pages
into his backpack.

"It's the least I could do," Sharon said. "I know I
wouldn't be able to keep my mind on school stuff if I saw
someone die."

Clark shrugged, his expression troubled. "I was just sorry I couldn't do something to save Mr. Stoner."

"Maybe it was hopeless," Sharon offered as consolation. "Does anyone know what killed him?"

"Asphyxiation," Pete said, "but we won't know what caused that until Chloe gets the autopsy lab report."

Sharon blinked. "Chloe has an in with the medical examiner?"

"Chloe has sources everywhere," Pete said, then suddenly realized he might have said too much. He relaxed when he realized that Sharon's attention was locked on Clark.

When Pete first learned about Clark's gifts, he had been a little envious and a lot intimidated. Even though Clark didn't flaunt his abilities, how could he or any other red-blooded boy from this planet compete? Then Pete had realized that Clark was light-years behind him when it came to dealing with the opposite sex. He had made it his personal mission to improve Clark's love life— whether Clark approved or not.

And the immediate circumstances demand an instant intercession, Pete decided.

Clark wasn't picking up on Sharon's inept cues, but they both had a biology paper to write. Not much, but it was a starting point. More importantly, Clark didn't have a history of friendship to overcome with the new girl. There was no telling how long the "friends only" policy with Lana and Chloe would last, but for now, the pledge was in effect.

Still, swimming the Atlantic might be easier than playing Cupid for Clark. Pete sagged with dismay when Clark suddenly ended the conversation.

"Speaking of the *Torch*, I have to go explain to Chloe why I'm not done with the overdue library book list for the next issue." As Clark started to leave, the first bell rang. "Guess I'll have to catch her later."

Pete sighed as Clark shouldered his backpack and took off down the hall. His first class was in the opposite direction.

"Don't mind Clark, Sharon. He can be a little—" Pete's explanation hung in the air as he turned. "—manic."

Sharon was already walking away.

Chloe Sullivan sat back in her desk chair. She eyed Sharon Farley's earnest face with the suspicious mind of a reporter trying to peel layers of spin off the facts. "You seriously won't mind doing cafeteria polls?"

"Actually, I can't think of a better way to get to know some of the kids here." Sharon's gaze drifted around the *Torch* office, then snapped back to Chloe. "Because if I'm doing a poll, I'll have a *reason* to talk to people, you know?"

"Well, there is a certain logic to that." Chloe smiled, appearing more at ease than she was. She had been completely unprepared when the new girl walked in, practically begging to be on the school newspaper staff.

Chloe's only impressions of Sharon Farley were vague at best. She was cute in an all-American way, with a trim figure, short blond hair, and freckles, but she had stayed removed from Smallville's teen set during her three months at the high school. Since Clark typed up the lunch menu, sport schedules, club activity notices, and other miscellaneous filler pieces, almost every cub reporter assignment on the *Torch* required face time with people—students and teachers. A timid new kid wasn't really a good fit.

As though sensing her uncertainty, Sharon edged her chair closer to the desk. She leaned forward with a white-knuckled grip on the notebook in her lap. "What about a trial period?"

"Like probation?" The idea hadn't occurred to Chloe, but she liked it. She also admired Sharon's tenacity, even though the go-get-it personality was incongruous with the rabbit rep Sharon had acquired.

"Yes, for a week? Maybe, two?" Sharon asked hopefully. "Then, if I don't meet your high standards for the *Torch*, I'll bow out without a fuss. Promise." She crossed her heart.

Chloe's baloney detector red-lined. She didn't mind being known as a hard taskmaster, but performance and attitude were what counted, not suck-up compliments. Still, a trial week seemed fair. Besides, if Sharon spent her lunch periods asking students how they really felt about the new principal's closed campus policy, she wouldn't have to.

"All right, we'll give it a try." Chloe held out her hand to shake on it. "I've got a student survey I want to start during lunch on Monday, so rest up over the weekend."

"Great!" Sharon beamed. "This is so exciting. I've never told anyone this, but I love solving mysteries, getting down to the bare bones of what's what."

"Really?" Chloe tried to look interested.

"But I'm thinking about going into journalism, as a career," Sharon went on, "instead of law enforcement. Being a cop would be way too dangerous."

Journalism in Smallville is way too dangerous. Chloe nodded to cover her dismay. After months of isolation, Sharon obviously had reams of pent-up conversation ready and waiting to roll off her tongue. *And, apparently, I just opened the floodgate.*

"Like that dead farmer Clark Kent found." Sharon shuddered and lowered her voice. "How come nobody thinks it might have been foul play? How often do people die in the middle of fields around here?"

More often than we like to admit.

Chloe sighed. The *Smallville Ledger* hadn't published Clark's name because he was a minor, but everyone in town had known he found Mr. Stoner before that edition hit the streets. The truth was, Chloe hadn't dismissed the possibility of foul play. She was just waiting for hard evidence.

A good reporter doesn't jump to conclusions, Chloe reminded herself. *She just explores all the angles on the QT. Then, if it turns out that Mr. Stoner had a heart attack, I won't have to grovel or apologize or print a retraction.*

Chloe repeated the new mantra frequently to keep from stepping over the line with Mr. Reynolds. In Smallville, foul play was always a possibility until something disproved it, but most people blamed the fertilizer plant for inexplicable illness and death. Very few thought the meteor-rocks caused the strange things that happened in the area, but that didn't make the theory untrue.

Sensing a potential ally, but wary out of habit, Chloe chose her words carefully. "I haven't dismissed the idea that Mr. Stoner might have died from something other than natural causes, Sharon. It's just that the school authorities tend to freak if the *Torch* speculates. We have to be able to prove what we print."

"See?" Clark elbowed Pete as they came through the door. "I told you Chloe was just being careful."

"Hi, Clark!" Sharon grinned.

Chloe noted the sparkle in the girl's green eyes as they followed Clark into the room. A hint of crimson bloomed on Sharon's cheeks, and her breath caught in her throat when he smiled.

All the symptoms of a Clark crush, Chloe observed.

Suddenly caught in the grip of conflicting emotions, Chloe rejected jealousy in favor of empathy. Sharon didn't yet know she had competition she couldn't beat.

Although she, Lana, and Clark had agreed to avoid complications that could ruin their friendships, Lana also needed time to grieve for her fallen ex-boyfriend. Clark was honoring that, but keeping his emotional distance didn't alter how he felt. He loved Lana.

And Chloe loved him. She had been overjoyed when Clark asked her to the Spring Formal. Then, after promising not to, he had abandoned her on the dance floor to check on Lana. Chloe was strong and resilient, but her self-respect wouldn't survive another botched attempt at romance with Clark Kent. In the end, it was easier to accept Lana's hold on his heart.

Eventually, Sharon would figure out that Clark wasn't tied down *or* available. In the meantime, Chloe would try to cushion the girl's inevitable appointment with heartbreak.

"Hey, Sharon." Clark sat down at the desk opposite Chloe. "I'm surprised to see you here."

"I'm not," Pete muttered as he pulled up an empty chair.

"Starting Monday, I'll be part of the *Torch* team," Sharon explained.

"Really?" Clark cocked an eyebrow at Chloe.

"You know those student polls you and Pete won't do?" Chloe asked. "Sharon will."

"I'll give it a shot, anyway." Sharon glanced at the large clock on the wall above the black filing cabinets. "I'd love to hang out, but I've got math this period."

"Take it easy." Clark turned back to Chloe before Sharon reached the door. "Any word from your man in the Medical Examiner's Office?"

"Not yet." Chloe frowned when she realized Sharon had paused in the doorway. "Was there something else, Sharon?"

"Uh—no, I was just wondering . . ." Sharon shook her head. "Nothing."

No one said anything until the girl was gone.

"Why would someone who quakes at the thought of talking to strangers *want* a job talking to strangers?" Pete asked.

"So they won't be strangers," Chloe said. "Or so she said."

"You don't believe that, either, do you?" Pete looked at Chloe.

"Nope. Not for a minute," Chloe said with a smug smile.

"Why not?" Clark frowned, puzzled. "Asking a survey

question seems like a great way to start a conversation with someone you don't know."

"Yeah, but getting to know the student body is not why Sharon Farley wants to work on the *Torch*." Chloe threw up her hands when Clark just looked at her. "She wants to get to know *you*, Clark. Specifically."

"You're kidding, right?" Clark's surprised glance flicked between his two friends.

"Not kidding." Pete slid off the table. "If you're seriously thinking about dating, Sharon Farley is primed to say yes when you call."

Dating? Stunned, Chloe stared as Pete handed Clark a folded paper.

"Sharon's phone number," Pete explained. "I took the liberty of calling information."

Chloe's heart sank when Clark put the paper in his shirt pocket and glanced toward the door. The curious interest in his eyes conveyed the gist of his thoughts.

Clark was going to make that call.

"Don't forget to turn out the lights when you come up, Clark." Martha paused halfway up the stairs.

"I won't." Clark smiled. "Goodnight, Mom."

"See you in the morning." Yawning, Martha hurried up to the second floor.

When he heard the bedroom door close, Clark got up from the kitchen table. His father had been asleep for an hour, and his mother had just finished her ironing. He had changed his mind about calling Sharon Farley three times while he waited for his mom to go to bed. If he decided to ask Sharon out, he didn't want anyone listening to his side of the conversation.

Clark sighed as he put the cordless handset on the table and sat back down. Pete and Chloe had tried to act as though going to the movies with someone was no big deal. He knew better. They really thought that spending a Saturday night with Sharon would be a breakthrough event. His parents would probably have a similar reaction.

It's like I'm finally putting Lana behind me.

Exhaling again, Clark rested his chin on his folded arms. He loved Lana, in the truest sense of the word, but also in a way that transcended the mundane. She would always be a part of his life, as important to his existence as breathing. But destiny, for reasons real or imagined, seemed bent on making sure they never became a couple.

Whitney's death had put Lana's obsession with Clark's secrets into a more realistic perspective, but the lack of trust remained an obstacle. A close relationship couldn't survive without honesty. Intuitively, they both seemed to know that any mutual romantic interest was best left alone, at least for now. Instead, they clung to the long friendship, which would survive time and circumstance.

Including taking Sharon Farley to see the latest Jackie Chan film.

Taking a deep breath, Clark unfolded the paper Pete had given him with Sharon's number, picked up the phone, and dialed her house.

Sharon answered on the third ring. "Hello?"

"Hi, Sharon. This is Clark Kent."

◆◆◆

After Clark hung up, Sharon sat back with a smile. This was the first social telephone call she had gotten since moving into the rented house on the outskirts of Smallville.

"Who was that?" Her father peered over the top of his newspaper.

The headline of the *Smallville Ledger* read: Farmer Suffocates in Field. Sharon had read the story earlier. The reporter who wrote it didn't know anything more than Chloe and probably didn't have the junior journalist's connections. As Lana had pointed out yesterday, the local paper had mistakenly reported the time Clark made his startling discovery.

"Clark Kent," Sharon answered. Setting the cordless back in its cradle, she drew her knees up to her chest.

The corner of her father's left eye twitched, a sign that he was struggling with a "daughter dilemma," his code for her perplexing teenage problems. "The boy who found Howard Stoner?"

"That's the one." Sharon smiled. Fifty-three and graying at the temples, Dr. Lawrence Farley looked like a stiff, out-of-touch scientist in his starched white shirt and blue, herringbone tie. He *was* totally uptight, and she couldn't help teasing him. "We're going to the movies tomorrow night."

Dr. Farley flinched. "On a date?"

"Yes, on a date." Noting the tension in his neck, Sharon hastened to reassure him before he had a stroke. "Can you think of a better way to get a teenage boy talking about his exciting adventures?"

"Perhaps, not." Dr. Farley's perpetual frown deepened.

"Assuming boys are still prone to bragging about their exploits to girls."

"They are." Sharon decided not to mention that Clark Kent was not like other guys his age. Talking to her at the Talon had been a genuine gesture of friendship, not a put-down or a come-on. Clark had been honestly concerned that she had torn the evolution articles from someone else's magazines and might get into trouble, and he regretted not being able to save the dead farmer.

"Just be careful." Dr. Farley carefully folded the paper and placed it on the end table. "I could face criminal charges if anyone finds out what I'm doing here—"

"They won't," Sharon interrupted, recalling a snippet of conversation she had overheard between Clark and Lana at the Talon.

"I'm just guessing, based on what I saw," Clark had said.

Which was what exactly? Sharon wondered. Since Clark wasn't upset or spooked, it was probably nothing they had to worry about.

"I don't think there's a problem, Dad," Sharon said.

"I hope you're right." Dr. Farley glanced at his watch and sighed.

When he stood up, Sharon was once again grateful that she had inherited her mother's looks and physique. Her slender frame gave the illusion that she was taller than five-foot-five. Her father was only three inches taller and losing his fight with a steadily thickening middle. He had been tennis fit with a charming grin before her mom died of pneumonia eight years before. He rarely smiled now.

"Dinner in fifteen minutes." Dr. Farley removed his

glasses and slipped them into his shirt pocket. "Then I have to go back to work."

"Please, take the box back with you." Sharon glanced at the lead-lined container on the side table in the front foyer. Her father's fear of legal complications was nothing compared to her dread of having meteor-rocks in the house.

CHAPTER 5

Max Cutler paused on the edge of the woods to study the soft ground. It had rained recently, but Layton Crouse's tracks were not easy to spot, even though he knew what to look for. Knowing that the mutant hunted in a circular pattern helped.

Moving out slowly, Max swept his gaze back and forth across the terrain to both sides and straight ahead until he spotted a clump of feathers. He squatted to examine the dead bird and noticed the palm-sized depression nearby. The three other imprints that marked the expansive, lumbering stride were positioned right where he expected. Layton's reach measured just short of twelve feet at its extreme limits. By digging in with his hands, he could pull his body and legs forward in a fluid motion that resembled a running ape.

More efficient and elegant, but apelike nonetheless, Max thought. The leisurely four-beat gait was only one of Layton's exotic modes of movement.

Rising, Max sighed with annoyed exasperation. Given his contributions to the project, being left alone to watch golf on Saturday afternoons didn't seem like too much to ask. However, Dr. Farley could neither find nor control the escapee.

Max did not negate his partner's value. There wouldn't be a project without Lawrence Farley's theories and scientific expertise. Still, acting on connections he had established while working for the CIA, Max had contacted Continental Sciences and arranged the financing. He had also supplied the required function data for the proto-types, recruited the volunteers, found the ideal location to conduct the experimental phase, then designed and supervised the installation of a high-tech security system worthy of a black ops facility.

But Farley was anxious about his daughter's impending date with the Kent kid and had forgotten to secure the entry hatch before he entered the elevator. While the scientist could contain and sedate the other failed experiments, Layton was unaffected by drugs and had a predator's need to prowl. Plus, Layton's control was improving, and he was learning to squeeze through smaller and smaller openings. So instead of watching the final holes in today's PGA tournament round, Max was chasing down a psychotic killer.

Max kicked the limp body of the bird aside with a snort of disgust. Espionage professionals wouldn't have hesitated to terminate a liability such as Layton had become. But, even though Farley was responsible for turning him and four others into genetic monstrosities, his warped ethics wouldn't tolerate permanent disposal.

"These are men, not lab rats!"

That was true. The men Farley had modified in the early human experimental phase passed the time cowering in corners, staring at the walls, pacing, weeping, or making as much noise as possible. Their bizarre behaviors were in constant flux and too numerous for anyone but the scientist to catalog.

When the rats went insane, they ate their own tails before they tore each other apart. Prior to that, they were perfect little subjects with a variety of engineered abilities. At least the latest batch of his precursors had been.

But the missing Layton and fate of his sanity weren't his only problems at the moment.

A shiver traced the curve of Max's spine as the sun dipped behind the LexCorp fertilizer plant on the far side of the cornfield. He had an hour at most before sunset, and judging by the pattern of prints, Layton had cut back into the woods instead of completing the circle.

Something had caught his attention and lured him off course.

Layton's senses had been enhanced as an unintended side effect of the molecular transformation process. Any living thing within range of the madman's ability to smell, see, or hear would satisfy his crazed desire to kill something. Layton seemed to achieve the same blood-thirsty high from ripping rosebushes out by the roots as he did from strangling cows.

Cursing, Max moved into the trees. Since Max's own alter-form wasn't appropriate for a capture mission, Layton had the advantage. The fugitive's ability to shift bone and muscle into an elastic rubbery state made him harder, if not impossible, to track. He could stretch or swing from tree to tree without touching down. As the project progressed, Farley hoped to re-create Layton's physical properties without the mental deviations.

A chorus of animal squeals shattered the twilight stillness.

Homing in on the high-pitched screams, Max raced through the dense woods. The urgency that empowered his legs had nothing to do with the senseless slaughter of wild woodland creatures, however. The killing spree was a reminder of what terrified him most: Farley had not isolated the cause for the loss of mental acuity in Layton and the others.

They had all been derelicts scrounging out an existence in the alleys of the Metropolis warehouse district. Feeble-minded, drunks, and addicts, they had signed their lives away in exchange for an unending supply of their chosen poison. Farley was convinced their moronic mentalities and damaged brains simply couldn't adapt to the stresses of transformation. The doctor had made some adjust-ments to the process, and the altered rats had thrived.

Consequently, when Layton first escaped three weeks ago, they had accelerated the schedule for Max's proce-dure. That he would undergo the process had always been part of the plan. Max had to be an alter-form to command them. Layton had proven that necessity repeatedly. Even in the delirium of a feeding frenzy, the elastic mutant obeyed him.

Since Max was strong in body with a disciplined mind, and the rats appeared stable, Farley had been confident that he wouldn't suffer any mental deterioration. Then a week ago the rodents had gone berserk, and Max had for-gotten the password to access his computer files.

Max stopped abruptly, stricken with the shakes as the memory of that traumatic moment rushed back. The trees seemed to close in around him, and he closed his eyes to shut out the claustrophobic illusion. He concentrated on breathing, trying to still his racing pulse as the horror of that fatal instant battered him again.

Max still didn't know how long he had stared at the blank rectangular box in the password access window on the computer screen before he stood up to get a cup of coffee. He had glanced at the lone rat left in the labora-

tory cage as he picked up the pot. The pitiful animal was
running in circles, chasing its tail, and slamming its head
into the glass.

Glass had always formed the boundaries of the rat's
world, and yet, it had forgotten the glass was there.

Just as he had forgotten the password he had been
using since they had set up shop in the old missile silo.

Max didn't forget things—ever. In that flash of insight
seven days ago, he had realized that his mind was failing,
too.

Layton was the key to whether or not the process of his
mental deterioration could be slowed, stopped, and perhaps reversed. The elastic mutant's mental and physical
condition was stable, which Farley insisted made him important to finding a fix. That, not the scientist's sensibili-
ties, was the only reason the lunatic Layton was still
alive.

"What's going on here?"

The sound of a man's voice brought Max to a halt just
before he broke from the trees. Hanging back, he peered
through a natural mesh of twig and leaf. A young man
wearing a CEP cap and jacket hurried across the field.
Max identified him as Gary Mundy, the environmental
agent mentioned in the newspaper article about Stoner's
death. Mundy must have been conducting tests in the
fallen farmer's field when he heard the animal squeals.
Max was too late to intercept the agent before he saw the
pile of mutilated rabbits.

Shocked into mute paralysis by the carnage, Mundy
didn't see Layton emerge from a hole in the ground behind him. The mutant had apparently slithered right into
the rabbits' burrows to grab them from their nests. Elon-

gated from head to toe and streaked with dirt, he still looked vaguely human as he shot across the furrowed ground.

Mundy yelped and dropped his soil sample tube as one of Layton's spaghetti-thin arms wrapped around his ankles. The agent toppled like a felled tree, and Layton's other arm snaked into his mouth, cutting off his air. The young man struggled for an agonizing moment before Layton crushed his ribs and tore into his flesh with his teeth.

As a precaution, Max waited until the mutant's murderous impulses had completely abated. He stepped out of the trees as Layton tossed Mundy's lacerated body onto the heap of dead rabbits.

Layton's stretched limbs and torso snapped back to normal when he saw Max. Knobby-kneed and gaunt, with stooped shoulders and a sunken stomach, the man's naked body was almost as grotesque as his misshapen alter-form.

"Come on, Layton. Time to get back inside." Max considered hiding Mundy's corpse but thought better of it. If the agent vanished, the authorities would mount a search of the area as soon as someone reported him missing. A broken body might prompt an investigation, but he could easily misdirect the search for evidence. With luck, the death would ultimately be classified as another unsolved, Smallville mystery.

"Hi, Max." Layton's words were slightly garbled, an effect of the mutation's diminished intelligence. "You mad?"

"No, I'm not mad." Max shook his head. Since Mundy had seen too much, Layton had saved him the trouble of killing the agent himself. "But I need you to do me a favor."

"Okay, Max." Dirty and docile, Layton patiently waited for instructions.

Instead of heading straight toward the chain-link fence that enclosed the old missile launch facility, Max retraced his path. He instructed Layton to slither behind and erase his footprints. With the sun sinking in the western sky, Max hurried on a circuitous route through the woods to Stoner's gravel driveway. Once there, he had Layton reform. As they headed across the field to the dirt access road, he walked in the naked man's tracks to obscure the impressions made by bare feet. His own boot prints were lost in the dozens left by the sheriff's deputies and paramedics the afternoon Stoner died.

Not all his bases had been covered yet, however. They still didn't know how much Clark Kent had actually seen that day that Stoner died.

"I didn't realize Jackie Chan was so funny." With both hands on the steering wheel and her attention on the road, Sharon laughed softly. "I thought his movies were just kung fu fights and stuff."

"You haven't seen a Jackie Chan film before?" Clark asked. He had suggested going to the martial arts comedy because it would be simple, entertaining fun. No depth, sap, or gory mayhem that would make either of them uncomfortable. He was uncomfortable enough without any external help.

"No, but I guess I should have," Sharon said. "Does he really do all his own stunts?"

"That's what they say." Clark shrugged. "I'm not sure."

For the first time since he had asked Sharon out, Clark started to relax. His parents' attempts to pry, without seeming to pry, had just added to his misgivings. He had been blunt, limiting his responses to Sharon's name, their destination, and estimated time of return. To avoid a full-scale interrogation, he had let Sharon drive instead of asking to borrow the family pickup. He had dashed outside the instant she pulled into the driveway, but his mom had not been able to resist peeking through the curtains. As they drove off in Sharon's 1987 Audi sedan, Martha Kent's curious gaze had burned into his neck with the intensity of an alien heat ray.

Clark couldn't tell if his mother and father were glad or sorry that he was making an effort to move beyond Lana. He hadn't known the answer to that himself—until now, after he had gone on an actual date with someone else.

Once Sharon Farley got over being shy, she was intelligent and pleasant with a witty sense of humor. He had enjoyed her company, but . . . she wasn't Lana.

Everyone close to him thought his infatuation with Lana was futile. Maybe it was, but he couldn't help how he felt. Eventually, he would resolve the emotional dilemma one way or another. He might even fall in love with someone else, but Sharon wasn't that someone.

Sharon sighed, as though she had just made a tough decision. "I'm not sure how to say this, Clark, but I was wondering—"

"About what?" Clark asked, anticipating an awkward

scene. He didn't want to hurt Sharon's feelings, but if she hinted about "doing this again," he'd have to be honest. It wouldn't be fair to lead her on.

Sharon sighed again, heavily. "Chloe's Wall of Weird."

Surprised, Clark hesitated. "Yeah?" He started. "What about it?"

"It's just so—creepy!" Sharon shivered with dread. "Don't you worry that something awful might happen to you?"

"Like growing an extra thumb or waking up covered with green spots?" Clark smiled, with relief, to put Sharon at ease, and to cover his unspoken lie. Unless fate was sitting on some additional surprises, being an alien who got sick around green meteor-rocks and mean around red ones seemed to be the extent of his Smallville maladies. "Not really."

"I wish I was that sure." Troubled, Sharon caught her lower lip in her teeth. "There're too many instances of strange things in this town to be coincidence. There must be a reason, some common denominator."

"Most people blame the fertilizer plant," Clark said. He didn't mention that his father was one of them.

Sharon frowned. "If chemicals got into the ground-water or something, that might account for some of the sicknesses."

"Except the county tests the water regularly, and no one's ever found proof of seepage from the plant," Clark explained. It wasn't right to give Sharon the impression that LexCorp was responsible for the strange things documented on Chloe's Wall of Weird.

"That doesn't exactly make me feel safer," Sharon said.

Clark understood her fear, but it was probably groundless. "You live in town, Sharon, a long way from the fertilizer plant."

Since Sharon had just moved into Lowell County, her susceptibility to the mutating effects of the meteor-rocks was minimal, too. The more severe molecular anomalies occurred in people who had lived through the meteor shower, particularly as young children. As long as she wasn't exposed to meteor-rocks for any length of time, Sharon should be okay. Unfortunately, he couldn't explain that without explaining Chloe's meteor theory, which might be more upsetting than reassuring.

"The Sheriff's Office here doesn't exactly instill confidence, either." Sharon's gaze flicked to Clark's face for an instant. "I did some checking. There have been dozens of unexplained deaths in Lowell County over the past several years, but it's like the local cops don't care."

"They care," Clark said. "It's just that this is a small farming community with limited resources. Unless it's an obvious murder, the sheriff can't afford to investigate."

"Well, Chloe hasn't ruled out foul play." Sharon's tone was casual, but she flashed him an impish smile. "And apparently, neither have you."

"What gave you that idea?" Clark was completely taken aback. He hadn't even considered murder as a possibility. He definitely hadn't said anything to suggest it.

"Mr. Stoner's autopsy lab report!" Sharon rolled her eyes. "You're obviously anxious to get the results."

"I'm curious," Clark admitted, with a shrug to mask his anxiety.

"Right." Sharon scoffed. "Chloe told me she has to be able to back up all her *Torch* stories with proof. I'm sure the high school newspaper doesn't have an eyewitness exclusive for very many dead guy articles."

More than you could possibly know.

"We've actually solved a couple cases at the *Torch*," Clark said with a touch of bravado. Sharon didn't seem to have a motive beyond idle curiosity, but he couldn't be sure. Instead of denying his interest, he tried to dilute the significance with mild bragging and truth that sounded like a lame excuse. "We just can't always print what we know or take credit."

"So you *do* think someone killed Mr. Stoner," Sharon said.

"I didn't say that," Clark hedged.

Sharon, however, was fixated on the idea of murder. She frowned as she mulled over the possibilities. "If someone slipped him poison, it would show up in the lab work."

"Yeah, but if the medical examiner suspected that, he would have asked the lab to do the work stat," Clark said. "Besides, if Chloe honestly thought Mr. Stoner had been murdered, she wouldn't care if Mr. Reynolds disapproved. She'd be hounding her friend for the lab results every hour on the hour."

"Chloe's interested," Sharon insisted. "I could tell."

Clark gave up trying to dissuade Sharon from her line of thought. However, she wasn't even warm about his interest in the case. Wondering if he could have saved Mr. Stoner was part of it, but that also served as a feasible cover story for Chloe. He couldn't tell Chloe he thought meteor material would turn up in Mr. Stoner's stomach because he couldn't explain why. Chloe didn't know meteor-rocks made him sick. The nausea he had felt near the farmer's body couldn't have been anything else, but he hadn't found any meteor fragments in Mr. Stoner's clothing. After the body was loaded into the ambulance, he had gone back to check the spot where the farmer had fallen. He had not gotten ill.

If Howard Stoner had died of natural causes or meteor-rock ingestion, then his father wouldn't have grounds to sue Lex. Clark hadn't mentioned that to Chloe or Pete, either. He was hoping his dad would give up the idea of a lawsuit before Lex found out about it through the local grapevine.

"I've never had a chance to work on something this important before, Clark." Sharon slowed the car as they approached the turn off onto Hickory Lane. "Chloe won't have a problem with that, will she?"

Since he wasn't sure how Chloe would feel, Clark glossed over the question. "Provided there *is* a story, it's hard to say. I know Chloe will be grateful if you do a good job on that cafeteria poll."

Sharon turned left onto Hickory Lane without asking if he wanted a coffee nightcap at the Talon. Clark's ego wasn't bruised because she didn't want to prolong the date. That was actually a relief. But it was marred by the suspicion that Sharon had ulterior motives for going on this date.

CHAPTER 6

Monday after school, Clark ran home by an alternate route to avoid the being seen by the CEP agent working at Stoner's farm. He wanted to get his chores out of the way before he met Chloe back at the *Torch*, and riding the bus took too long. Chad had promised to call her by five with an update on Howard Stoner's lab work.

Since the pickup wasn't parked in the driveway, Clark was surprised to see his father sitting at the kitchen table.

"Did Mom go somewhere?" Clark dropped his books on the stairs on his way to the refrigerator.

Jonathan frowned. "She's at Mrs. Bronson's having her secondhand clothes altered."

"Oh." Clark winced as he searched the open fridge for a quick snack.

Since they needed his mother's paycheck from Lionel to keep the farm going, she had refused to invest in a new business wardrobe. She was a capable seamstress, but she no longer had time to make her own clothes. Instead, she spent an occasional Saturday shopping at thrift stores and outlet malls in the Metropolis suburbs. On her last outing, she had been thrilled to find three outfits that were practically new and only needed minimal alterations.

Martha Kent viewed the bargain-hunting expeditions as a challenging game. His dad felt humiliated by the necessity but tried not to show it. He didn't always succeed.

Jonathan answered the phone as Clark emptied the milk carton into a glass.

"Mr. Small! Thanks for returning my call." Jonathan sat back. "Henry, then."

Clark listened as he made himself a cheese and peanut butter sandwich, a flavor combination no one else on Earth seemed to enjoy as much as he did.

Henry Small, a direct descendant of the town's founding family, was an attorney, environmental activist, and outspoken opponent of the Luthor corporations' unchecked polluting practices. He was also Lana's biological father. According to her, Mr. Small had forsaken the prestige of editing a law journal to handle hopeless cause cases from his home.

Clark sat down with his milk and sandwich as his dad finished outlining the situation.

"I've talked to every lawyer in Smallville and Metropolis who isn't on a Luthor payroll, Henry," Jonathan explained. "Most of them don't want to be on the Luthors' black list for any price. The rest want more money than I make in a year as a retainer."

Chewing slowly, Clark felt a ray of hope. Maybe he was worried for no reason. His father *couldn't* sue Lex-Corp if he couldn't find a lawyer to take the case.

Jonathan wouldn't be much better off if Mr. Small agreed to represent him. According to Mrs. Small, the lost cause advocate had the attention span of a gnat. His interest in anything was subject to abrupt shifts that left his clients and cases hanging. Lana wasn't convinced his wife's assessment was accurate, but the jury on that one was still out.

Clark fine-tuned his hearing to pick up the lawyer's voice.

"Have you thought about mounting a class action

suit?" Mr. Small asked. "That would reduce the amount each individual has to pay."

"I thought of that and made some calls." Jonathan picked up his pen and tapped the pad in front of him. The repetitive motion helped defuse his anger. "Nobody will join a case against the town's main employer."

"I know." Mr. Small sighed. "I have a hard time getting anyone to sign a petition that involves the plant. Can't say that I blame them."

Clark couldn't, either. With the possible exception of the weather, the LexCorp fertilizer plant was the single most important factor in Smallville's economy.

"Except that people are dying." Jonathan's expression had shifted from hopeful to discouraged to grave during the course of the discussion. Now his jaw flexed with determination.

Clark washed down the sandwich with the last swallow of milk. The look on his father's face did not bode well for the Kents's meager fortunes. In spite of the obstacles, his dad wasn't even close to giving up.

It isn't just the possibility of losing the farm that bothers me, either, Clark realized. He hated being torn between Lex and his father, and a legal dispute was too important to avoid choosing sides. And this time, unless irrefutable proof of Lex's guilt turned up, he was afraid his father was on the wrong side.

"Something killed Howard Stoner, Henry," Jonathan continued, "and that farm is a little too close to mine not to be concerned."

"Did the medical examiner find anything that supports chemical poisoning as the cause of death?" Mr. Small asked.

"The lab reports won't be in until later today or tomorrow," Jonathan said.

And with any luck they'll get Lex and me off the hook, Clark thought. He sped to put his glass and plate in the sink and returned to his seat without missing a word.

Mr. Small hesitated before suggesting, "You could give Joe Reisler a call."

"Reisler? That name sounds familiar." Jonathan wedged the phone between his shoulder and chin as he jotted it on the pad.

"Football." Mr. Small laughed. "Joe played defense for Middleton back in the late eighties. He blew out a knee his senior year at Kansas State and couldn't go pro."

"I'm sorry," Jonathan said, his expression puzzled.

"So was he, but he got student loans to finance the rest of his education," Mr. Small said. "His dad was a military man. Worked on missile maintenance as I recall."

"And why should I call Mr. Reisler?" Jonathan asked.

"Joe just passed the bar and opened a one-man law office on Bison Boulevard in Middleton," Mr. Small said. "I know he could use the work. I just don't know if he wants to kick off his career by taking on the Luthors."

Clark wasn't sure how to view being referred to another attorney by Mr. Small. It was possible he recognized his own limitations and honestly wanted Jonathan Kent to have decent legal representation in a fight against Lex Luthor. Or maybe he already knew the case was a lost cause.

"Nothing ventured." Jonathan smiled. "Thanks, Henry. I'll get in touch with him this afternoon."

"So you're really serious about suing Lex, huh?" Clark asked after his dad disconnected.

"Yes, Clark, I am," Jonathan said.

"Why now?" Clark was honestly perplexed. Other opportunities to file lawsuits against the Luthor corporations had come and gone for various reasons, usually lack of evidence. The difference this time eluded him.

"Because I'm tired of being a helpless bystander when disaster strikes." Weariness and stress accented the lines farm life had prematurely etched in Jonathan's face. "I can't fight tornadoes or a rotten economy or a political juggernaut that pays back agribusiness contributors at the expense of family farmers."

"What does that have to do with Lex?"

"Nothing and everything." Jonathan exhaled, as though struggling to find the right words. "Lionel didn't escape the tornado unscathed, but going blind didn't ruin his life. It's inconvenient, but not totally debilitating because he can afford every technological advance science develops. If money is the only thing standing between Lionel Luthor and a cure, he'll get the cure. How many other people do you know who could say the same thing?"

"None, but—"

Jonathan cut off Clark's argument. "The point is that they *are* responsible for some of the disasters that strike this town, Clark. And they'll just go on buying their way out of problems that ruin other people's lives unless someone takes a stand to stop them."

" 'Someone' meaning you."

"Apparently if I don't do it, no one will." Jonathan's bitter disappointment at the lack of community interest in joining a class action suit was evident in his clipped tone.

"And working through the courts is the only way to beat them."

"If Lex is guilty," Clark added. He couldn't betray truth and justice just to make a point, and neither could his father.

"That's up to a judge and jury to decide, isn't it?" Jonathan keyed the number for information into the phone. "Middleton, Kansas. New listing for Joe Reisler, Attorney-at-Law."

After his father finished writing down the telephone number, Clark gripped his arm to stop him from dialing. "Shouldn't we wait until the lab report comes back? Just in case Mr. Stoner died of some natural cause?"

"I might have to wait a couple days for an appointment, Clark. I can always cancel."

"Do we really want to pay for a cancellation?" Clark didn't know if Joe Reisler charged for consultations or broken appointments. He just wanted his dad to stop and think before he did something he couldn't undo. One thing wasn't in doubt. Within a few hours of making an appointment to see Joe Reisler, Lex would know that Jonathan Kent intended to sue him.

"All right. One more day can't hurt." Jonathan stood up and put the phone back on the base to recharge. "If you need me for anything, I'll be mending the fence in the back pasture."

Clark finished his chores before his father's tractor reached the crest of the hill. He was halfway to Smallville before Jonathan drove into the north pasture.

CHAPTER 7

"Hey, Chloe!" Sharon breezed into the *Torch* office. "Got a minute?"

Chloe noted the girl's perky attitude and forced a tight smile. In snug designer jeans with a T-top and matching bell-sleeved cover-up, Sharon defined casual style. If she knew she was knockout gorgeous, she didn't show it, which made it really hard to dislike her.

"Sure, Sharon," Chloe said. "What's up?"

"Nothing in particular." Sharon paused to read a flyer for the Public Library Book Fair tacked on the wall by the door. "Just thought I'd drop by, in case you needed help with anything."

"Oh, well—" Chloe shrugged. "Nothing comes to mind right now."

"Oh." Sharon sank into the chair where Clark usually sat. "Well, uh—maybe I could write a review of the movie Clark and I saw Saturday."

"There's an idea." Chloe nodded, her smile frozen. Sharon's sunny demeanor suggested to Chloe that the evening had not been a disaster. For a moment, Chloe was sorry she had given Sharon a trial week at the *Torch*, but she was a woman of her word, and that was that. Besides, Clark's love life was none of her business.

Not anymore, Chloe thought, trying not to glare at the girl with the telltale, bright-eyed glow. Sharon looked just as Chloe had felt while dancing with Clark at the Spring Formal.

A back issue I am not going to open—ever again. She

meant it. Clark Kent was old news in the Chloe Sullivan archives. *End of story, exclamation point.*

"Maybe it could be a regular thing," Sharon suggested in earnest. "A girl's take on guy flicks or something."

Chloe loved the idea, but she blurted out the other thought that popped into her mind. "Clark asked you out to the movies again next weekend?"

"No." Sharon shook her head, but she didn't seem upset.

Did that mean Sharon expected Clark to ask or that she didn't care if he didn't? Chloe didn't want to admit it, but she really hoped the Sharon/Clark thing fizzled quickly. Wondering about it was way too distracting.

"I was also wondering—" Sharon hesitated, as though she didn't know how to phrase what she wanted to say.

"What?" Chloe inhaled sharply, expecting a bomb-shell. "Please, don't tell me you hate doing the cafeteria poll."

"The poll?" Sharon waved away Chloe's concern. "No, that went great. I must have asked over fifty kids about the closed campus thing today."

Not bad for a shy, retiring type, Chloe thought. For someone who had tried to fade into the walls for three months, Sharon was demonstrating a remarkable gift for gab.

"The results aren't exactly a surprise," Sharon added.

"Everyone hates it, right?" Chloe hadn't chosen the topic to find out what the student body thought. She had picked it to test how open-minded Principal Reynolds really was about *Torch* content. The lockdown policy had been his first official act when he had replaced Mr. Kwan as principal.

"Ninety percent opposed," Sharon said.

Chloe blinked. "Actually, that is a little surprising. What did the other ten percent say?"

"No comment." Sharon grinned. "I told everyone the poll was anonymous, but some people just didn't want to take a chance. I bet Mr. Reynolds isn't as tough as he looks, but—"

A tone on the computer cut Sharon off and alerted Chloe to incoming mail. As she was about to click the new mail icon, Sharon abruptly changed the subject.

"Do you know what time Clark called 911 when he found Mr. Stoner?"

"Around four-thirty, wasn't it?" Curious, Chloe minimized the Internet program and opened her Howard Stoner file. She had saved every reference she had collected on the incident. "According to the dispatcher's report, he called at four-forty. Why?"

"Wow. You really do have sources everywhere." When Chloe arched a questioning eyebrow, Sharon added, "Pete mentioned it." She suddenly glanced at the clock and gasped. "Uh-oh. I didn't realize it was so late. I've got to get home."

"But—" Chloe rose as Sharon dashed for the door. The girl hadn't explained why she was interested in Clark's 911 call. "Clark will be here any minute if there's something else you want to know."

"Can't." Sharon paused in the doorway. "I promised Dad I'd stop at the store. Tell Clark I'll see him tomorrow!" She vanished from view, then ducked back. "He can call me tonight—or I'll call him. Either way."

"Uh-huh." Chloe settled into her chair again with the uneasy feeling that something about Sharon was off. The girl seemed to switch personalities as often as other people changed clothes. The once shy, overly curious, and suddenly ditzy shtick reeked of phony. Chloe was so deep in thought she didn't hear Clark come in.

"Clark to Chloe. Come in, Chloe."

"Huh?" Chloe looked up to see Clark waving at her. She did not mince words or beat around the bush. "Why would Sharon Farley want to know what time you called 911 about Mr. Stoner?"

"She probably thinks it works into her murder theory somehow." Clark shrugged with a tolerant smile. "She's got investigative reporter-itis as bad as you do."

"What makes you say that?" Chloe asked, curious.

Clark sat in the chair Sharon had just vacated. "I think she went out with me to get close to you. Because you call the shots at the *Torch*."

"No way." Chloe kept her expression neutral. Clark didn't need to know she was glad that Sharon's motives might not be romantic.

"I swear." Clark held up his right hand. "She wants to work on the story with your blessing."

Chloe was flattered, relieved, and annoyed. Wanting into the inner circles of the *Torch* explained Sharon's incongruous personality shifts and why she had become so friendly so fast. Chloe didn't necessarily approve of Sharon's using Clark to advance her journalism career at Smallville High, but she understood it.

"Does Sharon know something we don't?" Chloe asked.

Clark shook his head. "Don't think so. She wants to be a reporter, and she hasn't lived here long enough to know that Mr. Stoner's death is probably just a—death."

"Maybe, maybe not." Chloe had lived in Smallville long enough to know that most things weren't as obvious as they seemed on the surface.

"Any word from Chad?" Clark asked.

"Oh!" Chloe's head snapped up. "I just got an e-mail from someone. One sec."

Chloe brought the Internet screen back up and clicked for her e-mail listings. The new message wasn't from her friend at the Medical Examiner's Office, however. It was a Breaking News memo from Paul Treadwell, the morning news guy at KTOW. The local AM station sent bulletins to subscribers when newsworthy events happened in Lowell County.

"Oh, my God." Chloe stared at the screen. "That CEP agent was found dead in Stoner's field this afternoon."

"Gary Mundy?" Jumping up, Clark rounded the desk. He rested his arm on the back of her chair and read over her shoulder.

Chloe's detective synapses fired up as she skimmed the text. The sheriff had gone out to the farm after the Center for Environmental Protection in Metropolis had notified him that Gary Mundy was missing. The agent hadn't checked in since Saturday noon, right before he left for the field.

Chloe read the last sentence aloud. " 'The badly bruised and lacerated body was lying on a mound of dead rabbits.' "

"That doesn't happen every day," Clark said.

"No, it doesn't." Frowning, Chloe minimized the e-mail window and opened another bookmarked file. "And neither do a couple of other weird things that have happened around here in the past three weeks."

"Like what?" Clark asked.

"Like all of Wilma Roman's rosebushes were pulled up by the roots and torn apart." Chloe clicked links to the relevant *Smallville Ledger* articles as she talked. "Bob Gunderson found two cows dead one morning. Their windpipes were crushed. Donna Bell's apple tree was stripped of fruit, and Marvin Cates found dead snakes in his shed."

Clark whistled. "Not a typical crime spree."

"Nope." Chloe blew a lock of hair off her forehead. "And now we've got *two* guys who died in the same field."

Clark glanced at the time. "It's almost 5:00 P.M. Can you get in touch with Chad?"

"If I don't hear from him before he leaves work, I can call him at home later," Chloe said as she leaned back. She had been speaking in generalities when she had told Sharon she hadn't ruled out foul play in Mr. Stoner's death. For one thing, there hadn't been an apparent motive. However, if the rabbits were a hint, maybe motive didn't apply. Maybe the killer just liked to kill stuff.

"Do you have to go anywhere right now?" Chloe asked.

"No, I've got some free time," Clark said. "Why?"

"Two computers doing an Internet search are faster than one," Chloe explained. Although the recent wave of destruction had the stamp of Smallville strange all over it, it would help to know if a similar pattern of crimes had happened anywhere else.

Clark sat back down at the other desk and stretched to limber up. "What do you want to know?"

Are you going to ask Sharon out again?

"Start with these and see what turns up." Chloe scribbled several search reference phrases on a piece of paper and handed it to him.

"Hi, Lana."

Lana didn't recognize the voice until she turned and saw the new girl sitting at a table near the cash register. "Hi, Sharon."

"You remembered my name!" Sharon grinned, pleased. "Are you busy?"

"Well, I, uh—" Lana faltered.

She hadn't seen Clark all weekend, but Chloe had filled her in on the latest, disturbing developments. Sharon had a crush on Clark, and Pete had convinced him to ask her out. Lana knew she couldn't complain because Clark had taken someone to the movies. Since she hadn't come to terms with Whitney's death or sorted out her feelings for Clark, their relationship had been stuck in friendship limbo. She had no right to interfere with his personal life. *And I have nothing to say to his new girl-friend.*

"I just wanted to apologize," Sharon said.

"What for?" Lana frowned, puzzled.

"For seeming like a totally conceited snob." Sharon glanced around the nearly empty restaurant. "Can you sit a minute?"

"Sure." Lana couldn't bring herself to be rude. As Chloe had pointed out, Sharon didn't know about her long, sometimes tense, never boring, often awkward friendship with Clark Kent. Besides, the Talon was in an obvious lull between the after-school rush and the after-dinner coffee-and-dessert crowd. She couldn't use being busy as an excuse. "For a minute."

"Thanks." Sharon took a deep breath. "I didn't mean to ignore everyone. It just takes me a while to get to know people. Like my father, I guess. We moved to Smallville because he wanted to write in 'quiet obscurity.'"

"Being the new kid in town must be hard," Lana said, smiling. "I should be the one apologizing—for not trying to get to know you."

"I miss my old friends, but—" Sharon shrugged. "I'm just glad we're getting acquainted now. I know you and Chloe and Clark and Pete have all been friends like forever."

"Seems that way sometimes." Lana started to rise. "We'll have to talk again soon, but right now, I really should—"

"I'm working on a story for the *Torch*," Sharon announced. "I never expected to find anyone in Smallville that wants to be a reporter as much as I do."

"Clark?" Lana knew he was thinking about studying journalism in college. She just hadn't realized he had made up his mind.

"No, Chloe." Sharon exhaled. "I'm really going to have to hustle to keep up with her."

"Oh, right." Nodding, Lana settled back. Sharon wanted to talk, and since she hadn't made an effort to be friendly before, the least Lana could do was listen for a few minutes.

"Clark is nice," Sharon said. "A little closed off, though."

"You noticed?" Lana quipped.

"Hard not to." Sharon shook her head slightly. "I tried getting him to talk about finding Mr. Stoner for my article, but he didn't have a lot to say."

"Maybe there isn't much to tell," Lana suggested.

"That's probably it, but you just never know where you're going to end up once you start stringing the facts together." Sharon sipped her soda. "Are you sure he left here at four-twenty-five that day?"

"Yes, positive—" Lana hesitated. She didn't appreciate being pumped for information on the pretense of friendship. However, before she could get up to leave, Sharon suddenly remembered that she was in a hurry to get home.

"When my dad gets into his writing, he forgets to eat." Sharon grabbed her books and stood up. "Seriously. I've got to go. Thanks, Lana."

Lana watched the girl leave feeling slightly stunned. Except for the fact that she hadn't given away any deep dark secrets, the encounter left her with a sense of having been scammed.

Or maybe jealousy was clouding her judgment. *That* was a secret she had no intention of sharing with anyone.

CHAPTER 8

Pete grimaced at his plate. "I am so tired of eating hamburgers that could pass as hockey pucks."

"It's Tuesday, Pete." Clark pulled two tuna sandwiches out of the brown bag lunch his mom had prepared that morning.

"Exactly." Pete threw up his hands. "Every other Tuesday it's the same thing: hamburgers on stale buns with beans and fries. How come they never change the menu?"

"So I won't have to retype it every other week," Clark replied, grinning as he handed Pete one of his mother's homemade chocolate chip cookies. "Whenever you get tired of Tuesday hamburgers just remember that white-paste glop they gave us last Wednesday."

"Actually, except for the burned toast, I didn't think it was that bad." Pete took the cookie and set it aside. "My great-uncle Willie used to make something just like it."

Clark shuddered. "Must be an acquired taste, then."

"Must be." Pete took a bite of hamburger and scanned the cafeteria as he chewed. "I see Sharon's still conducting Chloe's closed campus policy poll."

Clark nodded as he followed Pete's gaze. Sharon was moving from person to person with a smile and a clipboard. He wondered how she remembered the people she had already asked and how much Chloe cared about accuracy.

"I told her the way to Chloe's editorial heart was through the student survey," Clark said.

"I don't think it's *Chloe's* heart she cares about." Pete grinned and picked up a fry.

Anticipating another interrogation about past or future dates, Clark tried to cap Pete's curiosity with the same ploy he had used on Chloe. "Sharon's an aspiring news hound. She's more interested in getting in good with Chloe than going out with me."

"Oh, yeah, right." Pete rolled his eyes, then nodded toward the door. "Looks like something lit a fire under our fearless *Torch* editor."

Clark turned to look as Chloe rushed into the cafeteria. Sharon noticed her, too, and followed.

"News conference. Right now." Chloe stopped at the head of the table, unaware that the other girl was behind her. It was too late to retract.

"Is this about Mr. Stoner?" Sharon's eyes shone with excitement as she sat in the chair beside Clark.

"Uh—yeah, but it's not for public consumption." Chloe shot Clark a helpless look.

"Oh, right." Sharon snapped a clean piece of paper over the poll on her clipboard and whispered. "Is it okay if I take notes?"

Clark shrugged. He didn't see any gracious way to cut Sharon out of the discussion. However, it was Chloe's call to hold back whatever she had learned until later or bring Sharon in now. She opted to bring Sharon in.

"I got the lab results back from Chad," Chloe said.

"And?" Sharon leaned forward.

Chloe lowered her voice. "They found meteor dust in Howard Stoner's lungs."

Sharon inhaled softly.

"Really?" Clark acted mildly surprised, but that's what

he had expected. The presence of meteor particles in Mr. Stoner's lungs explained why he had felt sick when he tried to resuscitate the dead farmer.

"How does someone get meteor dust in his lungs?" Pete asked.

"The dust must be in the field," Sharon said. "Those clippings on Chloe's Wall of Weird said the meteors hit all around Smallville."

Although Clark hadn't felt sick anywhere except near the body, he also hadn't walked every square inch of the field. So Sharon's theory was not outside the realm of possibility. Mr. Stoner hadn't grown anything in that particular field as far back as he could remember. Given the varied effects meteor material could have on living things, the farmer might have given up planting the field if his crops repeatedly died or rotted.

Pete squinted. "I suppose he could have kicked up a cloud of the stuff and inhaled it. Is that what killed him?"

"They don't know why he stopped breathing, but that's one theory." Chloe paused to look at each one in turn. "That's not all, though."

"What else?" Clark asked.

"They put a rush on the CEP agent's lab work because his death was so violent," Chloe continued. "They found meteor dust and traces of human saliva in Mr. Mundy's wounds. Someone used teeth to rip his body open after he choked to death."

"Oh, gross!" Sharon gagged and clutched her stomach as though she was going to be sick.

Clark sympathized, but he didn't try to temper Sharon's horrifying introduction to Smallville reality. Dealing with gruesome facts was common in the *Torch* regulars' experience. The newcomer would either drop out or learn to cope.

"Was there dust in his lungs, too?" Pete asked. The last bite of his hamburger vanished into his mouth.

"His throat, but that's not all." Chloe was bursting with her news. "There's an old missile silo just beyond Mr. Stoner's field, and guess who owns it?"

"Lex Luthor," Clark said. "It was actually a missile launch facility, but they never equipped it with launch keys. There was an armed Minuteman II in the silo for years, though, until 1994."

"Armageddon on our doorstep, and no one ever knew!" Pete quipped. "How come *you* know so much, Clark?"

"Yeah." Chloe was obviously annoyed that he had stolen her thunder about the military installation in Lex Luthor's corporate inventory. "Show off."

Sharon appeared to be in shock. Her face was ashen, and she swallowed hard. Apparently, the luster had suddenly worn off her romantic notions about reporting on murder and malice. Still, considering the serious, bizarre twists the situation had taken, Clark thought she was holding up fairly well.

"I checked it out a long time ago," Clark explained. "The land and the installation reverted to LuthorCorp when the government stripped the facility and moved out. Lex took possession when he bought the plant."

"Which doesn't explain how Chloe's nose for news caught the scent and tracked it down," Pete observed. "I mean, how do you make the leap from meteor dust in a dead farmer's lungs to a missile silo?"

Chloe's deflated ego was forgotten as she briefed Pete

and Sharon on the unusual vandalism occurring around Smallville the past couple weeks. "When Clark and I didn't turn up any other flora and fauna crime clusters, I started a random search for meteor references using some new key words, like 'military response.'"

"Those results must have been interesting." Pete pushed his plate aside and folded his arms on the table.

"Actually, not very." Chloe sighed. "NORAD knew the meteors were meteors, so they didn't even scramble jets to investigate."

Good thing. Clark shuddered to think what might have happened if the Air Force had found him and his spaceship instead of Martha and Jonathan Kent.

"There wouldn't have been much point to shooting rocks out of the sky," Chloe added.

"Probably not." Pete exchanged a quick glance with Clark before turning back to Chloe. "But I still don't get the interest in an old abandoned missile site."

"Lex owns it," Chloe said. "What if LexCorp is using the old launch facility for some dangerous new project?"

"Wait a minute." Sharon sat back, raising her hands in a braking gesture. "Isn't that jumping to conclusions? You're talking about a corporation with a whole lot to lose and tons of resources, Chloe. We're just high school kids! Even if you're right, how could we possibly prove it?"

"I agree," Clark said. He held Chloe's gaze, hoping she got the message to tone it down. The preconceived notions of Luthor guilt that dominated much of Smallville's thinking hadn't influenced Sharon's perspective.

Chloe glared at Clark, bristling. "Tackling the tough stories separates the pros from the amateurs."

Chloe's reaction took Clark by surprise. He hadn't meant to insult her. He was just tired of the knee-jerk accusations against Lex every time something weird happened.

"Maybe," Sharon countered defensively, not realizing that Chloe's barbed comment had been aimed at him, not her. "But if people get sick and die around meteor-rocks, I don't want to go anywhere near them."

So much for protecting Sharon from Chloe's theory. Clark hadn't said a word about it, but the girl was sharp. She had connected the dots between the Wall of Weird and the dual meteor dust references in the autopsy lab reports to make a logical—albeit flawed—assumption.

"Unless you drink meteor-grown vegetable shakes like someone we used to know," Pete explained, "you don't have to worry, Sharon."

"Right." Chloe made an effort to sound positive. "The meteor-rocks are safe unless you're mega-exposed somehow."

"Like a lot of kids who grew up here, who were little kids when the meteors struck in 1989," Pete added.

"But even *that's* just a theory," Clark said. Although the growing body of evidence supported Chloe's conclusions, Sharon was already worried about chemical contamination from the plant. Since she had to live in Smallville, it seemed cruel to scare her without cause. Her dad's rented house was located in a neighborhood that hadn't sustained a direct meteor hit.

"If it'll make everyone feel better," Clark said, "I'll ask Lex if anything's happening at the old silo."

"Would he tell you?" Sharon asked.

"No way!" Pete scoffed. "If something's going on nobody knows about, it's probably illegal. Believe me, Lex Luthor won't say or do anything that might hurt Lex Luthor."

"But it can't hurt to try, Clark," Chloe said. "I wouldn't bet money, but you're probably the only one Lex would tell."

Clark didn't bother arguing, but he was plagued by some troubling thoughts as he headed to class.

He didn't take the route past Stoner's farm home very often, not unless he had to avoid being seen by someone like the surveyor. Lex could have moved half the plant into the launch facility without his knowing it. Last Thursday he hadn't seen anything that indicated the silo was being used—except the flattened weeds in the dirt access road. That was probably worth checking out, regardless of what Lex had to say.

Although Clark didn't dwell on it, neither he nor Lex had perfect records when it came to honesty. The difference was that Lex's personal survival didn't depend on his lies. Lex knew he had come close to losing Clark's trust and friendship when he had hired Roger Nixon to investigate the Old Mill Bridge accident and the Kents' family history. Clark wanted to believe that Lex wouldn't risk lying to him again.

Asking about the silo wasn't the only reason Clark wanted to visit the Luthor mansion. If Lex hadn't yet heard about Jonathan Kent's plan to sue, Clark had to decide whether or not to tell him. As the discussion with Chloe had just shown, the presence of meteor dust in the bodies cast doubt, but did not eliminate Lex as a suspect. However, since the lab reports hadn't provided absolute proof, he hoped to talk his father out of filing the lawsuit.

And if he couldn't?

Clark wondered how he'd feel.

He was certain that if the roles were reversed, he'd rather find out he was being sued from the friend who was suing him than from a stranger.

Wouldn't he?

Martha Kent kept the heavy roll of fencing wire standing upright while her husband stretched an unwound portion between posts. The spring tornado had torn out miles of fence on the Kent farm. Insurance had covered the cost of new materials and labor, but they had elected to do the work themselves rather than hire a contractor. Although it had taken months longer, replacement would be complete within a week or two. The money they saved had gone into Clark's college fund.

"Such as it is," Martha muttered. Every night she prayed that Clark would earn an academic scholarship. He could not accept one for athletics because of his unearthly, natural advantage.

"Did you say something, Martha?" Jonathan wiped his forehead with the back of his leather-gloved hand as he glanced back.

"Just muttering to myself, Jonathan." Beyond him, Martha saw a hyperwind cut a path through the corn. "There's Clark!"

Jonathan and Martha both held on to their hats as Clark braked between them.

"Hey, son." Jonathan waved at the wire. "Give me a hand with this, will you?"

"Sure." Clark grabbed the wire in his bare hands and pulled it taut between posts. He held it in place while his father secured it with U-shaped brads. "The lab report on Mr. Stoner came back today."

Jonathan nodded. "I heard. Mr. Mundy, too. Both bodies contained meteor particles."

"Right." Clark took a breath. "So it probably isn't Lex's fault."

"Clark—" Martha smiled tightly. Things were tense enough without having additional strain between father and son. "We've already discussed it."

The look of hopeful relief on Clark's face became worried frustration when he caught her meaning. Martha understood. Nothing she had said all afternoon had made a dent in Jonathan's stubborn determination to proceed with the lawsuit.

"I'm calling Joe Reisler tomorrow." Jonathan gave the first brad a final whack with the hammer.

Martha saw Clark's jaw flex and sighed. Jonathan and his adopted child did not have a single drop of blood in common, yet they were so much alike in so many ways. Jonathan always tightened his jaw when he had made up his mind to do something he knew he shouldn't.

Like sue Lex Luthor.

Clark had decided to dig in his heels on the other side of the argument.

"Lex didn't drop the meteor-rocks on Smallville, Dad," Clark said with commendable calm. "So I don't understand how you expect to connect him to Mr. Stoner's death."

"Two words, Clark." Jonathan held another brad in place and swung the hammer with a steady hand. Whack!

A second swing embedded the curved top of the brad in the wooden post. He reached into his pocket, pulled out another brad, and held the prongs against the post. "Level Three." Whack!

The hammer hit the brad with such force, Martha could almost feel her teeth rattle in her head. Clark didn't flinch, but his frown indicated his dad had scored a point.

When Lionel Luthor was running the fertilizer plant, he had authorized experiments on corn in a secret, underground level of the plant. Earl Jenkins, a family friend who had once worked on the Kent farm, had been working in the area when an explosion occurred. The blast left Earl with thousands of meteor particles embedded in his skin. He still suffered from violent shaking episodes as his body attempted to purge the foreign substance.

"It's not out of the question, Clark," Martha said gently.

She knew how much her son valued his friendship with Lex. While she didn't trust the young Luthor as implicitly as Clark, she respected the bond. However, now that she knew firsthand how Lionel operated, she couldn't deny that both men were probably capable of despicable things.

"What if it isn't Lex?" Clark looked up, his expression hopeful. "What if the dust is in the field? Some of the meteors were pulverized when they hit."

Martha suspected he was grasping at straws in a desperate attempt to put his father's intentions on hold. She didn't interfere.

Jonathan nodded. "I suppose that's possible."

Clark jumped through the verbal opening. "Just give me one more day to find proof—one way or another."

Martha saw a fleeting, uncertain frown cross Jonathan's face and crossed her fingers behind her back.

"How are you going to do that?" Jonathan's voice oozed skepticism, but Clark was undeterred.

"For starters, I'll ask Lex." Clark hastened to add, "I was going over there anyway, to ask about that old missile installation for Chloe."

"I'd forgotten all about the missile silo," Martha said. The launch facility was a chilling reminder of her terror the day of the meteor shower.

She and Jonathan had been driving along Route 19 when the first meteor hit. For a few seconds, she had thought the United States was under attack, that the disintegrating Soviet Union had decided to collapse with a nuclear bang. She had cast a spilt-second glance across acres of corn toward the underground military installation, fully expecting to see the Minuteman II roar out of the ground on its unthinkable mission of mutual annihilation. The destruction wrought by the flaming rocks had been devastating, but the community had recovered.

Nothing would have survived the horror of the other scenario.

Jonathan walked to the tractor to refill his pocket with brads. He paused to stare across the pasture for a moment then looked back at Clark. "Howard Stoner had a thing about protecting that missile silo."

"Yeah, I know. He used to chase me away. I always thought it was funny because Mr. Stoner didn't know I could rip the entry hatch off its hinges." Clark laughed warmly at the memory of the farmer. "I guess he took his patriotic duty very seriously."

"He did." Martha agreed with a smile. "Although I

think he may have missed getting a monthly check from the government more."

"Check for what?" Clark asked.

Jonathan shook his head as he trudged back to the fence. "The government paid LuthorCorp and Howard Stoner *not* to use the fields that bordered the missile site. The money was just pocket change to Lionel, but it probably accounted for half of Howard's annual income."

"Losing it must have hurt," Clark said.

Martha nodded. "Yes, but it didn't stop Howard from making sure that local kids didn't break in and tear the place apart."

"So you'll give me another day?" Clark's dark eyes twinkled as he suddenly shifted course.

"He's just going to keep pestering you if you don't agree, Jonathan," Martha said.

Jonathan raised his eyes and hands to the sky in surrender. "All right! One more day." He pointed the hammer at Clark. "One!"

CHAPTER 9

Standing outside the closed door into Lex Luthor's office, Clark paused to cement his resolve. He could think of fifty other places he'd rather be than the mahogany halls of his friend's home. The interior of the Scottish castle, which Lionel had transported across the Atlantic and half the North American continent in crates, was as imposing as the illusion of regal impregnability the structure's turreted design, stone façade, and sheer mass created.

Ordinarily, Clark enjoyed walking through the spacious rooms and down the long halls. He was always spotting some antique knickknack or carved design in the woodwork that he hadn't noticed before. Most days, however, he wasn't trying to find out if Lex was guilty of some horrendous misdeed. He needed a moment to compose the least offensive way to say what he had come to say.

Since he couldn't see through the decorative cut glass in the door with normal sight, Clark focused his X-ray vision.

Lex Luthor was seated at his desk with his feet propped up. He raised a glass to his mouth without turning his head from the laptop computer in front of him. Since alcohol dulled his mental edge, Lex didn't drink while he was working. At least Clark wouldn't be interrupting anything important.

"Come on in, Clark!" Lex called, his voice muted by the door.

Clark sighed. The current butler wasn't as lax as some

Lex had employed and had used the intercom to announce Clark's arrival. As he opened the door, Lex swung his feet to the floor.

"Did you get lost?" Lex arched an eyebrow. Beneath an expanse of scalp unadorned by hair, the subtle gesture seemed amplified.

"No. Just not in a hurry," Clark said.

"Because your father is thinking about suing me?" The calm timbre of Lex's voice held steady, but Clark did not mistake that for a clue regarding his mood. At their most vicious, both Luthors were portraits of quiet control.

Clark dropped into a chair and clasped his hands between his knees. "I was hoping you hadn't heard, yet."

"Jeff Carter of Carter and Swain in Metropolis called me yesterday." Lex swirled the ice in his glass. "Probably the instant your dad hung up. For the record, they'll have points deducted for betraying a prospective client's confidence."

"You don't seem upset." Clark sat back and rested his arms on the sides of the upholstered chair.

"I'm not." Lex pushed the laptop aside, clearing his view of Clark.

"Why not?" Clark knew better than to second-guess Lex Luthor's motives.

"For one thing, your father is an idealist, who believes that everyone is innocent until proven guilty," Lex said. "And while he may have an irrational dedication to principles that conflict with his own best interests at times, he is not a foolish man. Jonathan Kent won't sue me or anyone else without proof, and there isn't any."

"You saw the lab reports, too?" Clark asked.

"On advice of my attorneys, I can't discuss it." Lex

rose to top off his drink. "The CEP inquiry is still open, and LexCorp has other, unsettled complaints. My PR Department is already over budget for the year."

Clark just nodded. Trying to understand the complexities of Lex's financial empire would give him a headache, if he could get headaches.

"Would you like something?" Lex replaced the stopper in the decanter of Scotch. "Soft drink? Water?"

"No, thanks." Clark shook his head. "I have another question, though."

"What's on your mind?" Lex took a healthy swallow of the amber liquor, undaunted by the fiery bite.

Clark opted for blunt candor. "Have you expanded the plant's research and development operations into that old missile installation?"

"No."

Clark watched Lex's face, but there was no hesitation, no shift of the eyes or other sign that he was lying.

Lex's brows knit. "Why?"

"Just heard some casual speculation," Clark said. That was a partial truth, but he would be more specific if Lex asked.

Apparently satisfied, Lex didn't follow up. He walked back to his desk and turned the laptop toward Clark. A detailed graphic of a woodland scene complete with a mounted knight, horse-drawn coach, and wildlife was displayed on the screen.

"Have you ever tried one of these on-line role-playing games?" Lex asked.

"The monthly fee isn't in *our* budget." Clark stood up as Lex sat back down. "I thought you didn't like to play games, Lex. Of any kind."

"I don't, but millions of people *are* willing to pay for the privilege." A slow smile tugged at Lex's mouth as he sipped Scotch and watched the screen. "I have no doubt that there's an angle or an advance that no one has thought of, developed, or cashed in on, yet."

Clark had no doubt that he was right.

"Mrs. Kent?" Sharon paused at the white picket railing on the Kent porch when Clark's mother stopped a red pickup by the barn and turned off the engine. She had hoped to intercept Clark before he went to see Lex Luthor.

"Can I help you?" With auburn hair, blue eyes, freckles and a warm smile, Martha Kent was not at all what Sharon had pictured. Blue jeans, a short-sleeved tailored shirt, and a straw hat seemed like fashionable country wear on her trim figure.

"I'm Sharon Farley." Sharon extended her hand as she descended the porch steps.

Martha hesitated. "Oh, Sharon." She nodded, her smile widening when she realized her visitor was Clark's Saturday night movie date. Her handshake was firm and sincere. "How nice to meet you."

"You, too." Sharon smiled back. "I was looking for Clark. Is he here?"

"No, I'm sorry, he's not," Martha said.

"Oh." Sharon sighed with disappointment. There was a hint of regret in Martha's tone, but she didn't volunteer any information. Her brief answer made it clear she wouldn't divulge any details about her son's where-abouts.

Sharon, however, already had a good idea where Clark had gone. She just needed to know when.

"Long ago?" Sharon asked. Since Martha had the pickup, the Kent's only road vehicle, she also knew Clark was on foot. "If I catch him, I'll give him a ride back into town."

"It's been twenty minutes or so, but I don't know if he went back to town." Martha shrugged. "Sorry I can't be more help."

Sure you are, Sharon thought as she waved a polite good-bye and got back into her car. She turned right out of the driveway and headed toward the highway.

There wasn't anything in particular Sharon could put her finger on, but a subtle aura of mystery seemed to sur-round Clark Kent. Saturday night, she had had the dis-tinct feeling that he knew more than he wanted to say about meteor-rocks and Smallville's suspicious mortality rate. Martha and Lana were almost as reticent, as though they feared letting some awful secret or damaging piece of information slip.

Sharon turned onto Beresford Lane and slowed the Audi. Since Clark had promised Chloe to ask Lex Luthor about the status of the old missile installation, she was sure he had gone to the mansion. *She* wasn't going to ring the doorbell, but if she could connect with Clark when he left the estate, she might be able to find out what *he* had found out.

"That's what good reporters do, right?"

Sharon cruised the two-lane road, looking for a likely spot to park and wait. Even if Clark was running cross-country, he hadn't had nearly enough time to reach Lex's formidable home.

Unless, of course, the amount of time between when he left the Talon and called 911 last Thursday had really been fifteen minutes and not twenty-five or thirty as everyone assumed.

Two dirt drives cut into the woods and farm fields across from the Luthor property. Sharon pulled into the second drive a short distance down the road from the Luthor gate and turned the car so it was facing the road. While the trees weren't perfect cover, the silver Audi wouldn't be immediately apparent to anyone coming down the Luthor's winding drive.

The front entrance of the mansion was obscured by landscaping and stonework, but Sharon had a clear view of the grounds. She watched in amazement when Clark emerged from the house a few minutes later and ran across the manicured lawn into an expanse of dense woods.

Leaving Lex to figure out how to capitalize on virtual empires, Clark left the mansion grounds at an easy loping pace. He didn't head home when he ducked into the woods, but turned toward Stoner's farm. Although he hoped Lex hadn't lied, there were things he felt compelled to check out. After all, the dirt access road had been used recently, two men had died in the field near the silo within days of each other, and both bodies had contained traces of meteor dust.

Because Lex had previously financed Dr. Hamilton's

research before the mineralogist died from a lethal dose of meteor formula, Clark's suspicions weren't unfounded. He wasn't sure how much Lex knew about the potent properties of meteor-rocks, but the young entrepreneur knew enough to be dangerously curious about the untapped potential.

That was definitely true of Lionel. Clark and his parents would never have known that the senior Luthor was assembling a dossier on him if thieves hadn't broken into Lionel's vault and taken his mom hostage. Clark had burned the files with his heated gaze, but Lionel was a threat they could only guard against, not eliminate.

It wasn't outrageous to think that Lionel might be up to something that Lex knew nothing about. Lionel hadn't disclosed the existence of Level Three or the experiments he had authorized when Lex had taken over management of the Smallville plant. Considering the ongoing power struggle between father and son, Lionel was not above trying to humiliate and demoralize Lex by operating a clandestine project in the missile silo on LexCorp property.

Certainly no one else was capable of keeping Lex in the dark, Clark realized.

Since new, innovative technologies and scientific advances were vital to the future of both Luthor corporations, continued research and development was imperative. However, to avoid a repeat of the Level Three fiasco, the more dangerous research projects would be moved to remote locations.

The abandoned missile installation was ideal for that purpose, too.

Clark ran at a normal pace until he was well beyond

sight of the road. At superspeed, he covered the remaining distance to Howard Stoner's farm in less than thirty seconds.

Clark came to a halt in the trees by the gravel driveway and cautiously stepped into the open. No one else was in sight or within range of his acute hearing. Yellow crime scene tape was the only sign that the sheriff's deputies and forensic teams had been at work. The tape was strung from the driveway through the woods to a spot that probably marked where Gary Mundy had fallen.

Starting to the left of Stoner's small farmhouse, Clark panned the entire area. His gaze moved right across the field, past the access road and woods, to the chain-link fence that enclosed the entrances into the launch facility and silo. He shifted to X-ray vision, which identified animal bones, a broken plow blade, other tools, and nonglowing rocks buried in the field. The large fenced-in yard had been cleared of all metal objects except for scattered nails and the hatch entrances into the silo shaft and launch center. From Clark's vantage point, the site looked undisturbed.

Finding the source of meteor dust was his first priority. He began jogging the field, postponing a closer inspection of the underground military installation, which had been built several years prior to 1989. That meant the government had been paying Stoner to let the field lie fallow long before the meteors hit. If meteor dust had rendered the land arid, the farmer wouldn't have known it until he tried to grow a crop—after the facility was decommissioned and the missile removed.

Maintaining a steady pace, Clark moved in a systematic pattern back and forth between the access road and the dense woods on the field's western edge. At high speed, he could have covered the rutted acreage in a few minutes rather than thirty, but he couldn't take the chance that someone on the official investigative team might show up.

When Clark completed the final leg, he knew the field was clean. Small pockets of meteor dust might be hidden beneath the surface, but Stoner's field had obviously not been a primary landing zone for a meteor that blew itself to smithereens on impact.

Clark glanced toward the LexCorp property to the south and west. A wide strip of woods hid the plant building and most of the intervening cornfield from view. The cornfield was the favored location for the ritual the Smallville football team enacted every fall for good luck in the Homecoming game, turning a freshman into a human scarecrow. When Clark was a freshman, they had picked him. Lana's meteor necklace had made him too weak to help himself, and Lex had freed him.

In 1989, a large, blazing meteor had landed in that same cornfield. The impact had robbed Lex of his hair, flattened every cornstalk, and probably strewn meteor residue over the entire field.

Clark had assumed Mr. Stoner was walking back to his house after checking the missile silo when he collapsed. Perhaps he had been coming back from the LexCorp field. Clark made a mental note to check there, too, after he explored the crime scene and the fenced enclosure.

Being careful not to disturb anything, Clark followed the yellow tape from the chalked outline of Gary Mundy's body into the woods. The tape paralleled a wide, shallow furrow. The snakelike trail looked as though something heavy had been dragged from the death scene to the gravel drive. *Like what?* Clark wondered. The body would have been taken out on a stretcher. *A bag of dead rabbits, maybe?*

Since he hadn't experienced any meteor sickness near the yellow tape or the drag depression, Clark pushed those speculations to the back of his mind and headed for the chain-link fence.

The enclosed area was roughly the size of a football field, and Clark took his time walking around it. While he hadn't paid close attention to the site since his initial discovery years before, his mind retained almost everything he saw in passing. If anything was different, he would notice.

Clark peered through the wire mesh at the huge, six-sided lid over the actual silo. The massive concrete cover measured ten feet across and three feet deep and weighed one hundred tons. It was mounted on rails and automatically slid away from the shaft opening during a launch countdown or when properly keyed during certain maintenance procedures. Sections of the metal railing that circled the lid were missing or broken. The shaft that housed the nuclear warhead and delivery system ran 140 feet straight down, 80 feet below the level of the launch control and equipment areas. A smaller, emergency exit hatch was positioned 10 feet from the lid.

Another personnel access hatch measuring 3 feet across was located 100 feet east of the silo lid. A four-foot-by-six-foot concrete slab and two ventilation openings, which were flush to the ground and covered with wire mesh, were the only other exterior signs of the subterranean military facility.

However, the weeds inside the fenced area had been mowed recently. *By Howard Stoner or someone else?*

As Clark's gaze swept the compound, everything he had learned about the installation when he was a kid instantly came back to him. The text, photos, and diagrams he had found in the public library so long ago were just as clear in his mind now as they had been when he first saw them.

A metal staircase spiraled downward around a central elevator to the facility 60 feet underground. The elevator opened into a spacious junction where the hundred-foot silo tunnel connected to form the stem of a T. The Launch Facility Equipment Building on the right and the Launch Control Center on the left of the elevator formed the top of the T and measured 120 feet from outer wall to outer wall.

Clark was glad he had memorized the layout. His X-ray vision couldn't penetrate the lead-lined silo lid and smaller access hatches or 60 feet of dirt, rock and concrete.

The Launch Control Facility had been a completely self-contained environment when it was operational. Buried cables had supplied electrical power, but in the event the commercial source was cut off, the Launch Facility Equipment Building had been equipped with a diesel generator as backup. The emergency engine was fueled from a fourteen-thousand-gallon storage tank buried outside the steel and concrete walls of the LFEB.

Clark jogged to the gate on the southern side of the fence. The dirt drive that connected the installation to the access road ran through another densely wooded area. The wheel ruts in the drive were overgrown with grass and weeds that had not been driven over lately. However, the chain that held the two gate panels together had been outfitted with a new padlock.

Clark stared at the lock and considered his options. Only two scenarios made any sense: Howard Stoner had been maintaining the grounds and buying new locks as needed or someone else had access.

Either way, Clark had to know. If Lex was lying or being lied to and the missile site was in use, it was probably being used for illegal and dangerous purposes.

Clark knew that Lionel equipped himself and his surroundings with state-of-the-art security technology. His X-ray vision hadn't located any cameras, and he didn't see any sensor wires attached to the fence, which was designed to keep trespassers out. The chain-link portion was ten feet high and topped with three strands of razor wire angled to the outside.

Though Clark could easily jump the fence, he wouldn't be able to explain how he had gotten inside without breaking the lock if someone found him. He pulled the body of the lock down hard, breaking the inner lock mechanism. After slipping through the gate, he put the chain back in place so the panels wouldn't swing open and looped the lock's U through the links.

Once inside the fence, Clark still didn't see anything that struck him as unusual. Mr. Stoner could have kept the path between the gate and the personnel hatch worn down, especially if he had been adhering to a regular maintenance schedule since 1994. Except for the tire marks made by a riding mower, there were no vehicle tracks.

Clark walked around the large silo lid, which appeared

to be firmly in place. Like the lid and the primary personnel hatch, the bulk of the secondary exit hatch was above ground. He wondered if Lex was still paying for power, if only to lock and open the automatic entry mechanisms. Then he noticed that the heavy, raised gasket between the above- and below-ground segments of the thick cover was not properly aligned. The hatch was not completely closed.

Curious, Clark grabbed the edge. The balance mechanisms, which allowed a normal man to open the hatch, were broken, but he lifted it with ease. The steel-and-concrete cover swung up against and rested on a metal brace, which supported its weight. Clark braced himself to look down into the pitch-black darkness of a narrow, sixty-foot tube. Instead, he was surprised to discover that the tube had been filled with cement.

"Nobody's getting in or out that way," he muttered as he lowered the circular cover.

The blocked hatch just raised more questions. Had Lex filled in all the hatches to eliminate the risk of liability? Other abandoned launch facilities, some dating back to the era of Atlas and Titan missiles in the 1960s, had been used for unauthorized parties and campsites or had been vandalized. One silo he had read about was half-filled with water. By their nature and design, the abandoned missile complexes held many dangerous traps for unsuspecting teenagers. In the interest of lower insurance premiums, preventing anyone from getting in—ever—made sense.

Except that Howard Stoner would never have let such desecration occur without a fight, and the *Smallville*

Ledger would never have passed on a dispute between a local and a Luthor.

There was only one way to be certain. Clark had to check if the elevator shaft and platform area had also been filled in with concrete.

As Clark approached the main personnel hatch, he thought he heard a faint, almost imperceptible hum. It reminded him of the vibration in the wire fence when his father had hit the brads with his hammer, just smoother and quieter.

Working machinery 60 feet down could send a vibration through pipes and other conduits to the ground. He alone on Earth would be able to detect it.

With his senses focused on the ground and the hatch, everything else became perceptual white noise. Something was humming below. Clark slipped his hand under the handle and prepared to break the electronic lock. Was Lex paying for power to keep the interior equipment functional and the installation locked? Or was someone else?

"Hi, Clark," a girl said. "What are you doing?"

CHAPTER 10

Clark's head snapped around as he straightened. "Sharon! What are you doing here?"

"Looking for you." Sharon smiled with a sheepish shrug and adjusted the bag slung over her shoulder. "And I asked you first. What are you doing?"

Clark quickly devised a reasonable cover for his shocked reaction. Since truth often camouflaged itself, he was honest with an embarrassed grin. "Getting caught trying to break into Lex Luthor's missile silo."

"Any luck?" Sharon smiled, folding her arms tightly over her chest. She clutched a bulky cell phone and seemed nervous. Clark wasn't sure why.

"Nope. It's locked." Clark shrugged and mentally retraced his actions.

He could only guess how long Sharon had been watching him. He glanced across the field, but the silver Audi wasn't parked in the gravel drive by Stoner's house. Since she hadn't walked to the farm from town, she must have driven up and parked on the access road when he was focused on the vibration by the primary hatch. There was no other window of opportunity in which she could have sneaked up on him. He was certain she had not seen him lift the broken hatch cover.

"Caught, huh? I guess that means Lex didn't give you permission to poke around," Sharon stated flatly.

"I didn't ask," Clark said, still puzzling over her obvious distress. Was she nervous because they were both trespassing?

"Oh." Sharon glanced around the yard.

"You said you were looking for me," Clark said to distract her. He'd have to come back another time to continue his investigation. Until he determined the nature of the threat, if there was a threat, he couldn't involve anyone else. Not directly.

"Oh! Duh." Sharon laughed. "It's just that, well—all that talk about meteor dust with magic powers and stuff is, well—"

"I don't think anyone said 'magic,'" Clark corrected when she paused.

"Not exactly, no." Sharon sighed. "The thing is, Chloe's meteor theory is way too out there to be believed."

Clark didn't comment. The idea that meteor-rocks were dangerous had upset Sharon at lunch. Her denial might be a subconscious defense to alleviate her fear, but it was better to say nothing until he knew for certain.

"I don't want to pull the permit on anyone's parade, but I just can't buy the idea that a bunch of rocks from outer space are killing people." With a tight grip on the cell phone and her arms still folded, Sharon stared at the ground. When she looked up, she spoke hurriedly, as though trying to convince herself. "Even you said it was just a theory."

"It is," Clark agreed. His family and the *Torch* team knew from experience that the theory had proven out, but no hard evidence existed. It seemed pointless for Sharon to lose sleep over something that probably wouldn't affect her.

"So then the problem *is* chemical contamination from Lex's plant," Sharon said.

"Not necessarily," Clark countered.

Sharon's eyes narrowed and her arms tightened. "Chemical pollution makes more sense to me."

It would make more sense anywhere but Smallville, but to say so would just drive the discussion in an endless circle.

Clark's attention zeroed in on her fear instead. If she was so worried about chemical seepage or meteor dust, why was she on the site of two suspicious deaths? And why had she decided to look for him there? In fact, she still hadn't explained why she wanted to see him.

"So why were you looking for me again?" Clark asked as he started walking toward the gate.

"Uh—" With a glance over her shoulder, Sharon turned to walk beside him. "Actually, I went looking for you at your house, Clark. I didn't expect to find you here, beating me to the scoop."

Clark looked at her askance. "What scoop is that?"

Sharon rolled her eyes in disbelief. "That chemicals from the plant killed Mr. Stoner and that environmental agent."

Clark felt as though he was stuck in an endless loop. "There isn't any evidence."

"Not yet." Sharon looked annoyed. "I came here to find some."

With what? Clark wondered if she had left her specimen collection equipment in her car. A science kit wouldn't fit in her shoulder bag. He began to doubt the rest of her story, but rather than challenge her, he let her talk.

"Chloe was right," Sharon said. After they slipped out

the gate, she stared past Clark into the yard as he pulled the swinging panels closed.

"About what?" Clark secured the panels with the chain and broken lock.

"What separates the amateurs from the pros in the newspaper business." Sharon dropped the phone in her bag and flipped it back over her shoulder. "The pros don't let their fears stop them from getting the story."

"That comment was directed at me, not you." Smiling, Clark's gaze scanned the woods between the enclosure and the access road. "Where are you parked?"

"Over there." Sharon pointed down the drive, but she had walked through a cleared area between the trees and the boundary of Stoner's field.

"You probably think I take this whole reporter thing too seriously." Sharon carefully stepped around a tall, prickly thistle. The purple flowers were beautiful, but difficult to remove when they snagged in animal fur or fabric.

"No, I'm thinking about going into journalism, too." Clark spotted a small cloud shadow ahead. He hadn't noticed any clouds in the sky and started to look up. A twinge of meteor nausea suddenly gripped his stomach. Assuming a rock or pocket of meteor fragments was buried in the dirt, he moved to the side. The symptoms began to subside.

"Do you have your professional sites set on the *Daily Planet* like Chloe?" Sharon asked.

"I'd probably be happy at the *Ledger*—" Clark faltered as his temples began to throb with a dull ache. The veins in his hands twisted, and he stumbled. Through blurring vision, he saw the shadow flow toward him and over the toes of his boots.

His last coherent thought before the agony overwhelmed him was that the air around him was still and the cloud was riding currents high above.

"Clark?" Sharon put her hand on his arm. "What's wrong? Are you sick?"

Clark doubled over in pain, unable to answer. For an instant before he collapsed and faded out, he saw the darkness creep up his jeans and envelop his legs.

Time slowed as he hovered in an undulating nexus between the torment of awareness and merciful unconsciousness. Sharp pains erupted in his chest and sent burning spasms of pain through his body. Waves of nausea roiled in his stomach and every muscle screamed. When the agony began to recede, Sharon's hysterical voice penetrated the pounding in his ears.

"Clark! What's happening?"

The pain faded, yet lingered.

Clark groaned as frantic hands closed on his arm and rolled him on his back off the meteor material in the ground. The debilitating symptoms of his sickness abated quickly, but not completely.

"Clark?" Relief flooded Sharon's frightened green eyes when he opened his. "What the hell just happened?"

Still groggy, Clark dragged himself farther from the infested spot. He didn't see any green rocks or flakes, but dirt couldn't protect him from meteor fragments buried just beneath the surface. When the fuzzy feeling in his head didn't go away, he wondered if he had just found what he had been looking for: an area near Mr. Stoner's field that was permeated with meteor dust.

"Sorry about that." Clark struggled to his feet, but the effects didn't dissipate when he was standing up. He swayed slightly as he brushed dirt and dried grass off his clothes. That helped, but he was still not back to Clark Kent normal.

Except for a brief period when a lightning strike had transferred his gifts to Eric Summers, Clark's only experiences with physical vulnerability were his violent reactions to meteor-rocks. The magnitude of the effects and how much he suffered depended on the amount of meteor he was exposed to, at what distance, and for how long. The symptoms usually passed as soon as he was out of range of the alien radiation. At the moment, he was still suffering from low-level exposure.

"Can we get out of here?" Clark asked.

"Sure, but—are you sure you're okay?" The smattering of freckles across Sharon's nose and cheeks stood out in stark relief against her pale skin. She tightened her grip on his arm to keep her hand from shaking.

Clark nodded and offered the first plausible explanation that came to mind. "Maybe I just got a whiff of whatever killed Mr. Stoner."

Sharon gasped and pulled him toward the road. "Come on, Clark! Move!"

Clark was not proud of misleading the girl, but he couldn't explain that he was allergic to meteors in any form. For now, it wouldn't hurt to let her believe that something unknown was to blame. It seemed unlikely that the green particles had shown up in both bodies by coincidence. That didn't mean the alien material had killed Howard Stoner and Gary Mundy, but the dust had to be related.

Sharon had turned the Audi around before she parked on the road near the rutted drive into the missile compound. As soon as they were inside and buckled up, she fired up the engine, jammed the gearshift into drive, and took off in a spray of gravel and dirt.

Still feeling dizzy, Clark fumbled with the doorknob. The door banged open as he stumbled into the Kent kitchen.

"Clark?" Martha set aside the shirt she was mending.

Clark didn't want to upset his mom, but he had used up his reserve energies on the drive home with Sharon. He had briefly considered refusing a ride, but that had two major drawbacks. There wasn't a reason to walk rather than ride that would make sense to Sharon, and superspeeding cross-country would have required him to run naked through the woods. He couldn't speed wearing clothes that were contaminated with meteor dust.

Having to act as though he was fine all the way home had been hard, but not impossible. Sharon was so freaked by the idea that she had been exposed to some unknown poison, he had struggled to maintain the pretense. Short of confessing that he was a superhuman being with a deadly response to meteor-rocks, he had tried to convince her that the danger was minimal. She had finally agreed that Mr. Stoner might have died because of prolonged exposure to the mysterious toxin.

If they finally determined that meteor dust was the lethal substance, he could argue that he was more susceptible to the radiation than she was. The people who were allergic to bee stings and thousands of ordinary foods or substances were the exception, not the rule. It was the best he could do under the circumstances.

Unaware that anything was amiss, Martha rose from the rocker. She glanced out the window as Sharon peeled out of the driveway. "Was that Sharon?"

"Yeah." Clark pulled his shirt over his head, dropped it on the floor, unbuckled his belt, and kicked off his shoes.

"She came by earlier," Martha said.

"She told me." Clark shed his jeans, pulled off his socks and tossed them on the shirt. The instant he kicked the pile of clothes across the floor, he felt better.

His mother paused in the opening between the kitchen and the living room. Her expression was casually curious. "Is this a hormonal thing?"

"No." Clark sped halfway up the stairs and stopped.

There had been many moments in Clark's life when he was especially grateful that Martha Kent was his mom. A few stood out, such as the day he had hit a baseball clear across the front pasture, through the kitchen window, and into a freshly baked pie cooling on the table.

He had been seven and terrified that the woman he loved so much would finally decide she just couldn't deal with a one-boy wrecking crew. He had already broken a milking machine that week. His father had gently admonished him to be more careful. His mother had calmly observed that at least the cow's udder hadn't been in the suction tube when he accidentally squeezed it closed. That afternoon, she had washed the apple filling off his baseball and handed it back with a smile. Not a word about the ruined pie—ever.

Now was a moment like that. Martha Kent took it for

granted that her son had a good reason for stripping to his shorts in the kitchen.

"Would you do me a favor, Mom?"

"Sure." She waited, unperturbed, to hear what he had to say.

"I think there's meteor dust in my clothes," Clark explained. "Would you mind shaking them out to check?"

"No, of course not." Martha gathered up the pile to take it outside. "Are you all right?"

"I was a little light-headed on the way home, but that's mostly gone now," Clark said. "I'm sure a shower will wash away anything that's still clinging to my skin."

Martha glanced at Clark's clothes with distaste. "Maybe I should just burn these and bury the ashes."

"No, don't do that!" Clark hadn't meant to snap and softened his tone to explain. "I need a sample of the dust for Chloe's forensic friend to analyze. I picked it up near the field where Mr. Stoner died."

"Where exactly?" Martha's brow furrowed.

"Between the access road and the missile silo," Clark said. "If a meteor hit hard enough, it might have exploded into dust and powder that filtered deep down into the soil—except for a few pockets of concentrated particles."

Nodding, Martha moved to the counter and reached for a grocery bag in the cabinet under the sink.

Clark continued. "If the dust in my clothes is a match for the dust they found in Mr. Stoner and Mr. Mundy, then Dad's Level Three theory will be a no-go."

"Because the dust is in the ground and not part of a LexCorp research project," Martha added for clarification. She carefully put Clark's clothes in the brown paper bag.

Or a LuthorCorp project, Clark thought. "Right."

"That's an interesting theory, Clark," Martha said. "Except for one thing."

Clark frowned, hoping he wasn't going to get a lecture about sticking together as a family. He didn't like working at cross-purposes with his dad, but he couldn't shake the feeling that his father was making a huge mistake. Jonathan had been wrong about Lex's business activities and motives before. He was just too stubborn to admit it.

"After you left, I came back here and did some checking." Martha sighed. "Immediately after the meteor shower, NASA and several universities used radar tracking records and on-site inspections to map every impact they could identify."

"And?" Clark prompted.

"The meteor hit on the plant property was the only one close to the Stoner Farm," Martha said. "The debris radius was measured and confirmed with accurate and extensive tests. If there's meteor dust on the Stoner side of that old missile launch facility, it didn't come from an original impact."

CHAPTER 11

"Clark?" Jonathan stuffed his gloves in his back pocket as he called up to the loft in the old barn. The porous wood had absorbed the pungent odors of old hay, horse, and harness over the decades, and the familiar scent soothed him as no manufactured tranquilizer could.

"Up here, Dad!" Clark called back.

Jonathan paused, hesitant to disturb the dust motes suspended in the morning sunlight streaming down the stairs. The sight reminded him of the many hours he had spent sitting and staring out the upper-level door when he was a kid. In spite of Hiram Kent's no-nonsense personality, he had honored his son's need for personal space. As long as his chores were done, his father had left him alone.

When Clark was old enough, Jonathan had blocked off the lower section of the door to form a window. He had added railings and shelves, moved in an old desk and sofa, scrounged a radio and bought a telescope so his adopted boy would have a special place to call his own. Clark spent so much time in the loft at first he had started calling the hideaway his son's Fortress of Solitude. The designation had stuck even though Clark entertained more company in a month than Jonathan had in a lifetime.

"You're up early, son."

"Just trying to get ahead on my homework." Clark shuffled magazine articles and printed Internet reference pages into a neat pile and slid them into his binder notebook. The notebook went into his backpack, which he zipped with lightning speed.

"If you don't get moving, you're going to miss the bus," Jonathan said.

"Chloe's picking me up." Clark glanced at his watch. "Any minute."

"I thought only seniors were allowed to drive to school under the Reynolds regime," Jonathan said.

"Those are the rules," Clark muttered, "until he decides to change them."

Clark's sour expression revealed a normal objection to authority that Jonathan found oddly reassuring. Although Clark had never mentioned it, he suspected his unbelievably well behaved son had had some kind of run-in with the new principal. But, until the school started calling to complain or sending home notes, he wasn't going to worry about it.

"Lana said she could park at the Talon," Clark went on. "We're dropping that meteor dust sample off at the medical examiner's on our way in."

Jonathan frowned. They didn't know whether or not prolonged or repeated exposure to the alien radiation was having a cumulative effect on Clark. The less time he spent around the green poison the better. Although the thimbleful of meteor dust Martha had shaken out of his clothes yesterday had made him more uncomfortable than sick, a word of caution seemed advised.

"Did you put a lead lining in your backpack?" Jonathan quipped.

"No." Clark grinned. "The dust is in a plastic bag on the porch. Don't worry, Dad. I can handle being a little dizzy on the ride into town."

Jonathan nodded, but the lab test was probably irrelevant. "I thought your mother explained that meteor dust couldn't have gotten that close to Stoner's field when the meteors hit."

"She did, but I'm working on another theory." Clark slung his backpack over his shoulder. "I know you only promised to wait one more day before calling the lawyer, Dad, but—"

"Joe Reisler called me last night," Jonathan said. "Henry Small gave him my number."

"Dad!" Clark's face darkened with disappointment and frustration.

Jonathan had lain awake past midnight thinking about what to do. As certain as he was that Lex and Lionel Luthor had caused more health and environmental harm in Lowell County than anyone realized, he couldn't avoid another, more disturbing truth—not if he was being totally honest with himself.

He *did* resent Clark's friendship with Lex, but it wasn't a matter of jealousy. It was knowing that no matter how hard Lex tried to reject or deny it, he was his father's son. Sooner or later the bond between the two young lions would be ripped apart because they were who they were—one the product of Lionel's relentless challenge and calculated cunning and the other molded by Martha's trust and unconditional love. The only uncertainties were what would cause the rift and when.

When he rose at dawn, Jonathan knew the catalyst wouldn't be him and the breakup wouldn't be now.

Before he could make his position clear, Clark's feelings boiled over.

"Look, Dad, I know you don't trust Lex and you don't

think I should, either, but I'm not against this lawsuit because I'm blind to the facts. It's because I think you are!"

"Clark—" When Clark's rant continued uninterrupted,
Jonathan let it run its course.

"I felt this weird vibration at the old missile silo yesterday so I *do* think there's something going on. I'm just
not sure what, or that Lex is behind it." Clark's stare was
hard and unflinching. "So do what you want about getting a lawyer and filing a lawsuit, Dad, but I really wish
you trusted me enough to wait."

"I do trust you, Clark," Jonathan said. "That's why I
told Mr. Reisler I'd call back when and *if* I need a
lawyer."

Jonathan rarely stunned his son into speechless amazement. Having *that* role reversed was a rush. Now Clark
knew how his father must have felt the first time he saw
his five-year-old son using metal pipes and tractor tires as
Tinkertoys.

"Chad said he'd take the sample over to the lab right
away." Chloe braked the car at the four-way stop and
checked for oncoming traffic. "He's pretty sure we'll
have an answer this afternoon."

"Great." Clark tried to sound enthusiastic, but it wasn't
easy. His head buzzed with a thousand pinpricks, as
though his brain had fallen asleep from lack of circula-
tion. Sitting in the back seat wasn't much protection from
the plastic bag of meteor dust in Chloe's shoulder bag.
The only advantage was that the two girls up front
seemed unaware of his sickly state.

"Is Chad always this cooperative?" Lana sat in the passenger seat.

"I promised to do his makeup shopping at Arlene's the next time I'm in Metropolis." Chloe turned left onto the county highway that cut through the north side of town.

"Why?" Lana asked, amused. "Chad goes Goth day and night in Smallville so he can't be too embarrassed to buy makeup."

"No, but it's a huge hassle getting anyone to wait on him," Chloe said in disgust. "Wearing basic black in broad daylight may be out for the fashion sensitive set, but the dark side of style isn't contagious."

"I think most people can accept basic black. It's the pierced tongue they can't deal with," Lana said.

"Probably," Chloe agreed. "You don't want to stare, but you just can't help it."

Lana glanced back with a concerned frown. "You're awfully quiet, Clark."

"Just thinking about my biology paper," Clark said.

"What did you settle on for a topic?" Chloe flipped the signal lever on and turned right.

"Whether or not multicellular organisms evolved from single-celled organisms or arose independently." Clark closed his eyes for a second, but that just made the chaos inside his skull worse.

"Really?" Lana sat back with a nod. "Where'd you get that idea?"

"From Sharon." Clark wished Chloe would get to the county medical building soon. Once the meteor dust was out of the car, he wouldn't sound like he was gargling nails.

"Sharon came into the Talon the other day." Lana hesitated then smiled. "She seems—nice. A little curious."

"She's new," Clark said, economizing on words until the spinning stopped.

"Just beware of getting too bosom buddy with her," Chloe said. "Once Sharon gets over being shy, she doesn't stop talking."

"She's trying to impress you, Chloe," Lana said.

"Impress me?" Chloe was genuinely surprised. "Why?"

"Because you edit the *Torch*." Clark's voice cracked with the strain of covering the slight but steady draining effects of the meteor dust. "She told me the same thing yesterday at the missile silo."

Lana frowned and faced forward as Chloe drove into the business complex where Lowell County had annex offices.

"You took Sharon to the missile silo?" Chloe pulled into a spot, shifted into park, and turned to glare at him.

"I didn't *take* her," Clark said, suddenly irritated. "She just showed up. You pretty much dared her to prove herself with that remark about pros and amateurs."

"How much of a pro does she want to be?" Chloe asked, alarmed. "And how much does she *know*? Enough to beat me to the *Smallville Ledger* with a story?"

"Sharon wants to be the new star reporter at the *Torch*, Chloe." Talking was an effort, but the sooner Clark said what needed saying, the sooner Chloe would take the dust sample inside. "And she thinks chemical contamination from the plant makes more sense than killer rocks, so you don't have to worry about being scooped."

Chloe scowled. "Only because the *Ledger* doesn't buy plant conspiracy articles."

Not unless the evidence to back them up is ironclad and libel-proof, Clark thought wearily. *Which is never.*

"I don't know why you told Sharon about my meteor theory in the first place." Chloe pushed open the door and grabbed her bag.

"I didn't," Clark objected.

"Well, neither did I." Chloe slid out, closed the door, and pulled the plastic specimen bag from her bag as she stalked toward the front door.

Lana winced. "I think you touched a nerve."

Clark began feeling better the instant the meteor dust was out of the car. He nodded as his head cleared. "Apparently, but I don't think Sharon is trying to unseat Chloe as the intrepid defender of truth at Smallville High."

"I'm not so sure," Lana said softly. When she caught Clark's quizzical look, she started to explain. "It's just a feeling, but—" Her smile tightened. "It's probably nothing."

Clark's clarity of mind sharpened as his body recovered from the meteor sickness. He slipped into pensive thought as he settled back. Lana seemed unsure about Sharon, and Chloe felt threatened. He didn't know why they had formed their opinions, but something about Sharon bothered him, too. He just couldn't figure out what. She had an explanation for everything she did, assuming she really wanted to be a reporter. What if she was just using the *Torch* as an excuse to gather information? About the people she wanted as friends, the Stoner story, or both?

Clark gave everyone the benefit of the doubt—until they gave him reason to doubt.

He had noticed inconsistencies with Sharon's story yesterday, particularly the absence of specimen collection equipment in her car. In spite of being groggy from the meteor dust clinging to his clothes, he had mustered enough energy to focus his X-ray vision on the Audi's trunk. The contents had been easy to identify: books, a jacket, a flashlight, a boom box, and a case of CDs.

Unless Sharon had planned to collect soil samples in CD jewel cases, she had nothing suitable in the car.

Clark cupped his chin as his thoughts flowed in logical progression. If Sharon hadn't gone to the silo to look for evidence, what was she doing there? Even if his mom had known his plans, she wouldn't have told a girl he had just met where he had gone. Sharon knew from the conversation at lunch that he intended to see Lex, but he hadn't said a word about going to the missile launch facility.

Stumped, Clark leaned forward. "What is it about Sharon that doesn't feel right, Lana?"

"Nothing." Lana shrugged. "Really." She seemed relieved when Chloe rushed out of the building and down the walk.

Chloe jumped back in the car and slammed the door. "According to county time, my watch is five minutes slow. If you guys want to get to school in one piece before lockdown, sit back, hang on, and let me drive."

"I am *so* glad Mr. Reynolds gave me an exemption because I work." Lana braced with a hand on the dash as the car shot backward.

Clark knew Mr. Reynolds wasn't dispensing special favors. Lana used her free periods to keep up with Talon business, a responsibility the principal supported.

"Right." Chloe yanked the steering wheel hard to the left. "You'd think being the editor of the *Torch* would qualify me for the prisoner work release program, too, but no."

Clark sighed as Chloe gunned the engine, and the car sped down the drive. Lana had obviously wanted to say something about Sharon and had thought better of it. He didn't know what or why, but he didn't have the patience for guessing games or the emotional fortitude to press. If it was important, she'd tell him when she was ready.

CHAPTER 12

"I assure you, Dr. Farley, I haven't said a word to anyone." Lex swiveled his desk chair toward the window, away from the medieval virtual world displayed on the computer screen. He did not appreciate having his train of thought interrupted for trivial matters. "I honor my agreements, including the privacy clause in our contract."

"Then explain why that Kent boy was trying to break into this installation after leaving your mansion?" The geneticist was furious, but with the wrong person.

"I don't know," Lex said with steely calm. He was incensed by the insinuation, intrigued by Clark's interest, and annoyed by the man's bluster. Farley's security measures had made teenage breaking and entering difficult to the point of impossible. "Perhaps, you should ask your daughter."

The irate father sputtered. "Sharon has nothing to do with this, Mr. Luthor."

"Quite the contrary, Dr. Farley." Lex's modulated voice did not betray the depth of his displeasure. When he wasn't busy adding to his wealth, he enjoyed toying with people. He always held the winning hand—except with his father. That would change, sooner rather than later if his assumptions about Farley's work were correct.

Although Max Cutler, Lawrence Farley's partner, was ex-CIA and an expert in matters of surveillance and security, Lex was confident the mansion system was superior. Another clause in the lease agreement gave Farley the right to refurbish the underground facility to suit his needs, including the installation of security equipment at his own expense. However, while Lex knew exactly when and where Sharon Farley had parked to watch his estate yesterday afternoon, the doctor could not have known Clark was on the missile silo site unless his daughter had told him.

Lex prided himself on his powers of deduction, which the scientist was grossly underestimating. The lease had been written to give him final approval of Cutler's plans and a LexCorp security team inspection after the modifications were completed. The lack of surveillance equipment above ground was deliberate. There were no cameras or sensors that would alert the casually curious or the educated professional that the underground installation was occupied. Even Howard Stoner, a potential problem, had been utilized to Farley's advantage.

Since everyone in Smallville knew that Stoner was the missile site's self-appointed sentinel, Cutler doubled what Lex had been paying the farmer to keep watching and to keep quiet. To all outward appearances, nothing had changed. In the two months since Farley and Cutler had finished moving in, all evidence of their activities had been removed. Even the weeds on the road, drive, and yard had grown back. For an extra twenty dollars a week, Stoner had mowed the enclosure to hide the footprints and trampled vegetation that marked Farley's and Cutler's comings and goings.

If either man had emerged from the facility to apprehend a trespasser, Clark would have returned to the mansion to report that someone *was* using the old missile silo—with or without Lex's knowledge.

The only way Farley could possibly have found out

that Clark was in the enclosure was if someone Clark knew, but didn't associate with the facility, had told him.

"If Sharon hadn't been spying on me, she wouldn't have known Clark was here," Lex said. "She obviously followed him."

"No, she didn't," Farley huffed. "He was here when Sharon arrived to warn me that some of the local kids were getting too curious about this place."

Exactly, Lex thought. Seeing Howard Stoner drop dead must have aroused Clark's interest in the old missile site nearby. Clark had an uncanny knack of finding trouble that didn't find him first.

An accusatory edge crept into Farley's tone. "Apparently, you and the Kent boy are friends."

"My friendship with Clark is irrelevant," Lex said coldly. "The local kids, who know that old military installation is there, have *always* been curious about it. That's why *I* paid Howard Stoner to watch the place. Now, he's dead. Why is that, Dr. Farley?"

"I have no idea." Farley matched Lex's icy calm.

Lex didn't know if Farley was implicated in the deaths of Howard Stoner and Gary Mundy or not. The presence of meteor dust in both bodies was odd since Stoner's field hadn't sustained a direct meteor hit in 1989. Perhaps the burrowing rabbit population had unearthed an undiscovered impact pocket of pulverized dust. That would explain the presence of the green particles in the dead rabbits, but not why they had been battered and left in a pile. And meteor dust couldn't account for Mundy's death, either.

Stranger things had happened in Smallville, especially since the meteor shower. Before Dr. Hamilton died, he had proposed an interesting theory about the ability of meteor material to change some organisms at the molecular level. Lex's and many other original victims' blood had extraordinarily high white cell counts. Although Lex had gone bald, his asthma had been cured, and he hadn't been sick since that October day. Not even a sniffle.

But the meteor-rocks didn't have an effect on everyone, and those who were susceptible reacted in different ways and to varying degrees. His experience with the extraterrestrial rocks was limited, but he was sure of one thing. The mutating properties couldn't be harnessed to produce a controlled, calculated result—except death.

None of that was his concern, however. He had legally insulated himself and LexCorp from any liability resulting from the rental lease.

"Is there anything else I can do for you, Dr. Farley?" Lex asked as a courtesy. There was only so much he was willing to do to pacify his outraged tenant.

"I told you I needed peace and quiet before I signed the lease, Mr. Luthor. You assured me I would have it."

Lex chose not to argue. Keeping the young and curious away from the property was a reasonable request under the circumstances.

"I'll have a word with Clark," Lex said. "Now if you'll excuse me—"

Lex glanced at the precise Swiss clock on his desk as he hung up. Classes at Smallville High wouldn't be over for a few hours. Since time was money, he turned his attention back to the computer adventure game.

It was necessary to understand how something worked before making a significant investment. He had recognized the relaxing escape qualities of the ongoing scenar-

ios immediately. However, he wasn't playing to relieve
the stress of an everyday life. He was playing for real, for
keeps, and for much higher stakes. He was focused on
conquering the real-world masters who were making fortunes providing realistic role-playing games for paying
adults. He had already ascertained that the gaming community could be induced to abandon current realms for a
more intricate and exciting virtual world. He just had to
identify and incorporate that elusive, missing element
they all wanted and couldn't find—yet.

Which involved spending a few dollars and some time
talking to people within the context of their alternate,
cyberlives.

Lex fitted a headset over his ears and adjusted the
mike. "Kilya? Are you there?"

"Hi, Dome. Thought I lost you."

"You did. I had to leave for a few minutes, and someone killed me." Lex knew nothing about the real woman
who had befriended his pathetic character, but he had
grown rather fond of Kilya Warcrest, the brazen lady bar-
barian who had taken pity on a new player. "I still have
five gold pieces hidden away, though."

"Good. You'll need them to buy a Lazarus ritual."
Kilya laughed.

"So I'm not really dead?" Lex asked.

"Only temporarily," Kilya said, then added, "Unless
we can't find a priest before your window of renewal ex-
pires."

Lex made a note to push his accountants. If the numbers added up, a new subsidiary of LexCorp would be in
the works before he finished breakfast tomorrow. He'd

have the best graphic artists, programmers, and fantasy writers in the country on the payroll by noon.

Chloe breezed into the *Torch* offices and keyed the computer to sign on to the Internet before she even sat down. Although Mr. Reynolds wouldn't give her a campus exemption like Lana's, he had given her permission to work on the newspaper before and after school and during study halls. She had spent most of the last period in the library getting the research for her biology paper out of the way so she could concentrate on the important stuff.

"Like finding out what the hell Sharon Farley is really up to." Chloe dropped her books on the side desk and popped the top on a cold soda she had just gotten from the machine outside the cafeteria.

Something Clark said that morning had jump-started her investigative instincts.

Chloe hadn't told Sharon that meteor-rocks might be responsible for many of the strange ailments and deaths in Smallville, and neither had Clark. Although Sharon had spent quite a long time perusing the Wall of Weird, was she smart enough to make a connection that the best EPA and NASA scientists rejected? Were the new girl's powers of observation and deduction good enough to make the leap from meteor dust in two bodies to "killer rocks"?

Clark seemed certain that Sharon didn't buy the meteor theory. Chloe wasn't so sure, but that wasn't the only thing that disturbed her. Since Sharon had argued against investigating Lex Luthor's missile silo site, why had she gone there? Although Chloe couldn't discount the possibility that Sharon was just going after a story, she couldn't ignore the gut feeling that something wasn't right, either.

Clark and Pete came in as Chloe sat down and pulled up her incoming e-mail menu. They took their usual positions at the desks behind and in front of her.

"Heard back from Chad, yet?" Clark asked.

Chloe scanned the e-mail list and shook her head. "Not yet, but it's only three. I've got something else that's pretty darn interesting, though."

"The cafeteria hired a new cook?" Pete asked hopefully.

"No, but this came up at dinner last night, when I mentioned the missile silo to my dad." Chloe shifted her gaze from Pete to Clark. "I was just making conversation. I didn't expect to find out that one of his best friends wrote an insurance policy on the site three months ago."

Clark sat up. "What kind of policy?"

Chloe loved it when she got Clark's attention with an information coup. Her father only knew about the policy because Wayne Baum had called to crow about scoring a LexCorp account. For a small insurance agency trying to compete in Metropolis, doing any business with a Luthor was a professional and financial boon.

"All the usual damage coverage for a property," Chloe explained. "But the main thing is that it protects Lex and LexCorp from any liability resulting from renter activity."

"So someone is definitely using the place." Clark frowned.

"We don't know that," Chloe cautioned. Sometimes she had to play devil's advocate to keep people on track with the facts. "Maybe Lex is just covering all his bases before he tries to rent it."

Clark didn't argue with her logic.

"Who would want it?" Pete pegged the obvious question.

Chloe voiced the obvious answer. "Someone who's doing something they don't want anyone to know about?"

"Something they'd kill to protect?" Pete scowled. "We've got two dead guys and a pile of broken rabbits, remember."

"Slaughtered snakes and two strangled cows," Clark added.

"Don't forget the rosebush massacre," Chloe said. "All incidents that probably qualify for Wall of Weird status."

"Is the sheriff making any progress on the case?" Clark leaned back with his hands clasped behind his neck.

"They don't have a suspect," Chloe said. "I called my friend at the department this morning. The only thing they know is that the CEP agent was dead before someone took a few chunks out of him."

"But we still don't have a likely candidate for who," Pete said.

"What do we know about Sharon's father?" Clark asked.

"You don't think Sharon's dad munched a bunch of Mr. Mundy, do you?" Pete was aghast.

Clark laughed. "No, but he might have rented Lex's missile silo."

"You think?" Chloe raised an eyebrow. Their thoughts

were obviously running in similar circles. Sharon's insufficiently explained trip to the missile silo yesterday was apparently bugging Clark, too.

"A missile silo instead of a cabin in the woods." Pete shrugged. "I suppose if someone wanted to be left alone to write a novel, that would work."

"Maybe," Clark said, "but before he decided to write science fiction, Dr. Farley did some kind of scientific research at a university."

Pete pointed as his memory sparked. "Until he lost his grant!"

"I'm on it." Chloe turned to the computer to begin an Internet search for anything she could find on Dr. Lawrence Farley. When her cell phone rang, she answered absently, "Chloe."

"Sorry to bother you, Chloe," Lex Luthor said, "but I need to get in touch with Clark. Will you give him a message?"

"Uh—he's right here. Hang on." Mouthing Lex's name, Chloe thrust the phone at Clark.

"Hey, Lex. What's up?" Clark nodded as he listened, then glanced at the time. "The last bell rings in five minutes. As soon as the gate's unlocked, I'll go right over."

"Right over where?" Chloe asked when Clark handed the phone back.

"The Talon to meet Lex. He didn't say why, but I wanted to see Lana anyway." Clark stood up with a pensive frown. "Do you know if something happened between her and Sharon, Chloe? Something she wouldn't want to talk about?"

"She hasn't said anything to me." Chloe looked up from the keyboard. "But you'll have to wait to ask her.

One of the other waitresses needed tonight off, so Lana changed shifts."

"What time will she be in?" Clark picked up his books.

"Five?" Chloe shrugged. "I didn't ask. I wasn't worried about getting my car back because I have so much to do here. And now that I'm researching Sharon's dad, I've got even more."

"I'll help." Pete slid into Clark's chair and turned on the computer.

"I'll check back later." Clark paused at the door. "Can you find out if the missile silo is plugged into Kansas State Water and Power, and who's paying the bill?"

"Probably." Chloe waved without taking her gaze off the monitor. Every journalistic synapse fired up as she clicked on the first link. The Stoner story had finally gotten hot.

CHAPTER 13

Clark sorted through everything he knew as he walked to the Talon. Lex had called from the road and wouldn't arrive for a few minutes, yet.

From what he heard at the site, he was certain that machinery of some sort was being used in the underground installation. He couldn't tell Chloe and Pete how he knew, but he had more than a slight vibration to support that someone was down there. Lex was extravagant, but he never wasted a dollar. He would not have bought insurance against renter damage unless he had rented the property.

Clark made a snap decision not to tell Lex that he knew about the policy. Wayne Baum shouldn't have disclosed his business dealings with LexCorp, but he had told Mr. Sullivan in confidence. Chloe's dad had told her without knowing the information might be relevant to a crime. Lex would have a legitimate complaint if he knew, but he might also retaliate in a manner more harsh than the indiscretion warranted. The leak was an unfortunate fluke. Clark wouldn't be indirectly responsible for ruining Mr. Baum's business.

As he approached the Talon, Clark slowed down again. He hadn't decided whether to confront Lex or not. Technically, Lex hadn't lied about using the missile silo, but he had deliberately misled him.

Based on the body of circumstantial evidence, Lawrence Farley was almost certainly Lex's tenant. Dr. Farley and his daughter had moved to Smallville three months ago, around the time Lex was having the insurance policy on the property drawn up. If Sharon's father had rented the silo, that would explain why she didn't have any soil sample gear with her yesterday. She hadn't gone to the site looking for evidence against LexCorp. She had gone to warn her father that the *Torch* staff was getting too curious about the place.

When he had asked Lex if the plant's research and development operations had expanded into the missile facility, Lex's answer in the negative had been correct. *Renting* the property wasn't the same thing. Since Lex wouldn't disclose anything if he was on the defensive, Clark had nothing to gain by bringing up the clever spin. Letting it slide, on the other hand, might be beneficial.

As usual right after school, the Talon was packed. Teenagers and shoppers had staked claims to every chair around every table. Laughter and shouted greetings rose above the steady drone of conversation and the clink of glasses, coffee cups, and plates.

Lex almost hit his head on a hanging plant when he stood and waved from a corner table.

Clark ducked under another plant to drop into the opposite chair. "I think Lana forgot that most people are taller than she is when she put these up."

"The dangling danger adds a certain charm." Lex flipped a trailing vine into the hanging basket, then raised his demitasse cup and nodded toward a frosty glass. "I ordered you a root beer, but feel free to get something else."

"Root beer's great. Thanks." Clark took a swallow, hoping Lex wouldn't waste time with small talk. He had called him here with a purpose, and Clark didn't want to sit for too long wondering why.

"This is rather awkward, but necessary." Lex stared into his dark espresso for a moment before meeting Clark's gaze. "I wouldn't even bring this up except that it involves a promise."

"What's going on?" Clark prodded.

"I know you were at the missile silo site yesterday," Lex said, "and I have to ask you to stay away."

"Okay." Clark nodded. "Why?"

A flicker of surprise registered in Lex's eyes, as though he hadn't expected Clark to agree so readily. "I've rented the property and privacy was part of the lease agreement."

"To Dr. Farley," Clark said matter-of-factly. Lex's stony expression didn't provide the confirmation he was hoping for, however.

"What makes you think that?" Lex asked after a prolonged pause.

"A couple of things," Clark said, "but mainly because I ran into his daughter out there yesterday. Either Sharon told you I was at the missile silo or her father did. There's no other way you could have known." The logic wasn't perfect, but it had the desired effect.

"You didn't hear that from me," Lex said pointedly.

Clark realized that the agreement must have a secrecy clause, too. Lex wasn't free to divulge his tenant's name, but he couldn't stop someone from guessing.

Clark took another swallow of soda and nodded to convey that he understood. However, he couldn't ignore the fact that people had died. An insurance policy might protect LexCorp from some liability, but it wouldn't stop his father from holding Lex responsible. If Dr. Farley was engaged in something criminal and Lex knew, he was an accomplice.

"Do you know what Dr. Farley is doing, Lex?" Clark tackled the situation head on. "Because if whatever it is had something to do with Mr. Stoner's death, and the sheriff finds out someone's there—"

Lex cut him off. "I don't know, Clark, but I have arrived at some educated guesses."

Clark's throat tightened, but he choked back his questions. Lex Luthor couldn't be pushed, but he might give. *Especially if he thinks it might discourage Dad's quest for legal satisfaction.*

Lex took a sip of espresso. "Dr. Lawrence Farley is a geneticist. He was researching stem cell manipulation in conjunction with engineered evolution potential during his tenure as a professor—until the government pulled his grant last year."

Clark's eyes widened with interest. No wonder Sharon knew so much about fringe theories of evolution. Since Lex had no qualms about discussing Dr. Farley's work, he didn't interrupt.

"His career should have been over," Lex continued, "but Europeans aren't nearly as squeamish as Americans regarding certain areas of medical curiosity and endeavor. Dr. Farley found a partner with a background in security and acquired private funding."

"From where?" Clark blurted out the question without thinking.

"There are financial consortia overseas that gamble on risky orphan projects," Lex explained.

Clark wasn't sure what Lex was trying to tell him. LuthorCorp, Lionel's umbrella corporation, had subsidiary medical companies that did not believe "do no harm" was a priority. Studies using human test subjects at Metron Pharmaceuticals had resulted in several deaths and complications for which there was no cure.

"Unfortunately for my father, the federal government has restricted stem cell research and therapeutic cloning in this country." Lex's brow furrowed slightly. "And, of course, both therapies show promise for repairing optic nerves, which would cure his blindness."

"That would be fantastic." Clark wanted to believe Lex's interest in Dr. Farley's research was motivated by altruism rather than profit.

Lex's enthusiasm was less than exuberant. "I'm responsible for my father's condition. Erasing that would be worth something to me."

The rare glimpse into Lex's emotional psyche surprised Clark. Lex was more concerned with being free of the guilt than whether or not his father's sight was restored. Apparently, he had agreed to the secrecy clause because he thought Dr. Farley was continuing his stem cell research. Lex could plead ignorance if the geneticist's illicit scientific work was discovered.

Does that work involve meteor dust? Clark wondered.

"Sharon said her father's writing a book," Clark said.

"I'm certain Dr. Farley is writing something he wants to protect until he can publish," Lex said.

Since Dr. Farley couldn't publish findings on illegal medical research, Clark realized Lex was sending him another guarded message.

"No doubt that's one reason why he asked permission to install a sophisticated security system and wishes to be left alone." Lex drained the small cup and set it down.

Warning noted, Clark thought, but filling an access tube with cement was not exactly state-of-the-art technology.

Dr. Lawrence Farley finished loading the wheeled utility cart and locked the cabinet door. The stock of chocolate, cheap wine, and cigarettes would last another week. Layton preferred fresh kill, but they could no longer trust him to hunt in the silo, tunnels, and equipment area of the facility. He had developed a taste for beef jerky, but Sharon had forgotten to buy more when she had done the grocery shopping. Today, Layton would have to settle for chocolate. There was no suitable substitute for morphine, but Hoover's time would run out before his supply of the drug.

Hoover had been Farley's first experimental human subject. Reduced to a mass of pulsating tumors that left him barely recognizable as a man, he would have died two months ago if not for his amazing immunity to toxins. The cancers adapted to and absorbed every poison Farley had tried except morphine. The drug's lethal effects were taking longer than he liked, but at least Hoover was in a constant stupor, removed from mental and physical pain.

Farley was beginning to agree with Max. Mercy killing would be humane for the four others who had preceded Layton Crouse.

Sighing, Farley left the lab complex. The sphere once called the Launch Control Center, Max had divided into a lounge, office, and combination laboratory and infirmary. He had also soundproofed the galley, latrine, and large storeroom outside the lab and muffled the forced-air conductors. Earplugs were no longer a necessity, saving time and trouble. The metal bridge that linked the habitation area to the six-ton door into the junction tunnel still clanked dreadfully, however.

When the Missile Launch Facility was operational, the massive door had been locked at all times. Strict procedures had been followed to prevent the authenticators and launch keys from being accessed by the wrong people. Only one LCC door in the Midwest network of ten Launch Control Facilities had been allowed to be open at any one time, and no individual could enter a sensitive LCC area alone. Once the two-man teams had been cleared and admitted to the Launch Control Center, they had been locked in until their relief arrived.

Farley left the massive door open. He and Max, and Sharon on her rare visits to the underground compound, ran in and out of the lab complex too often to deal with the locking mechanism.

The floor of the Launch Control Center, and the even larger Launch Facility Equipment Building across the tunnel, which housed the diesel generator and climate control systems, rested on huge shock absorbers. Metal ramps bridged the gap between the floor and the walls, which had been designed with flexibility to withstand a close nuclear hit.

Edgar began calling and banging on his cell door when he heard Farley's footsteps on the metal bridge.

"Max!" Farley called out as he exited the narrow passage through the thick wall into the spacious tunnel hub. The LCC, LFEB, and elevator all opened into the central area. Six cells had been built into the original space: three along the blank wall opposite the elevator doors and three on the wall between the equipment room door and the silo tunnel. Five of the six-foot-by-eight-foot cubicles were occupied. The sound of Farley's voice was drowned out by Edgar's thumps and demanding cries.

"Shhhmok! Now, Faley!"

"Settle down, Edgar, or you'll have to wait until last," Farley snapped.

The mutant-man shut up.

Farley glanced toward the open hatch behind the elevator. The extension tunnel ran one hundred feet west to the missile silo. The silo floor was eighty feet below the complex level, which was sixty feet underground. Until it had been removed in 1994, a Minuteman II had stood tall and proud in the shaft, ready to fly in defense of the country.

Now the deep, empty shaft was a hazard, and the connecting tunnel served as a jogging trail and exercise room for Max Cutler. The ex-CIA agent had been a dangerous man before he had submitted to the molecular enhancement procedure. Farley was now working to arrest the progress of the problematic side effects. If he could stop Max's decline into insanity, the result of accelerated deterioration of nonregenerating neurons in the brain, Max would be a spy unlike any ever known.

In his dark alter-form, Max was impervious to all toxic substances and conventional weapons. He could easily invade any lit place anywhere without being noticed, an ability that gave him unprecedented information-gathering potential. His ability to infiltrate and memorize data he heard or saw would command a high price from govern-

ment, corporate, and industrial sources. Some would pay
for the intelligence itself. In other cases, a force of engineered spies-for-hire would use what Max learned to
complete other difficult missions. There was no limit to
the possibilities or the wealth they would both acquire.

*If the unsolved mental problem doesn't doom Max and
the project first*, Farley thought with a sigh. He wiped
nervous sweat off his forehead as he unclipped his
walkie-talkie and pressed the call button. The installation
was too far below ground for cell phones to work.

"This is Max." The agent was breathing heavily.

"Time to pacify the patients."

"They're freaks, not patients," Max snapped.

"They still need their rations." Farley winced, anticipating Max's next response. The agent despised his eu-
phemistic code word, but that was too damn bad.

"Whatever," Max scoffed. "I'll be there as soon as I
finish my run."

Ignoring the distressed noises emanating from the
cells, Farley pocketed the comm-device and began por-
tioning the tranquilizing substances. Like the euphe-
mism, his carefree tone was a cover for a deep revulsion,
not just for the victims of his initial botched experiments,
but with himself for abandoning all sense of decency and
principle.

When the government canceled his research grant, he
had thought his future, and by extension Sharon's, had
been canceled, too. Others in his field had found legal, lu-
crative outlets for their uninspired expertise without too
much delay. He had been ostracized. His premise that
evolution could be engineered to specification and advanced on a molecular level was too preposterous to be

taken seriously. No one had understood the potential of the green meteor material he had found in Dr. Hamilton's old university lab. He had applied the unknown substance in his genetic manipulation of rats with erratic but fascinating results.

Outraged, indignant, and desperate after his dismissal, he had been anxious to talk when Max Cutler approached him with his super-spy project proposal. With Continental Sciences of Europe providing the funds, it was a once-in-a-lifetime chance to continue his work unhampered by academic ridicule or government oversight.

Now, everything depended on whether or not he could stabilize the cellular erosion in Max's brain.

Farley tried not to think about what would happen if he failed. Without Max Cutler to control and operate a fleet of specialized agents, there wouldn't be a financial empire. His work would be worthless and a threat. He would have no choice but to destroy all evidence of the project, including the bodies of his hapless volunteers.

All he had to do was turn a key and push a button.

But Farley wasn't the only person wondering, What if?

Trained to think of every possible contingency, Max had extrapolated and planned for several emergency scenarios.

If the power failed and the electronic locks on the cells opened before the generator came on-line, gas would be released from canisters to subdue the patients—except for Hoover, who was immune, but harmless. Gas masks were stored throughout the installation for his and Max's protection.

The self-destruct mechanism had been installed in a case by the elevator. If the mutant-men couldn't be con-

trolled or he and Max had to abandon the project to escape apprehension, the simple, two-step activation
process would initiate a five-minute countdown. The
agent had rigged the underground missile facility to im-
plode, making a search of the rubble impossible. If anything bad happened to Max, the explosive charges would
obliterate his existence, too.

They had thought of everything, except the insidious
madness.

"Damn!" Max rushed out of the silo tunnel and came
to a sudden stop. Breathless, he bent over with his hands
on his knees, his sweat towel dragging on the floor.

"What?" Farley's voice cracked, and his left eye began
to twitch. Max had always made him nervous, but his
anxiety response had gotten worse since the agent had
begun showing signs of mental deterioration. The slight
memory lapses and minor tantrums were not as worri-
some as Max's irrational fear of the dark.

"Lightbulb burned out." Flipping a towel over his
shoulder, Max joined Farley at the cart. "You'll take care
of that, right?"

"As soon as we're done here," Farley promised. He
loathed making the afternoon rounds to check the patients, but Max could not properly assess their conditions.
The agent's untrained eye might miss a subtle, yet critical
physiological change. It was enough that Max was willing to distribute the morning and evening meals without
his help.

"Shhhmok." Edgar's gnarled, hairy hand slipped
through the window bars of the first cell. "Pease, Faley."

"You can smoke after we see how you're doing,
Edgar." Farley waved the reluctant man back.

All Farley's modifications had been intended to enhance an espionage agent's performance: strength, immunities, reflexes, camouflage, and retention. When he and Max had first conceived the idea of designer spies, Farley thought he could create specific alterations in the first few volunteers. He had hoped to isolate the various genetic patterns so more than one attribute could be incorporated into future models.

Edgar had grown barbed hairs on his hands and feet that allowed him to scale walls and hang upside down from the ceiling. That was the intended result of Farley's engineering, except that the wiry hair had grown over the small man's entire body and face and was too tough to shave. Even if he hadn't degenerated mentally overnight, Edgar couldn't blend in with the general population.

When Edgar didn't obey, Max barked, "If you want your cigarette, you'd better move. Now!"

Pouting, Edgar sprang backward and stuck to the far wall.

"Excellent, Edgar." Farley smiled with an approving nod as he entered. With everyone except Hoover, who was always spaced on morphine, praise seemed to soothe the mutants' violent tendencies.

Max shook a cigarette from an open pack and held it up for Edgar to see.

Edgar hissed through rotted teeth, his version of a laugh.

Farley picked up the dirty bucket commode, set it outside the door, and moved a clean one in. He and Max made the exchange in every cell twice a day. Blankets, pillows, and air mattresses were cleaned or replaced as needed.

When the basic sanitary chores were done, Farley ran Edgar through his rudimentary paces. Except for the worsening speech impediment, he didn't detect any changes. Unlike the mental aberrations, the physical effects of the procedure manifested quickly and became permanent within a couple of weeks. Max's condition was following an identical physical pattern, but with a much slower rate of mental deterioration.

"Okay, Edgar." Farley backed out of the cell, smiling up at the bright eyes looking down. "Very good."

The instant Farley closed the door, Edgar dropped to the floor. He thrust his hand through the bars of the small, rectangular window set in the solid, steel door. "Shhhmok!"

"Here you go, pal." Max lit the cigarette and handed it to the addicted mutant.

Farley moved on to the next cell. The only humanity the volunteers had left was their habits and addictions. Out of pity at first, Farley had positioned a TV in the tunnel junction where all the subjects could see it. Max had taken it down when they realized no one was watching. The men's minds had become so primitive, they were content to rock, pace, whine, shout, or sit.

When Edgar wasn't smoking the cigarettes they rationed to keep him calm, he flitted from one wall to another—all day and most of the night.

"Hoover's not looking very good, Doc." Max peered through the bars of the next cell.

Farley nodded with a cursory glance at the human tumor. Hoover rested on a pile of blankets with his back braced in the corner. His empty eyes appeared sunken in the cauliflower growths that sprouted from his forehead and cheeks. The lumps, bulges, and festering sores that covered his grotesque body didn't exist in his drugged oblivion.

Farley eyeballed the IV bag hanging from a ceiling hook. The tubes were in place and the needle secured in the back of Hoover's enlarged hand. Farley decided to increase the drip rate when he replaced the morphine. If Hoover was lucky, his body would relinquish its tenacious hold on life by morning.

"Let's move on, Max." Farley stepped up to the third cell on the back wall. He took a plastic sipper filled with red wine off the cart and stood back while Max unlocked the door.

Cooper stood in the middle of the padded cell, swatting at the splotches of color that faded and blossomed on his skin. Pinks, greens, and yellows mingled with and overlapped shades of brown, tan, and gray. The camouflage shifted at random, completely beyond the madman's control. His appetite had dwindled along with his mental capacity, which had turned him into a kaleidoscopic, skin-and-bones caricature of a man. Wine was the only thing that diverted Cooper's attention from his futile attempts to catch the fleeting patterns.

"Get back, Cooper," Max ordered. When the Harlequin flailed his arms, Max shoved the wine sipper into his hands. The commode bucket sloshed when he yanked it away from the wall.

Max muttered something unintelligible.

Farley exchanged buckets without a word. Whenever Max complained about the unpleasant duty, he offered to bring someone else in for a third of the cut. Once the agent had dared to suggest that Sharon help out. Farley had threatened to walk. It was bad enough his daughter knew about the "Frankenstein project," as she called it, and that Max had used her to find out what the Kent boy knew about Stoner's sudden death. In spite of his assurances, she was convinced that her genetic structure could be damaged by casual exposure to the meteor material. The idea was ridiculous, but the last thing they needed was a hysterical girl in the lab.

Max slammed Cooper's door closed. "You'd better finish with these guys soon, Doc, 'cause my patience is running out."

Farley's eyes flashed. "Your only hope of avoiding the same fate as these guys is to let me work in peace."

"Yeah, yeah." Sighing, Max pushed the cart past the equipment room door.

Farley didn't mention that he was seriously considering putting the others out of their misery. He was not fond of the tedious chores, either, but the subjects hadn't outlived their usefulness, yet. One or all of them held the clue to Max's mental survival.

Max grabbed a large chocolate bar for the resident of the fourth cell. Nathan could condense and expand his cellular structure, which gave him a stunted ability to morph into crude, basic shapes. At the moment, he looked like a lumpy cube with his facial features squashed into a three-inch oval area. An arm shot out from his side to snatch the candy bar from Max's grasp.

Nathan was a crude version of the elegant elasticity Farley had achieved with Layton.

Farley nervously glanced past the empty fifth cell that had Max's name penciled in. They never acknowledged its presence.

The sixth cell had been elaborately modified for Layton Crouse's comfort and containment. In addition to the bucket, air mattress, pillow, and blanket, Layton had been given handheld video games, picture books, puzzles, and plastic building blocks to keep himself amused and entertained.

Compared to the other four, Layton was a resounding success. His ability to transform into a fluid, rubbery state showed enormous promise. His form had spontaneous shape memory, and even though he possessed the mental processes of a slow three-year-old, he had learned to fine-tune and control his malleable body, which had caused them more trouble than Max thought Layton was worth.

For a while, Layton had been content to hunt the wild rats that infested the Launch Facility Equipment Room and silo. He had also enjoyed racing back and forth in the long connecting tunnel. Max could control the child-like monster except when Layton's predatory bloodlust took over, as it had the first time he escaped. With his twelve-foot, loping gorilla stride, Layton had easily outrun Max down the connecting tunnel to the maintenance tube by the silo shaft. The hatch was broken and he had flowed to freedom through a wide crack between the ground and the cover. As soon as Max brought him back, they had filled in the access tube with cement.

For all the good that did us, Farley thought. Despite their efforts to contain him, Layton had repeatedly broken out of the installation. The mutant had refined his rubbery form to access smaller and smaller escape routes, which demonstrated Farley's success while endangering the project. However, until Gary Mundy had made the fatal mistake of interrupting his killing frenzy, Layton's victims had been plants and animals. The incidents had no doubt baffled the sheriff, but tracking down a vandal who stripped the apples off a tree hadn't become a priority.

Nobody was looking for a naked human rubber band, either,

They had been fortunate, Farley knew. Except for the kids who worked on the school newspaper, no one seemed inclined to try to figure out what had killed the farmer and the environmental agent or why.

That wouldn't happen again. Max had found every opening larger than half-inch PVC pipe and capped it. All the ventilation grates, ducts, and vents had been fitted with wire mesh. Layton would have to assume the size and shape of a spaghetti strand to escape his sealed cell now, and it was doubtful that he could. If he ever managed that, however, there was no foolproof way to contain him. Rather than go to the trouble and expense of a lockdown, which meant switching to emergency power, maybe they could bribe the mutant into behaving. The only alternative was elimination.

"Do you have jerky for Layton today?" Max locked Nathan's door.

"Chocolate," Farley said.

"Well, it's not rabbits or snakes, but—" Max looked through the shatterproof glass over Layton's window and froze.

Farley's heart lurched as he stepped up to the door.

Layton's cell was empty.

CHAPTER 14

Lana parked Chloe's car in a dirt-and-gravel area off the drive by the pasture fence. She hadn't planned to come to the stable today, but when Margo asked for the night off, she had gladly switched shifts. Cruising the Kansas countryside on horseback was the best way she knew to wrestle with problems. Riding cleared her head and helped her solve them.

Sighing, Lana stuffed her wallet under the driver's seat. She had been troubled all day because she hadn't given Clark an honest answer when he asked about Sharon Farley that morning.

At first, Lana thought she was just being fair to the new girl. Whether Sharon really was shy or just trying to decide what students she wanted as friends, it had taken her three months to open up. It didn't seem right to assume Sharon was up to something devious just because she seemed too curious.

However, as the day wore on, Lana couldn't deny the real reason she had clammed up. *And it wasn't out of consideration for Sharon.*

She had been afraid Clark would think she was jealous if she said Sharon was a phony. In fact, that's exactly what she *had* thought after Sharon left the Talon; that maybe she couldn't trust her judgment where Clark Kent was concerned.

Lana had decided to find Clark and explain before school let out, but then she had realized something else. Just because she and Chloe had mistaken Clark's warning about Ian as jealousy didn't mean that Clark would react to her warning about Sharon the same way. Even hinting that he might would be an insult.

So now the whole day is gone, and my chance to fix this is fading fast. Lana didn't know what to do, except go for a gallop and hope she could figure it out.

Lana locked the car door and slipped Chloe's keys into her jeans pocket. Three other cars were parked in the gravel parking area, but she didn't see anyone—or hear anyone. The black barn cat wasn't curled on the bench by the stable door soaking up the late-afternoon sun, and the stable manager's dog didn't run out to greet her.

Frowning, Lana scanned the carefully tended grounds. The white board fences around the show and practice rings gleamed against the meteor green of the surrounding meadow. A wren flew into the eaves of the raised judges' stand to tend her nest, and squirrels scampered around the permanent hedge-and-board jumps that formed the outside hunter course. The broodmares calmly grazed in the pasture, and the horses inside the barn were quiet.

Everything seemed normal, except that no one was around.

Then she noticed that the large horse van wasn't parked in its usual spot behind the barn.

"Oh, of course!" Lana suddenly remembered that Walter Holtz, the stable manager, had taken the barn's top show riders and their horses to the Equestrian Center in Metropolis.

The semiweekly outings had started last month and would continue until Mr. Holtz found a new hunter-jumper trainer to employ full-time. Rowdy James, the nearly deaf, cranky, aging stable hand, was probably taking a nap in the hayloft. The old man worked as little as possible and complained about everything constantly and loudly. The stable wouldn't be the same without him, but she was glad he wasn't around to talk her ear off now.

The tranquil setting had a soothing effect as Lana walked toward the barn. She noticed a black helmet and leather gloves lying on the stepped mounting block and wondered who had forgotten them. Everyone loved going to the enclosed arena in the city to train, and things often got left behind in the excitement. As soon as she could afford it, Lana intended to get back into serious training and competition, too.

The large double doors on the front of the stable were open, and she could see Coral Roman's gray mare, Fiona's Luck, in the first box stall. With ears perked forward and nostrils flaring, the mare's attention was on something unseen deeper within the barn. When Lana got closer, she understood why the horse was so fascinated. Someone was rummaging around in the feed room.

Lana's smile faded when she paused to glance through the vertical bars of Fiona's stall door. The mare's dappled gray coat glistened with sweat, and every muscle was spring-coiled. The horse wasn't anticipating her next meal. She was frightened and poised to fight or flee.

From something harmless, Lana wondered, or did the animal sense a definite danger?

Every instinct told Lana to run, but she couldn't abandon the horses in the stalls that lined the wide central aisle. The bay gelding on her left nervously paced a circle, and another farther down snorted and pawed the floor. Tension gripped every animal in the barn. If the threat was real and not hyper horse-imagination, she could open the stalls to free them.

If necessary, she thought with an anxious glance toward the feed room halfway down the aisle on the left. She was *not* leaving without her pinto, but he was stabled at the far end of the barn.

Lana considered circling around the outside of the building to avoid being seen by whoever—or whatever—had upset the horses. But she had to open the doors on the far end to get her horse out, and the hinges creaked. Her chances of making a quick, fast getaway would be better if she reached the horse first and opened the noisy doors to leave, rather than enter.

Lana moved to the wall just past the bay gelding's stall. On the right between Fiona's stall and the next stall down, a smaller aisle branched off. She paused to peer down the short, narrow corridor, but the doors into the office and tack room were closed.

Lana's mind raced through possible reasons for the prevalent tension as she inched toward the feed room. Grain and feed mixtures were stored in metal containers, and unopened bags were stacked until needed. The feed room and barn were swept or blown clean twice a day, and hay and straw were kept in the loft. No tinder material was left lying around to combust spontaneously. Fire seemed unlikely unless a wire had shorted out or an intruder had deliberately set one.

That thought gave Lana pause. Anyone despicable enough to risk killing a barnful of horses wouldn't think twice about hurting a teenage girl.

She had left her cell phone home so she wouldn't lose or break it, a decision that seemed foolish now. As other riders had learned, the small phones slipped from pockets or came unhooked and were impossible to find on wooded trails or open meadows. Annie Frame had been kicked with a cell phone in her pocket. Her hip was bruised, and the phone was smashed. The cell phone survival rate after being stepped on by fifteen hundred pounds of horse was also zero. Such accidents were rare, but Lana didn't need the unnecessary expense of replacing a phone. She obviously needed to rethink that—later.

Lana stopped and glanced around for anything she could use to defend herself. Metal hooks, rounded halter and bridle holders, and metal blanket bars were attached to the outside of each stall. Wooden boxes with sloping, hinged lids were spaced at intervals along the walls. Each box was filled with brushes and other grooming tools and products.

As she edged past Artax's empty stall, Lana quietly lifted a leather lead with a chain extension and heavy snap-clip off a hook. She wasn't strong enough to choke anyone with the shank, but she could throw an intruder off stride and buy time if she hit an eye with the snap. She coiled the leather and chain and folded her hand over the snap to muffle any metallic sound.

Next, she carefully sorted through the bristle brushes and rubber currycombs in the grooming box until she found a hoof pick. The hooked metal tool was used to remove collected dirt from the underside of a horse's hoof and could function as a weapon. Lana slipped it into her back pocket and slowly advanced on the feed room.

Thwhap!

The odd sound was followed by a squeal that was abruptly silenced.

Lana halted, swallowing a gasp, her heart pounding wildly in her chest. As much as she loved her horse, she suddenly questioned the wisdom of her actions. Perhaps, a better plan would be to back up and detour into the stable office, where she could use the phone to call for help.

Help with what? Lana took in a deep breath to calm her rattled nerves. She would feel like a complete fool if the sheriff or Clark raced to her rescue only to discover she had been spooked by—

"Yeow."

—the cat!

Sagging with relief, Lana exhaled slowly. The noise had signaled a bad end for a mouse that had not been quick enough to elude feline fang and claw. Mr. Holtz had let the black stray settle into the barn when he proved to be an adept mouser. The boarders called him Ninja Cat because he yowled as he attacked.

Disconcerting, but effective, Lana thought as she moved into the open doorway.

All the intellectual and emotional defenses Lana had built to insulate herself from shock shattered. She had honestly believed she'd been tempered by her experiences over the past couple of years to cope with anything. She had been cocooned as bug boy Arkin's future mate, turned into a sizzling, heartless vamp by an extinct flower, and forced to witness a bad cop's crimes through his eyes because she had been knocked unconscious in a gas-line explosion.

However, none of those bizarre and inexplicable events had prepared her for the gross scene in the stable feed room.

Time slowed as Lana's gaze swept the room, taking in

every significant detail. Ninja Cat crouched on a high shelf between large plastic jars of vitamin supplements, oils, and medicines. The fur on his tail and back bristled, and his fangs were bared in a silent hiss. Thirty or more dead mice were piled on the floor under the shelf.

A tall, attractive man with a muscular build and short, brown hair leaned on a cabinet storage counter, using his cell phone antenna to scratch his back. Lana recognized him from a brief conversation they had had at the Talon last week. Max Cutler had been introducing himself to businesspeople around town, claiming to be a real estate developer.

Mr. Cutler didn't notice her in that first split second because his gaze was fastened on the horrific creature sprawled on the floor. It looked like a human squid with four elongated appendages. One of the tendrils whipped out, stretching as it snapped across the room to snare one of the dead mice in a rubbery hand. The elastic arm snapped back to almost normal size and shape and shoved the furry body into an expanding mouth. It swallowed the animal whole, then giggled.

Lana clutched her stomach and covered her mouth to muffle a sickened gag. She didn't understand Mr. Cutler's connection to the monster, but he was definitely not in Smallville to buy large tracts of land.

"C'mon, Layton," the man muttered under his breath.

As Lana backed up a step, the metal snap slipped from her grasp. In her shock, the arm holding the leather and chain lead shank had gone limp at her side. When the large snap hit the floor, Max Cutler and Layton both turned to stare.

I am so dead. Still clutching the coiled lead shank, Lana turned and ran.

This time, Max didn't stop to think before making the transition to his alter-form. Since the girl hadn't come between Layton and his Mickey Mouse snack, the AWOL mutant had no interest in her.

It was up to Max to neutralize the threat. Lana Lang had seen too much, and she couldn't be allowed to escape.

Max's alter-form was activated an instant before the young manager of the Talon realized that she had inadvertently attracted his attention.

His body went numb. As it crumpled to the floor, his conscious mind was driven downward by processes he could not define and didn't comprehend. One moment he was looking at the girl through human eyes. Then his senses were part of the dark shadow that Max Cutler had become. He did not smell, hear, see, or feel in the traditional sense, but his perceptions were all-encompassing and acute.

Max sensed Lana running toward the door and focused on his target.

"Go, Max!" Layton cheered, laughing as the sentient shadow shot forward.

Max sped across the brick floor, fleeing the gray light in the barn for the brilliance of the late-afternoon sun. Once he was outside, chasing the terrified girl filled him with an ecstatic energy he hadn't felt since he had overwhelmed and killed Howard Stoner.

The farmer had become an expensive annoyance. Farley had doubled Stoner's salary to continue doing what he had been doing for Lex Luthor: keeping the locals away from the silo enclosure and keeping his mouth shut. They had paid extra to have the fenced-in area mowed, but that wasn't enough for the greedy hick. Howard Stoner had threatened to call the cops about Layton, the "creepy thing" he had seen ooze out of a buried cable trench.

Max had found the runaway before Layton started another extermination rampage. He had brought the naked mutant back immediately, but not before the farmer saw them. Continental Sciences had been generous, but Max had no intention of wasting good money on a blackmailing snitch.

As Stoner stomped across the field toward his house, shadow-Max had attacked him. A large segment of his shadow-self had flowed down the man's throat into his lungs, cutting off his air. When he was certain Stoner was dead, he had started to extract and retreat. He had just slipped off the body when the Kent kid had suddenly shown up.

Max hadn't a clue where Clark had come from or how he had gotten there so fast. When the teenager ran into the house to call 911, he had flowed away from the body and back to the underground installation.

The unplanned field test seemed to confirm Dr. Farley's assertion that no one would notice a shadow, not even if it was out of position in relation to the lighting. Max didn't think Clark Kent had seen him on the ground by Stoner's body, but he hadn't been certain. Since being certain was critical to the safety of everyone in the project, he had talked Sharon into finding out.

Lana ran, reaching into her pocket for her keys without breaking stride. Max wrapped around her ankles before she made it to the car.

Crying out in terror, the girl frantically tried to beat him off with a coiled strap, but leather and chain had no effect on the gossamer substance of his shadow-form. Unlike particles of light, he had miniscule mass that was impervious to injury. He could also exert force many times greater than should be possible for his size. As he tightened around Lana's legs, she lost her balance and fell over.

Sharon will be sorry she missed this. Usually, Max took perverse pleasure in thwarting Farley's spoiled brat. She had been a thorn in his side from the moment they had moved their operations to Smallville.

Even now, Sharon's whining complaints played in his mind like a CD caught in a defect loop.

"I hate it here! Everything smells like manure!"

"Why would I want to be friends with a bunch of farmers?"

"Shopping for clothes in this cow town? Not in this lifetime."

Dr. Farley made excuses for Sharon's petulance, but she was old enough to understand the dangers they faced and the rewards they stood to gain. Smallville *was* a cow town, which made it an ideal location for their illegal, clandestine enterprise. The world was full of worthless airheads Sharon could befriend *after* their fortunes and futures were secure.

Sharon had finally earned her keep when she agreed to

spy at the high school. Her decision had nothing to do with helping him, however. She had had her own reasons for accepting the mission: to relieve her self-inflicted boredom, because Clark Kent met her teenage standard for cute-enough-to-date, and she wanted to protect her father. As a bonus, she couldn't resist the challenge of snagging Clark away from the Lang girl, who had a secret thing for him. The thrill had only lasted through the movie date, but that was long enough to find out what the boy had seen the day Stoner died.

Sharon was convinced Clark Kent hadn't noticed anything strange. He *was* strange.

Max had thought Sharon was imagining things, until he brought the kid down as he was walking away from the silo site.

Sharon had found Clark snooping around the yard. They still hadn't figured out how he had managed to break the lock on the gate. While she had kept him talking, Sharon had held down the call button on the walkie-talkie she carried for use underground. That had alerted Farley to the problem above while preventing the scientists from returning the call, which would have alerted the boy to their presence. When Sharon had seen his shadow-form emerge through the wire mesh over a vent, she steered Clark away from the shaded woods.

Even at full strength in direct sunlight, Max had expected some resistance from the strapping young man, but he had felled Clark Kent with almost no effort. When he realized the kid was reacting to the meteor dust in his alter-form, he had aborted the mission.

Clark Kent was too valuable to kill.

Lana Lang was not.

She's just unlucky with a rotten sense of timing, Max thought as he spiraled up and around Lana's legs, tightening his hold.

When Max had begun tracking Layton, he quickly realized that the mutant was headed for a cluster of farms. The stable complex with its main barn, outbuildings, and manager's house had been the first source of abundant rodents in Layton's path. Max had emerged from a wooded area at the crest of a rise expecting to find horse and human carnage he could not possibly cover up. Instead, Layton had hunkered down by a tractor to wait until the truck loaded with horses and a minivan full of girls had driven away.

By the time Max reached the barn, the elastic escapee was merrily catching and crushing mice in a feed storage room. Because of the late hour and distance from the silo, he had called Sharon's cell to ask for a ride back to the underground installation. If Lana had arrived fifteen minutes later, Layton would have been finished feeding, and they would have been long gone. The pile of uneaten dead mice would have been just another unexplained Smallville curiosity.

Stunned after her fall, Lana hesitated for a moment before she tossed the useless leather shank aside and dug into the dirt with her fingers. Max flowed around her torso as she tried to drag herself closer to the car. When crawling proved futile, she clawed at her chest to pull him off, but she couldn't hold on to a substance that separated and re-formed beyond her grasp. Her struggle intensified as he contracted to cover her mouth and nostrils, muffling her screams and blocking her air.

The termination was necessary, but he respected the girl's desperate fight for life.

Max didn't want to die, either.

The Audi skidded as Sharon yanked the wheel to turn onto Rolling Hills Road. She had just turned into the Kents' drive when Max had called asking for a ride. She was getting really tired of being ordered around by Max Cutler, especially when he couldn't make up his mind.

"Go get Clark Kent, come get me." Sharon huffed with derision. She didn't care that Max had once been an experienced but underpaid field agent for the CIA. He was just another one of her father's less-than-perfect experiments now. He had probably forgotten he had sent her to find Clark. "Jerk."

Max wasn't the only one who wanted to find out why Clark Kent was totally normal except when he was exposed to meteor material.

Or how he gets from one place to another faster than a speeding car, Sharon thought.

She had become suspicious when she realized that neither Lana nor the *Smallville Ledger* had gotten the times wrong the day Clark had found Mr. Stoner's body. He had left the Talon at four-twenty-five and called 911 fifteen minutes later. Since he could have hitched a ride, which would account for the discrepancy, she had put it out of her mind. Then Clark had left Lex Luthor's mansion on foot and arrived at the missile silo faster than she had been able to drive. Even taking into account the shorter cross-country route, the feat was impossible unless his running ability had been artificially enhanced.

There was no doubt that the green meteor dust her father used to engineer his subjects altered cellular integrity, usually in ways he didn't anticipate. Although her dad could now induce specific physical changes that were stable, he hadn't conquered the problem of neuron deterioration, which would turn Max into a blithering idiot like Layton and the others within a couple of weeks, if not sooner.

Regarding Clark, Max and her father had finally reached the same conclusion she had. Since Smallville was the site of the 1989 meteor shower, Clark's superspeed was probably the result of meteor exposure. That together with all the incidents documented on Chloe's Wall of Weird proved *her* worst fear, which her father had been denying.

Casual exposure to the meteor-rocks could cause erratic, usually horrible, and perhaps fatal physiological changes.

Except in Clark Kent's case.

Clark seemed to have a meteor-induced, stable physical ability, and he was not a mental midget. They had to find out why.

He was Max Cutler's only hope, and maybe hers, too.

Sharon strongly suspected that her father's precautions with the meteor-rocks had been inadequate, and that she had been contaminated. She wasn't exhibiting any effects she could identify, but she was certain the vile radiation was busy scrambling her DNA.

Spotting the stable sign up ahead, Sharon slowed her car and turned down a tree-lined drive. The fences, barns, livestock, open fields, and stands of forest that everyone in Smallville treasured would never feel right to her. She missed the sprawling malls, country clubs, exclusive shops, and exotic restaurants of the East Coast suburbs.

When Sharon reached the circular drive in front of the barn, she slammed on the brakes. There was no sign of Layton, but Lana Lang was lying on the ground with Max's dark shadow wrapped around her face.

Throwing the gearshift into park and leaving the motor running, Sharon jumped out of the car and rushed to the fallen girl. "Get off her, Max!"

The shadow shimmered angrily, but Max didn't obey.

Lana's breathing was getting shallow, but for the moment, she was still alive. A leather strap with an attached chain and halter snap was on the ground beside her. If she had been going to the pasture to get a horse, why had Max attacked her? Was he becoming a mindless predator like Layton ahead of schedule? Sharon wondered, but Lana's predicament demanded her immediate attention.

"If you kill that girl, Max, you might kill your chances for a cure." Sharon stood back with her hands on her hips and relaxed when shadow-Max flowed off the girl onto the dirt drive.

Max's perceptions were so sensitive he could detect nuances of body language and expression. Although he couldn't speak in his alter-form, he understood everything and found innovative ways of communicating.

Sharon watched as Max's shadow shifted into a ribbon that formed the word, "Why?"

"Because we need Clark Kent, and Lana is one of his closest friends. We can use her as bait to snare him," Sharon snapped. A week ago, Max would have understood that without an explanation. Angry and afraid, she lashed out with snide disdain. "Run along and find your body, Max. Then round up Layton so we can get out of here."

Max's shadow rocketed toward the barn. He was upset, but it wasn't her fault he was less than the man he had been.

Lana moaned as she sat up and rubbed a bump on the bone ridge above her eye. She sprang to her feet, as though suddenly remembering why she was on the ground. Her fearful gaze settled on Sharon as she reached for something behind her back.

"What's going on, Sharon?"

"Nothing." Sharon pulled her fist back and hit Lana in the jaw.

Already weakened from her encounter with Max, Lana crumpled to her knees. A hooked metal tool fell out of her hand as Sharon kicked her in the skull, knocking her out. The girl collapsed as Max came storming out of the barn with Layton trailing behind him.

Sharon had seen Layton in all his glory once before, but that didn't diminish her revulsion.

The scrawny naked man waved with a toothless grin. "Hi, Sharn."

Sharon leveled Max with a piercing stare. "Do *not* let him touch me."

"Get a grip, Sharon." Max picked up Lana's limp body and nodded toward the car. "Open it."

Layton opened the back door and climbed inside.

Sharon smiled as the agent set Lana's unconscious body on the back seat beside Layton. "Why the hurry, Max? The sun won't set for another hour."

"Shut up." Max slid into the driver's seat and slammed the door.

Laughing, Sharon got in the passenger side and speed-dialed Clark. She let it ring, but no one answered.

CHAPTER 15

"You don't have to hang with me, Pete." Chloe glanced at the clock on the wall behind him. Three hours had passed since Clark had left the *Torch* offices. "It's almost six."

Chloe had drafted an article titled "Lockdown or Lockup" as a companion piece for the *Torch* cafeteria poll on the closed campus policy. Pete had patiently searched the Internet for information on Dr. Lawrence Farley. They were both starting to bog down in boredom.

"What?" Pete looked up sharply. "Well, that explains why my stomach is growling. Do you still have emergency rations stashed somewhere?"

"Oatmeal granola bars and a bag of Really Sour Jells." Chloe pointed toward the filing cabinet on the wall behind her. "Top drawer."

"That should take the edge off." Pete stood up and stretched.

Chloe looked back at her computer monitor. After Clark had called to report on his conversation with Lex Luthor, she had narrowed the Internet search parameters. She wasn't sure what Dr. Farley was up to in his missile silo, but she didn't think it involved legal, or even illegal, stem cell research.

"I thought Chad said he'd get back to you before he left work today." Pete paused behind her chair and ripped the wrapper off a granola bar.

"He did, and he will," Chloe said. "Chad never breaks his word. I'm staying until I hear from him."

"I am, too, then." Pete balled the wrapper and tossed it into a wastebasket across the room. "So what's your theory if Clark's dust matches the stuff they found in Mr. Stoner and the environmental guy?"

Chloe hedged. "I'd just be guessing."

"You're guesses are usually right." Pete popped a sour jelly candy into his mouth and pulled a chair up beside her.

"Okay, in a nutshell—" Leaning back, Chloe rattled off her conclusions. "For starters, Sharon wasn't ever interested in Clark."

"What?" Pete sat back so hard the chair almost tipped over. "No way! She was putting the moves on him, Chloe. I know it."

"She probably was," Chloe agreed, "but not because she liked him."

"And this is based on what?" Pete's skepticism was pointed. "A little residual Clark crush of your own, maybe?"

"Not!" Chloe's hand flew out and smacked him in the chest. "I think she knew that meteor-rocks have bizarre effects on some people before she suddenly decided to talk to us."

Pete frowned. "It was kind of sudden, wasn't it?"

"Very." Chloe picked up a pencil and nibbled the eraser. "Like two days after Clark saw Mr. Stoner die in the field next to the missile silo her scientist father is renting. Much too convenient, don't you think?"

"Yeah." Pete exhaled. "And I practically shoved Clark into Sharon's arms."

"No, you *did* shove Clark into her arms." Chloe

shrugged. "But since he wasn't suckered by Sharon's baby blues, you're forgiven."

"That makes my day," Pete quipped.

Rising, Chloe began to pace. "So tell me if you think this is a reach."

"Listening," Pete said.

"We've got a lunatic on the loose who kills snakes, and Mr. Mundy's body was found on a pile of dead rabbits. Sharon's father was a geneticist until the government pulled his research grant, and he rented Lex's missile silo because he doesn't want to be bothered. Plus, the saliva in Mr. Mundy's wounds was human."

Pete waited for the punch line.

"What if Dr. Farley is messing around with the effects of meteor dust on DNA?" Chloe asked.

"Making monsters?" Pete wasn't kidding.

"Maybe." Chloe frowned, tapping the pencil against her cheek. "Clark thought his meteor dust came from the ground, but what if he was in contact with something else and just didn't know it."

"Is that possible?" Pete asked.

"We're dealing with meteor-rocks, Pete. Anything is possible." Chloe dropped back in her chair. "Remember Amy Palmer's brother and the invisible skin cream?"

"Yeah. Smelled like a rose, but wasn't a rose." Pete's gaze flicked to her computer screen when the mail tone chimed. "Incoming."

Chloe was already bringing up the menu. The message was from Chad, and as usual, he didn't waste words.

New specimen matches Stoner and Mundy. Chad

"Guess that answers that." Pete rested his elbows on his knees. "So what do we do with it?"

"Call Clark for starters," Chloe said. "It's really looking like we've got two meteor murders."

As Chloe reached for her cell phone, it rang. She glanced at the Caller ID readout and hit *send* to connect her father. If his plans hadn't changed, he was working late filling a big order.

"Hi, Dad! Are you still at the plant?"

"Yes, why aren't you home, yet?" Mr. Sullivan asked.

"Homework and the *Torch*." Chloe cringed slightly. "I'll be leaving here soon."

"Is Lana there?" Her father asked abruptly.

"Lana? No," Chloe said. "She's working Margo's shift tonight. Try the Talon."

"The Talon called me," Mr. Sullivan explained. "Lana was supposed to be there at five. She didn't show, and it's after six. I've called the house and left messages on her cell, but she hasn't called me back."

Chloe frowned. Lana was infuriatingly punctual and considerate. She would have called the Talon to say she would be late—unless she went to the stable and left her cell behind again. That, in Chloe's opinion, was worse than not having one like Clark.

"I tried the barn. No answer there, either." Mr. Sullivan sighed. "We have to get this order out on schedule, Chloe. I can't leave work right now."

Her dad sounded frantic, which was easy to understand. Lana's Aunt Nell hadn't been wild about leaving her niece in Smallville when she moved away. She had only agreed because Chloe's father was a respected mem-

ber of the community and a wonderful parent. Now he
was responsible for Lana.

"Do you want me to go check the barn?" Chloe asked.
"It won't be dark for a while yet."

"The Kents are closer," Mr. Sullivan said. "I'll call the
farm and see if Clark or Jonathan will go."

"Call me back if you hear from Lana, okay?" Chloe
ended the call and frowned.

"That didn't sound good," Pete said.

"No, not good at all." Since Clark didn't have call
waiting, Chloe gave her father time to call first. After a
couple of minutes she speed-dialed Clark's number, but
the line was still busy.

Chloe jumped up again and paced around the two central desks. The line was busy so at least someone was
home at the Kent farm. She wanted to tell Clark that the
meteor dust he had picked up near the silo matched the
samples from the dead men.

With Lana missing and something running around
Smallville killing weird stuff on what seemed to be a
mindless whim, it was life-and-death important.

Clark also didn't know yet that LexCorp was still paying the bill to Kansas State Water and Power for the missile facility.

Clark sat at the kitchen table, making notes in a spiral
notebook. After coming home from meeting Lex at the
Talon, he had been helping his dad and mom with the last
section of fence in the back pasture. He had returned to
the house with his mother ten minutes ago. When she

went back to the pasture with coffee and snacks for his dad, he had stayed to finish his biology paper. It was almost done and ready to type into the *Torch* computer for printing, but he was having trouble concentrating.

He couldn't stop thinking about the old missile silo and why Sharon's father had paid for security modifications in a property he didn't own. Maybe he didn't understand because his family had to count every cent. To Lex, the expenditure made sense. If Dr. Farley's potential financial gain was big enough, a throwaway investment to secure the source of future wealth would be worth it.

Dropping his pen, Clark rocked back on the hind legs of his chair. If money was motivating Dr. Farley's activities, how sure of making a fortune was he? Would he kill to protect his secret cash cow until he was ready to cash in?

The theory was sound, but the only signs of a killer were the victims. Rosebushes and rabbits wouldn't threaten anyone's future revenues. Had Mr. Stoner and Mr. Mundy just been in the wrong place at the wrong time or had they stumbled on the valuable secret?

Clark sighed as he mulled over the facts. He had been sickened by meteor dust his clothes picked up from the ground. Sharon was too afraid of meteor-rocks to carry one, and no one else had been around.

But what if Sharon's father found the meteor property that produces invisibility? It had happened before, to Jeff Palmer.

When the phone rang, Clark sped into the living room to answer. He was surprised to hear Mr. Sullivan's voice and dismayed by his reason for calling. Lana had not shown up for work, and she had not called in.

"I don't know if Lana tried calling here, Mr. Sullivan." Clark didn't try to explain that their ancient answering machine had stopped working earlier that day and money was too tight to pay for a new one immediately. "Until ten minutes ago, no one was home to answer the phone."

His mother always carried her LuthorCorp cell phone, but none of his friends had the number.

"Could you or your Dad run over to the stable, Clark?" Mr. Sullivan asked. "Lana's probably there, but I'd feel better if I knew for sure."

"I'll go, Mr. Sullivan," Clark said. Hearing the worry in the older man's voice, he tried to reassure him. "Lana rides whenever she can. If she hasn't come back to the barn, I know some of the places she goes."

The cemetery came to mind. Not everyone knew how often Lana visited her parents' grave.

Clark sped out the door within a split second of hanging up from Mr. Sullivan.

He had been speeding around Smallville for as long as his parents had let him out of their sight. He had memorized less-traveled routes to every corner of the county and all major locations in between. However, in extreme emergencies, he used secondary roads and highways.

Lana was missing, and he knew she would never have ducked her shift without a good reason or calling to explain. He took the road.

Clark sped a mile down Hickory Lane then raced through the Gundersons' back cornfield to Jackson Road. After cutting the corner through Shaver Woods, he took a dirt road that came out on Rolling Hills Road. He crossed a pasture, then sped along the edge of the woods, leaping hunter brush jumps incorporated into fences. When he came into visual range of the stable, he slowed and walked out of the trees behind the tractor shed.

Mr. Holtz, the stable manager, stood in a large horse van in front of the barn. One horse was still waiting on the truck to be unloaded. A dark-haired girl walked another horse into the barn. Two blond girls were pulling riding gear out of a minivan that blocked Clark's view of the cars lined up behind it. His X-ray vision penetrated the minivan and three other cars before he recognized Chloe's. Lana had been here.

Clark seriously doubted Lana would have taken her pinto somewhere by truck without mentioning it, but he had to ask. He approached the horse van as Mr. Holtz snapped a lead shank on the charcoal bay's halter ring.

"What brings you out this way, Clark?" Mr. Holtz unhooked a metal bar in front of the horse and led the animal down the loading ramp. The ramp slid in and out of a floor slot in the side of the van. Safety railings folded up on either side and locked in place.

"I was looking for Lana," Clark said. "Is she here?"

"I haven't seen her." A wiry man of fifty with short, curly hair and twinkling eyes, Mr. Holtz smiled. "But I just got back from a training trip to Metropolis."

"I see that." Clark glanced toward the barn. If Lana was out riding, the pinto wouldn't be in his stall. "Mind if I look around?"

"Not at all." Mr. Holtz handed Clark the lead shank. "Take Domino inside with you. If Katie doesn't get him first, third stall down on the right."

The dark horse with one white sock and a white strip that angled off his nose, nuzzled Clark's chest.

"Let's go, Domino." Walking with the horse on his right, Clark entered the stable.

Micheline Jordan, a senior at Smallville High, was inside the second stall down on the left. A sign over the door read, Artax.

"Have you seen Katie, Micheline?" Clark asked.

"I think she's helping Kelly put the tack away." The girl slipped an unbuckled halter off her horse's nose and gave Artax a pat as she left the stall and secured the closer.

Everything in its proper place, Clark thought as he watched Micheline hang the halter and rope lead on a holder outside the stall. Mr. Holtz ran a tight stable with strict rules. Lana often teased Chloe that the show barn was neater and cleaner than their room. Chloe always retorted that a little clutter was a sign of a free spirit and didn't care.

"I can take Domino now." Katie Picken ducked out of a smaller aisle on the right. Slim and blond, with a warm smile, she took the horse's lead from Clark's hand.

"Thanks." As Clark started toward Lana's stall at the end of the barn, a girl screamed. Checking his impulse to speed, he hurried to the feed room. Jessica collided with him as she ran out the door. "What's the matter?"

"It's so awful!" Pale and shaking, Jessica pulled away and bolted for the office.

Fearing the worst, Clark jumped into the small storeroom. He was both revolted and relieved when he saw the pile of dead mice. A black cat sat nearby.

"Whoa! Ninja buddy!" Mr. Holtz paused in the doorway with an astonished grin. "There must be over fifty mice in that pile! Is that a great cat or what?"

"Unbelievable," Clark said. No cat could possibly kill that many mice. The mysterious rosebush and rodent killer was clearly the culprit, but it was easier to let the cat take credit. He was now faced with a more serious problem.

Ducking out of the feed room, Clark quickly confirmed that Lana's horse was still in his stall.

Bad news. Clark rushed back outside to check Chloe's car. A pile of dead mice and a pile of dead rabbits couldn't possibly be an unrelated coincidence. His thoughts skipped quickly from one fact to another, drawing ominous conclusions.

Judging by everyone's reactions, Lana had not yet arrived and the dead mice had not been in the feed room when Mr. Holtz and the girls left for Metropolis. Consequently, Lana might have been at the stable, probably alone, when the mouse murders had taken place. Clark's only ray of hope was the absence of a body in the feed room or in Chloe's locked car.

The second wave of relief passed as Clark scanned the parking area for clues and wondered what to do next. A metal hoof pick and a leather lead shank were lying on the ground. It was unlikely one of the other girls had dropped the items so far from the horse van and barn. Everyone associated with the show stable took meticulous care of the expensive equipment, especially Lana. Recent footprints and larger impressions in the dirt suggested that a struggle might have taken place, and that someone might have fallen.

Fearing the worst, Clark jogged up the drive.

The missile silo was the one thing that seemed to connect the various threads. Two men had died nearby, and both bodies had been contaminated with meteor dust. Although the series of vandalism incidents had taken place over a couple of weeks in different locations, the destructive similarities couldn't be ignored. He knew from Lex that Sharon's father was engaged in unknown work he didn't want disclosed. It wasn't outrageous to think Dr. Farley might be using meteor dust, some of which might have dropped on the ground where he had come in contact with it. If that were true, then it was possible the scientist had deliberately or unintentionally created an unpredictable predator.

What if Lana had seen something Dr. Farley didn't want her to see?

Would he kill to protect his secret cash cow until he was ready to cash in? Stoner and Mundy are both dead!

Clark's own thoughts about Dr. Farley's possible motives came back to haunt him as he ran across Rolling Hills Road and down another farm drive. If his hunch about the scientist was wrong, no one would be harmed. As he took off through the corn toward Stoner's farm, he realized that if he was right, it might already be too late to save Lana.

Pete glanced at Chloe as they drove down Hickory Lane toward the Kent farm. The top of his vintage blue convertible was down, but she wasn't fretting about having to push her windblown hair out of her eyes and mouth. Chloe was really worried.

"You'll run the battery down," Pete admonished when Chloe hit her cell phone redial again.

Chloe had been trying to reach Clark since her father had called to report that Lana was missing. She had gotten a little frantic when no one answered the Kents' phone after the initial busy signal. She'd tried calling her father back, but it was after six and she got an automated menu. Since Lana hadn't been found, she didn't leave a message on his voice mail.

They hadn't had much better luck at the stable. After repeated tries, someone named Kelly had answered the office phone. She hadn't seen Lana or Clark, but she made it clear she couldn't talk. The manager and several girls had just returned from Metropolis, and they were swamped with work.

Too upset to sit around doing nothing, Chloe had insisted on driving out to the Kent farm, Clark's last known location.

"Still no answer." Chloe signed off and pulled a charger cord out of her shoulder bag. She plugged it into Pete's cigarette lighter and connected the phone to recharge it. "Thanks for reminding me about the battery, Pete. I don't want to run out of juice if things get rough."

"Which they always do." Pete wasn't a wimp, but he had sustained more than his share of bumps, bruises, and contusions since he had become super Clark's stalwart, but strictly human sidekick.

As they passed under the Kent farm sign, Chloe pointed at a tractor moving slowly across the pasture. "There's somebody."

"Clark's mom," Pete observed. "Mr. Kent doesn't wear straw hats tied on with red scarves."

Rolling her eyes, Chloe stepped out as soon as Pete came to a stop. Pete followed her toward the barn.

Martha parked by the grain silo and turned off the tractor engine. She smiled as she climbed down. "Hi, Pete! Chloe. If you're here to see Clark, I think he's inside working on his biology paper."

"Wouldn't he answer the phone if he was in the house?" Chloe asked. "I've been calling for half an hour."

"Oh." Martha frowned as she pulled an empty basket from under the tractor seat. "Is it important?"

"Uh—well, we're just all have trouble connecting," Chloe said. "Lana, Clark, us—"

"Especially Lana." Pete didn't want to alarm Clark's mother, but people were starting to vanish without a trace. "We thought Clark was going to look for her—

"Maybe he went with Sharon," Martha said.

"Sharon?" Chloe asked, surprised.

"She drives a silver Audi, right?" Martha started walking toward the house. "I'm sure I saw her car pull into the drive on my way out to the pasture. Clark came back to the house right about then."

"Thanks, Mrs. Kent." Before Chloe could start grilling Clark's mom in earnest, Pete pulled her away. If something came up that required parental help or interference, they could call back. "Are you going to be here?"

"Somebody's got to make dinner," Mrs. Kent said.

Pete didn't broach the subject of a plan until he and Chloe were back in the car. "Where to now?"

"The stable," Chloe said without hesitation. "As far as we know, Dad got in touch with Clark and asked him to look for Lana. Maybe he hitched a ride with Sharon."

Pete didn't think so. Clark could have gotten to the horse farm quicker under his own power.

"What was Sharon doing at the Kent farm?" Chloe's eyes narrowed.

"Looking for Clark?" Pete suggested.

"Why?" Chloe's dark scowl deepened.

"I don't know," Pete answered honestly. "But if Clark and Lana aren't goofing off in the horse barn, I think we'd better check the old missile silo site."

The sun was sinking in the western sky when Clark stopped in the trees lining the old access road by Stoner's field. It was hard to believe only a week had passed since he had been here the last time, walking home from school with nothing on his mind but the everyday problems of an alien teenager with amazing abilities he had to keep secret.

Seeing Mr. Stoner die made his complaints seem trivial.

Clark thought back to the sequence of events that day, but with the exception of the farmer's sudden collapse, nothing unusual had happened.

Nothing that he knew of.

Clark scanned the surrounding terrain as he stepped out of hiding. He had thoroughly canvassed the missile site for surveillance equipment the other day and found none. Now, he was wary of human eyes or the unknown predator with a taste for snake. Although he didn't sense anything, staying under cover as long as possible seemed prudent. He jogged across the road and down the shoulder.

A thick stand of trees stood between the road and the

missile silo site a hundred yards in. Sharon's silver Audi was parked on the drive to the enclosure gate beside an older model SUV. *Her father's car, perhaps?* Clark paused to inspect both vehicles with his X-ray vision. Nothing inside the trunk of Sharon's car had changed since he had looked the last time. The SUV was littered with fast-food wrappers, magazines and newspapers, a toolbox, jumper cables, and assorted outerwear. He didn't see anything that suggested Lana might have been in either vehicle recently.

As Clark sped through the wooded section to the gate, he reminded himself that he was acting on gut feelings, making assumptions based on Lana's personality and circumstantial evidence that implicated Sharon and her dad. Not a whole lot was clear except that Lana Lang wouldn't flake out on her responsibilities or worry her friends and surrogate family.

Something was wrong.

In the gray twilight before sundown, the visible remains of the installation inside the chain-link and razor-wire fence seemed more sinister than in broad daylight. The broken lock on the gate hadn't been replaced, which surprised Clark—until he remembered that Dr. Farley's partner had a background in security. The broken lock and lack of cameras or sensing devices was probably deliberate. There were no aboveground signs that anyone was inhabiting the installation below.

Clever, Clark thought as he eased through the gate and replaced the chain. Farley's security expert couldn't have known that a local kid had the strength to lift the heavy broken hatch over an access tube that had been filled with cement. And that begged the question: Were they trying to keep the curious out or something terrible in?

Clark spun when a whirring noise sounded behind him. He quickly trashed the idea of jumping the fence and speeding into hiding as the automated primary hatch swung open onto the weight-brace. His X-ray vision couldn't penetrate the lead-lined silo lid or hatch cover to find out if Lana was in the facility below. He would have to break in or be invited.

As Sharon Farley climbed out, he decided to try for the invitation first. Although he wasn't positive, he didn't think she knew that he suspected her father of dangerous, criminal activity involving the dreaded meteor-rocks. If he forced his way inside, there would be no question that was what he thought.

And his suspicions could be wrong, Clark realized as Sharon palmed one cell phone and dialed another. Her father really *could* be an eccentric who was writing a science fiction novel locked in a missile silo. Or he could also be a paranoid scientist involved in legitimate research.

Clark didn't actually believe that, but he had nothing to lose by acting as though he did. *At least until my suspicions are confirmed and I find Lana.*

Given Sharon's fear, it was reasonable to assume that her father kept his meteor-rock supply locked in lead, if he actually had meteor-rocks. There was a minimal risk, but that was a chance Clark had to take. If Dr. Farley and his security man were responsible for the murders and assorted mayhem, he felt confident he could rescue Lana and escape to tell the authorities.

Sharon didn't realize that someone else was in the

compound when her speed-dialed call went through. "Hi! Is Clark there?"

Clark stiffened at the sound of his name. He didn't know whether to be alarmed or not, but the fact that Sharon wanted to talk to him would make his charade easier to pull off.

"I'm right here." Clark walked toward her with an impish smile.

Sharon snapped the compact flip-phone closed as she turned to stare. "What are you doing here, Clark?"

"Just looking around." Clark paused beside her to glance through the hatch. A metal ladder descended to an elevator platform eight feet down.

Sharon deliberately moved between him and the opening. "Looking for what?"

"I thought that was obvious yesterday. I want to get a look inside this old launch facility." Clark took a cue from Pete and told the truth. "I've been fascinated with this place since I was a kid."

Sharon frowned. "That doesn't explain why here and now."

"I didn't believe that you were here to get evidence against LexCorp yesterday." Clark shrugged. "Lex told me to stay away because he had rented the place. It wasn't hard to figure out that your father was the tenant."

"Uh-huh." Sharon eyed him uncertainly.

Clark glanced at the cell phone. "Must be lousy reception down there. No phone line?"

"Yes, and no." Sharon stepped away from the hatch and folded her arms in the same apprehensive manner as she had the day before.

The nervous gesture drew Clark's attention. Sharon

had *two* devices: the cell phone and another, slightly larger black case that she had been carrying the day before. "Two phones?"

Sharon held up the larger device. "Walkie-talkie."

Clark realized she was holding down the CALL button, opening the line to someone with a similar device below. He thought he had considered every contingency, but apparently not. Their entire conversation, from the moment he had stepped forward, had been overheard.

The nausea caught Clark off guard just as he made the decision to speed to safety to reconsider his options.

A sickening sensation spread up his legs. Fighting a losing battle against the debilitating effects of meteor material, Clark glanced down as he began to fade out.

A dark shadow twined around his legs as hands attached to deformed, elastic arms wrapped around his torso and pulled him into the hatch.

CHAPTER 16

Clark fell 8 feet down onto the metal floor outside the elevator. The bands circling his chest tightened. It felt as if a thousand cactus spines filled with acid had pierced his shirt. White-hot knives seemed to slice through muscle, tendon, and bone trapped under the dark shadow binding his legs. The pain was excruciating, but it helped him fight the haze that was dragging him into unconsciousness. His captors were infested with meteor dust, and he was helpless to break their grip. Still, he wouldn't be completely lost if he could stay awake and focused.

Information was his only chance and ally.

"Watch it, Max!" Sharon snapped. "I wasn't going to lock you out, so just chill! It's not even dark, yet."

Sharon's comment implied that the shadow was afraid of the dark. However, the elevator platform was too brightly lit for Max's phobia to help Clark now.

Everything suddenly became irrelevant when a tentacle whipped out and flattened over his face. Already breathless from the jolts of electric pain stabbing his heart and lungs, Clark gasped when his oxygen was cut off.

"Stop it, Layton!" Sharon screamed. "Get off!"

The mask of rubbery flesh trembled, but it didn't loosen its smothering hold. Running out of air and blinded, with his X-ray vision rendered useless, Clark could only listen.

"Max! That idiot is supposed to carry Clark, not strangle him! Do something!" Sharon sounded frantic.

Assuming Max was the shadow, Clark had no idea what Sharon expected him to do. Apparently, neither did Max.

"How should I know!" Sharon stamped her foot with an angry, frustrated grunt then paused. "Wait a minute."

I don't have a minute, Clark thought, as a numbing fog settled over his mind. If Sharon's annoyed attitude was a clue, she didn't want him to die. He clung to that dismal hope as he started to black out.

"Listen, Layton. I just bought a whole bunch of beef jerky." Sharon spoke with the exaggerated sweetness adults used to coax a child. "I'll give you some as soon as we get down to the lab, if you let the man go."

The suffocating hand zipped off Clark's face, but he couldn't breathe until the constricting bands slipped off his chest. Clark's normal vision cleared as he drank in labored gulps of air. His legs were still imprisoned by the meteor-shadow, but he had a reprieve from imminent death.

He could not escape an analysis of his miscalculations.

It was obvious now that this shadow had attacked him when he left the enclosure yesterday. Sharon had deduced that he reacted with violent illness to meteor dust. When she saw him in the enclosure, her nervous concern had been an act. She had called his house to lure him into a trap. He had saved her the trouble and walked right into it. Max and Layton, creatures of Dr. Farley's mad experiments with meteor-rocks, had been lying in wait to capture him.

Sharon had clearly been confident she could entice him to the silo site, which meant she had something he couldn't ignore.

Lana.

Rather than dwell on his past mistakes, Clark concentrated on the problems at hand. He couldn't move with Max wrapped around his legs, but as long as he was conscious, the meteor-enhanced entities had no power over his perceptions or wits.

Sighing, Sharon hit a button on a control panel by the ladder. The heavy hatch whirred as it slowly closed, and the electronic lock engaged. She stepped up to the elevator and pulled a lever to open the metal-mesh doors that covered the ordinary elevator doors. She punched the button to open the lift and turned to the naked man squatting in a corner.

Except for his immodest "altogethers," Martha Kent's polite term for nudity, Layton looked like a normal, skinny, old guy. He would take some getting used to, Clark realized when the man's arm suddenly snaked toward Sharon's boot.

Sharon jumped back, wagging a stern finger. "Don't do that. If you want your snack, help me move Clark into the elevator."

"Kay, Sharn." Layton grabbed on to the railing at the top of the metal stairs that curved down around the elevator shaft. He pulled himself across the platform like a monkey swinging from vine to vine.

As Sharon and Layton dragged him into the elevator, Clark pretended to be groggy, but he was memorizing every detail of the layout for reference later. When the lift doors closed, and they started downward, another question popped into his head.

Why had Sharon *wanted* to capture him?

Clark had a sinking feeling that he would find out soon, and he probably wouldn't like it.

When the elevator doors opened 60 feet down, Clark had a floor level view of the tunnel junction. Straight across, the door into a small room stood open. A man of average height and weight with graying hair came out, carrying an empty plastic bag.

Dr. Farley, I presume.

What Clark saw beyond the scientist was an outrage against science and humanity. The monstrosity in the corner of the cell was a bloated mass of tumors, sedentary and spaced out on whatever dripped from an IV.

Dr. Farley closed the cell door and dropped the empty IV bag into a bucket by the wall.

"I thought Hoover died," Sharon said, as her father walked toward them.

"It won't be long." Dr. Farley stopped just outside the open lift doors.

Not even a flicker of interest shone in Clark's eyes as the scientist stared down at him. If they thought the meteor-rocks affected him mentally as well as physically, they might let down their guard at an opportune moment. He had to be prepared to take advantage of any opening. However, he did not underestimate the intelligence and cunning of his adversaries. He could not count on Dr. Farley or his mutated minions to be careless, but survival always trumped greed as a motivator.

Sharon hugged the elevator wall as Layton jumped out. Surprised by the rubber man's unexpected move, shadow-Max slipped down around Clark's ankles. His symptoms abated to a degree, but Clark made no move that betrayed his improved condition.

"What is it, Layton?" A tremor shook Dr. Farley's voice.

"I promised to give him some jerky when we got down here, Dad." Sharon turned a key to keep the elevator doors open and stepped over Clark to exit. "We should probably lock Layton up—while we can. I'll wait."

"Yes, of course." Nodding, the scientist turned and disappeared behind a thick wall.

With Sharon's attention on Layton, Clark studied his surroundings. The basic layout of the interior matched the references he had read: tunnel to the missile silo behind the elevator, Equipment Building on the right, and the Launch Control Center on the left.

The Launch Facility Equipment Building, or LFEB, was a huge room that housed the emergency diesel generator, the power distribution system, and an air conditioner that weighed twenty tons. A fourteen-thousand-gallon fuel tank was buried outside the steel-and-concrete walls.

Clark's gaze jumped to the Launch Control Facility on the left, where Dr. Farley had gone. That section had been home for the two-man missile launch teams on duty when the Minuteman II was in the silo. They had been locked inside for the duration of their watch. A curved yellow line painted on the floor outside the LCC indicated the swing arc of the massive door. Now, the door was standing open.

Six rooms like the one holding Hoover had been added in the tunnel junction: three along the far wall and three on the wall between the Equipment Room door and the silo connection tunnel. The small, rectangular windows in each door were barred. The victims of Dr. Farley's early experiments were apparently confined in the small rooms. Clark was certain the men could not have known what fate awaited them when they had agreed to join the insidious project.

Through the small window, Clark caught a glimpse of the man in the cell to the left of Hoover. Swirls of color faded and shifted on his skin, apparently driving him crazy. *Like a chameleon*, Clark thought.

Despite Max being looped around his feet and ankles, Clark was able to muster enough X-ray vision to see through the fourth metal door. The density of that subject's bones was different than the skeletons he usually saw. As he watched, the man's bones shifted shape and position, changing from a crude cube into an oval.

Max and Layton were obviously more advanced, with relatively stable physiologies by comparison.

Dr. Farley returned with a jar of beef jerky. When Layton lunged for his treat, the scientist barked, "Back in your room first!"

Layton hissed, but he ran through the sixth door. He grabbed the sticks of jerky Dr. Farley offered and squatted on an air mattress covered with a blanket.

Sharon visibly relaxed when her father slammed the door. A green light on the electronic lock turned red.

"Shhhmok!" The man in the cell closest to the LCC door clung to the inside of his door and rattled the window bars. He was covered in stiff, barbed hair and resembled a porcupine. "Now, Faley!"

"No smoke now, Edgar." Dr. Farley pulled a canister from his lab coat pocket. He dashed to the first cell and threatened to spray the man. "Be quiet or no cigarette later, either."

Pepper spray or Mace? Clark wondered.

Edgar smashed his fist against the door and leaped onto the ceiling.

"C'mon, Dad." Sharon rolled her eyes and grabbed Clark under his left arm. Her father lifted him on the right, and together they dragged him through the installation.

Clark let his head loll to one side, but he was aware of everything. He was facing backward and noted the emergency box on the wall by the elevator. It reminded him of the glass boxes that contained fire alarms at school. A key was inserted in a slot beside a single button inside this red-trimmed glass case.

As they moved farther from the elevator, the open, metal stairs that spiraled up around the central shaft became visible. Six feet farther on and Clark could see the entrance to the connecting tunnel. The hatch, which locked from both sides, was open. The tunnel was 100 feet long and connected to a maintenance area attached to the silo shaft. The secondary access tube had opened in the maintenance room—before it had been filled with cement.

The cemented crew exit was impassable, but Clark doubted they had filled in the actual silo. The shaft was 10 feet across by 140 feet deep and the automated concrete, steel, and lead-lined lid weighed one hundred tons. Away from the sickening influence of meteor material, he could easily climb the metal rungs recessed into the silo walls. But even he might break a sweat trying to manually slide the massive lid aside.

"Wait a second, Dad." Sharon paused at the curved yellow line to catch her breath. "He's heavier than I thought."

Clark glanced at the door into the Launch Facility Equipment Room across the wide tunnel junction. He strained to hear, but didn't detect the rumble of the emergency generator. The facility was operating on commercial power. The wheel on the door was probably locked, which wouldn't be a problem if he was functioning at full strength. However, since there wasn't another way out of the room, the equipment room couldn't be used as an escape route, only as a place to hide and evade.

"Let's go, Sharon," Dr. Farley urged. "Max has been separated from his body long enough."

Max changed position to rest on Clark's shins, giving the impression he had heard, understood, and agreed. The shift wasn't a definitive indicator, but his actions supported the theory. Every move the shadow made was calculated.

Clark's arsenal of information about Max had just doubled. Now he knew two of his weaknesses: separation from his actual body and the darkness.

The wall into the LCC was so thick it was more like a short tunnel than a doorway. The heels of Clark's boots clattered over the metal bridge that spanned the gap between the wall and floor, which was mounted on twenty-foot-tall shock absorbers. The doorway at the end of the bridge had not been part of the original design. Soundproofed walls had been added to enclose the kitchen, latrine facilities, and a storeroom positioned outside the actual control center.

When Dr. Farley paused to key the electronic lock on the storeroom door, Clark risked a glance into the LCC. The section visible through the open door had been converted from a missile launch command post into a laboratory and infirmary.

Being dragged by the arms was not the way Clark had always envisioned taking a tour of the underground military complex, but it had served the purpose. When he broke free and found Lana, he would know how to get out.

And, in spite of the sharp pains shooting up his legs and the steady throbbing in his hands and head, that break was coming soon. Sharon and Dr. Farley knew that meteor-rocks made him sick, but they couldn't know about his gifts. He could act only when Max stopped functioning as manacles and reunited with his human body.

Dr. Farley pushed the door open. As he and Sharon dragged Clark inside, he let his head fall back to get a quick take on the room.

The only illumination came from a single lightbulb in a protective wire cage on the ceiling. The light was turned on. The cage's dimensions were roughly ten by twelve. Locked metal storage cabinets lined the walls on the right, left, and along the back. The body of a tall, muscular man was slumped on the floor to the left of the door.

Lana Lang was unconscious with her hands and feet tied.

Clark's throat constricted at the sight of her petite frame sprawled in the back, right corner. Lana was breathing, but probably drugged. Her jeans and tailored print shirt were rumpled and dusty. Dirt was lodged under broken fingernails, and a red abrasion blazed on her pale cheek. She hadn't been taken prisoner without a fight.

When Sharon and her father dropped Clark in the opposite corner, the shadow grew restless. It flowed upward, as though Max knew his feather-light touch was a torture and was taking out his separation anxiety on Clark.

"One more minute, Max." Dr. Farley left again, leaving Sharon standing in the doorway.

The shadow settled on Clark's stomach.

Despite the agony that twisted his intestines, Clark carefully planned his moves. The meteor dust that powered Max's dark essence would be incorporated into his solid body when the shadow merged. Clark would have to avoid close contact with Max in human form, too. He would also need a few minutes to regain his strength once the meteor dust was removed, especially after the lengthy exposure. His best bet was to wait until he and Lana were alone and locked in.

Dr. Farley had other plans.

The instant the scientist returned carrying a heavy, locked box, Clark knew that escape would not be easy. He cringed when Dr. Farley set the box on the floor by the wall just to his left. The doctor keyed the numbered combination and opened the lid to reveal six meteor-rocks. The smallest was the size of a baseball, the largest a brick.

"Is that absolutely necessary?" Sharon's fear of the alien rocks flared as she backed out the door.

"Yes," her father answered impatiently. "How many times do I have to tell you? Unless the element is injected directly into your system, the stones are perfectly safe."

"Then how come they turn Clark into jelly?" Sharon stubbornly hung back.

"That's what we want to find out, isn't it?" He pulled several lengths of rope from his pocket and shook them at her. "Tie him up, Sharon, as a precaution."

Clark was in so much pain he couldn't fight when Sharon wrapped a rope around his wrists.

At the stable, Chloe tried the driver's side door of her car then threw up her hands. It was locked, and Lana had the keys.

Wherever Lana is.

"So let's see if I've got this straight." Pete leaned on the hood. "We know Lana was here because your car is here, but nobody saw her. She's not here now, but her horse is, so she's not out riding. Clark came here looking for Lana and everybody saw him except Kelly."

"Right," Chloe said. "Because Kelly was in the tack room when Clark was in the barn."

"And nobody saw him leave." Pete braced his chin on his hand. "You'd think they'd be totally freaked about all those dead mice."

"They think the cat did it." Chloe sighed and ran her hand over her tangled hair. They only had one option left. "Next stop, the missile silo."

"Okay." Pete turned and jumped into the convertible without opening the door. "I've got a baseball bat and a can of fly spray in the backseat."

"What for?" Chloe asked as she opened the passenger door and got in.

"Just in case we run into the Big Creepy, and it wants a people or two for dessert." Pete shuddered and started the car.

"I'll take the fly spray." Chloe settled back and held her hair down with both hands.

In close proximity to a concentrated supply of meteor-rocks, Clark's ability to withstand the pain without blacking out was in jeopardy. It was not in his nature to surrender, no matter how hopeless a situation seemed, but he only had one weapon at his disposal now, his ability to think. He had to stay awake and cognizant.

Every nerve felt as though it had been set on fire. Yet, somehow, Clark managed to care when shadow-Max fled his body to return to his own. The pain didn't decrease when the meteor-enhanced darkness was gone, but the reunion diverted Dr. Farley's attention. The scientist hovered over the anxious shadow essence, which darted back and forth by Max's feet.

"Relax, Max. Your mind knows where it belongs," Dr. Farley said.

"It gets worse every time." Sharon watched from the doorway, where she had retreated as soon as Clark's hands and feet were tied. She chewed on her knuckle, her gaze riveted on the confused shadow.

Her father shot her a warning look.

Clark made a note and turned his attention to putting a little distance between himself and the box of meteorrocks. He usually suffered in silence, but he hoped a few moans would disguise that fact that his agonized writhing had a purpose.

Groaning, Clark pulled his knees up, rolled to alter his angle, then straightened in a faked convulsion. He aimed his feet at the box. When he hit it, the box turned so the open lead lid acted as a shield, blocking some of the radiation. He waited a few seconds then tried the maneuver again to position the box for maximum effect.

"Knock it off, Clark!" Sharon hissed with a quick glance in his direction.

Ignoring her, Clark doubled up, moaned softly, and inched toward the center of the room. Adjusting the positions of the box and his body was not a perfect solution, but it made the agony tolerable.

On the plus side, Sharon and her father were oblivious to the enormous benefits of the subtle corrections.

But Lana hadn't moved.

"That's it, Max." Dr. Farley took a step back as the shadow suddenly attached to Max's feet.

A wave of darkness rolled over the body and was absorbed in his head. Max sat up and began to rock, holding his head in his hands. "Empty, empty, nothing there."

Dr. Farley placed a tentative hand on the man's shoulder. "You're fine, Max. Remember who you are."

Max nodded, fighting a panicked disorientation. "Cutler. CIA. Once. Not now."

Max Cutler was not someone he should take lightly, Clark realized. He couldn't fathom why someone with the ex-CIA agent's looks and skills would volunteer for such a dangerous experiment. No amount of money could possibly be worth the threat to sanity and life.

Dr. Farley helped Max to his feet. He turned to Sharon as he ushered the shaken man through the door. "Keep an eye on them. I'll be right back to get the lab samples."

"How long before Max can take over the watch?" Sharon was not worried about Max Cutler's health and welfare, but about her own. Her fear of meteor-rocks could be used against her. Clark just had to figure out how.

"When he feels like it," Dr. Farley retorted sharply. He closed the door as he left. A small green light blinked to red on the locking mechanism.

Sharon leaned against the doorjamb, her stony gaze fastened on the box of meteor-rocks. When Clark chanced another glance at Lana, she caught it.

"She's just heavily sedated, Clark." Sharon's tone was cold and devoid of sympathy. "It's harmless stuff, and it'll wear off."

"Why?" Talking was a struggle, but necessary to verbally manipulate the situation.

"Are you here?" Sharon seemed to welcome the chance to talk. "Because you're a stable meteor-mutation, Clark. It is absolutely imperative that my father finds out why and how to duplicate the effect. In case you hadn't noticed, all his patients are bonkers—or soon will be."

"But I'm not a—"

"Don't even try to lie, Clark." Sharon cut him off. "You have unnatural speed, and you fall apart when you're around meteor-rocks. So don't deny what you are when the evidence is so obvious."

Her knowledge of his ability to speed surprised him. He had taken all the usual precautions since getting to know her. However, he hadn't taken into account that her interest in him had nothing to do with dating.

"You may not believe it," Sharon continued, "but I'm not happy about how this has to end."

"How is that exactly?" Clark had the uncomfortable feeling that the girl was trying to mess with his mind, to terrorize him with a fate she thought he couldn't avert.

Sharon hesitated then shrugged. "After my father has what he needs, Shadow-Max will enter your windpipe. You and Lana will die of asphyxiation with meteor-dust residue in your lungs—just like Howard Stoner. We'll even leave your bodies in Stoner's field to divert the investigation from ourselves."

"Like Gary Mundy?" Clark hated loose ends. He needed all the information he could get.

Sharon shook her head. "Mundy got between Layton and his rabbit food. Bad move. Either way, you and Lana will just be two more mysterious Smallville deaths that no one can explain."

"You may be making a big mistake," Clark said, throwing the first stone of his verbal attack.

"Don't think so. We can't afford to leave any witnesses." Sharon's gaze flicked from Clark to Lana and back. "It's you and Lana or us, so you lose."

Don't count on it, Sharon.

CHAPTER 17

Chloe left her bag in the trunk of Pete's car. She was still dressed in her school clothes, a tan blazer over a stylish blouse, black slacks, and ankle boots. It wasn't ideal attire for sneaking about in the woods, even worse for breaking into an underground missile silo, but at least she wasn't wearing shoes with awkward heels.

"Here." Pete shoved the aerosol can of fly spray into Chloe's hand and shouldered the baseball bat.

Chloe slipped her cell phone into her jacket pocket along with the capless fly spray can. The makeshift weapon would only be as effective as her ability to use it quickly. With her finger on the nozzle button, she whispered, "Ready?"

Pete nodded and tightened his grip on the bat.

Chloe led the way down the drive, through a dense thicket of trees, past an SUV and Sharon's silver Audi. It was darker in the wooded area than in the open, and she stayed on the drive. She had vetoed bringing a flashlight in case someone was watching.

Clark hadn't noticed any surveillance equipment when he had cased the fenced enclosure the day before. That had been enough to convince Pete they wouldn't be seen, but she wasn't so sure. Anyone who was conducting shady research in an old military installation wouldn't rely on luck for security.

"Ow." Chloe winced as she tripped over a tree root. She and Pete both froze at the edge of the woods, twenty feet from the double, chain-link gate.

The gray of twilight deepened into night as the sun slipped below the horizon. Nothing stirred except birds settling into nests and nocturnal animals venturing out to forage.

No alarms blared, and no guards leaped from hiding to surround them.

"See? There's nothing to worry about," Pete said.

Chloe frowned as she scanned the fenced-in yard. It was too dark to see much. Cameras and sensors could be equipped with night vision, but the technology probably couldn't be easily hidden. Clark hadn't noticed any devices attached to the fence, the ventilation pipes, silo cover, or entry hatch.

Maybe the best security *was* not having any that announced there was something worth guarding.

She had to make a decision. Once they stepped out of the trees, there was nowhere to hide. No trees or brush grew in the area around the outside of the high fence or inside the enclosure, and the weeds had been mowed. Either they risked getting caught or they turned around and left.

"How sure was Clark?" Chloe whispered the question.

"Trust me, Chloe," Pete said. "If Clark said he didn't find any snooper cams, there aren't any."

"Okay." Chloe sighed. Pete was so positive that she dropped her objections and walked quickly toward the gate.

At first glance, it looked as though the chain holding the two panels closed was padlocked. They quickly discovered that the lock was broken and looped through the links to give the appearance of being secure.

"That was easy," Pete said, once they were inside.

"Too easy." Chloe replaced the lock as Pete moved toward the first raised hatch. In spite of the cloaking darkness and his security assurances, she felt exposed and vulnerable. However, they were committed and someone had to find Clark and Lana. No one else knew they were *both* missing.

"Should we call Clark's parents?" Chloe asked as she joined Pete by the entry hatch into the underground facility.

"Probably," Pete said. "But we might want to call Lex first."

"Lex?" Chloe was startled by the suggestion. "Just because Lex told Clark he's not involved with whatever's going on here doesn't mean he's not involved."

"True." Pete nodded. "So if we call and ask him for the combination to unlock this hatch and he doesn't give it to us, we'll know he was lying."

Chloe dialed the Luthor mansion. An assistant answered and politely asked her to wait a moment. Seconds passed before Lex picked up. "Lex, it's Chloe."

"Yes, Chloe." Lex sounded preoccupied. "What can I do for you?"

Like his father, Lex Luthor had no use for hemming and hawing. Chloe was blunt. "I think your tenants may be holding Lana Lang and Clark Kent prisoner in the missile silo. Can I get the lock combination for the entry hatch?"

Clark found little satisfaction in Dr. Farley's failed attempts to draw blood from his impenetrable skin. When the befuddled doctor couldn't even secure a dermal sample with a puncture instrument used to extract biopsy specimens, he settled for a swab from inside Clark's mouth.

Been there, done that, Clark thought with a sigh. The court had ordered a DNA test to prove whether or not he was Rachel Dunleavy's son. A bizarre series of coincidences had made that seem possible to everyone except Pete and his parents. To protect his alien identity, he had broken into the lab, taken the sample, and replaced it with a swab from Pete.

Now Clark not only had to free himself and rescue Lana, he had to destroy Dr. Farley's swab specimen and records.

At the moment, he could barely manage to breathe and talk at the same time. Both basic activities were essential to survival.

Clark glanced at Lana again, looking for changes in her condition. A few minutes ago, she had frowned and shifted position, but she had shown no other signs of waking up.

Sharon sat in the front right corner, as far from the open box of meteor-rocks as she could get in the small room.

"He's lying to you," Clark said.

"Shut up." Scowling, Sharon wrapped her arms around her drawn-up knees. The abrupt response was indicative of intense fear.

Clark had struck a chord, and he had no problem lying to a liar who intended to kill him and one of his best friends. "Suit yourself, Sharon, but I know from experience that those green rocks aren't safe. One day you're fine, and the next—"

"What?" Sharon asked when he didn't continue.

"This stuff doesn't have to be injected to create massive changes," Clark explained. He was surprised at how easily he fabricated fibs, but he didn't have a variety of tactics to choose from. "You don't even have to be exposed over a long period time."

"I want to know what happened to *you*," Sharon pressed.

Clark thought about asking her to close the lead box before he answered but decided against it. She was too sharp not to see through the ploy. She had to decide on her own, with no prompting.

"I went swimming in Crater Lake," Clark said, still lying. "Once."

"Crater Lake as in meteor crater?" Sharon asked. "It has meteors in it?"

"Technically it has meteor*ites* in it," Clark explained. "Meteoroids become meteors when they hit the atmosphere and start burning up. After they hit, they're meteorites. Everyone around here just calls them meteor-rocks, though."

"I don't need a science lesson, Clark!" Sharon's eyes flashed. She made an effort to calm down when Clark managed a weak shrug. "What happened after you went swimming?"

"I was fine when I went to bed that night. When I woke up, I could dodge a speeding bullet. And as you know, I get really weak around meteor-rocks."

"Overnight?" Sharon was skeptical.

"Overnight," Clark insisted. He gambled, and asked, "How long did your father's victims take to mutate?"

"Not very long," Sharon admitted, with a worried glance at the box. "How old were you?"

"Eleven." Clark chose a number at random and went on, combining fact and fiction. "Not everyone reacts to meteor material the same way. Most people who live in Smallville are in denial, like Pete and Chloe. Nobody can live day after day thinking they could wake up one morning with insect mandibles instead of teeth."

Sharon inhaled, her eyes widening.

"Instant mutations," Clark said. "Happens all the time."

"That's it." Jumping to her feet, Sharon punched four numbers into the electronic lock. When the red digital light turned green, she opened the storage room door and shouted toward the lab. "Max! I need you!"

Clark's bolstered spirits deflated. He had missed his chance to bully her into closing the lead box while they were still alone. Now, she was plotting her moves with the same care he had taken. There was no question that Sharon was going to remove the meteor-rocks, just not before Max was there to make sure the prisoner stayed too sick to move.

"What is it?" Max Cutler appeared in the doorway.

The ex-agent had the slightly haunted look of someone who was being stalked by an unspeakable horror. In Max's case, the horror was his own swift decline into madness. He knew that without a medical miracle he was condemned to become a moronic freak locked in one of Dr. Farley's cells. The certainty was wreaking havoc with the shadow-man's emotional equilibrium.

"You have to separate again, Max," Sharon said, "to keep Clark under control."

"Forget it." Max angrily turned to leave.

"No!" Sharon grabbed his arm. "You do what I say, Max, or I swear, I'll convince my father not to give you the cure when he finds it. And he will find it. Just look at Clark. He's the key."

Max cast a questioning glance toward Clark. From his own observations, the agent knew that Clark seemed to be a normal kid—with a velocity anomaly and a meteor allergy.

"Clark's been like this since he was eleven!" Sharon drew Max's gaze back to make her point. "Years, Max, and he's perfectly stable. He gets A's in school because there's no neuron loss in his brain. He's your only hope."

"Unless your shadow-self takes over before Dr. Farley finds the cure," Clark interjected. He might not be able to outwit Sharon, but Max was on the edge and susceptible to suggestion.

"What do you mean?" Max asked, frowning.

Sharon fumed. "One more word, Clark, and I'll feed Lana to Layton."

Clark knew Sharon wasn't bluffing. He had seen fear manifest itself in many ways since he had started investigating local meteor mishaps with Chloe and Pete. Fear could reduce a tough guy to tears and turn a physical weakling into an emotional giant. Some people became stronger and more determined. Sharon Farley was one of those, but with a mean streak.

"Dad is already testing the specimen he took from Clark, Max," Sharon said. "He'll have an answer soon, I'm sure. Then after Clark and his girlfriend are gone, you can stay connected to your body until Dad stabilizes your condition."

Max hesitated, swayed by her arguments.

"In the meantime"—Sharon's voice rose with hysteria—"*nobody* is safe if those rocks are radiating their poison into the whole installation!"

Max looked toward the glowing green rocks in the lead box on the floor and shielded his eyes. The gesture was an unnecessary, but instinctive response to a known danger.

Sharon eased up. "I can't close the box until shadow-Max is making certain that Clark can't go anywhere."

Exhaling, Max nodded. He sat down and closed his eyes. Within a few seconds, a shimmering dark emerged through his facial pores and flowed toward his feet. As the dark essence combined with his actual shadow, Max's body slumped. It fell on its side when shadow-Max separated. The sentient substance did not have to be told to encircle Clark's legs.

"Great, Max. Thanks." Sharon kicked the top of the meteor box closed and picked it up.

Before she reached the door, Clark was feeling a slight lessening of the debilitating effects. Still, the only thing his fast-talk maneuvering had accomplished was to exchange one source of meteor contamination for another. However, since the meteor dust in shadow-Max wasn't as potent as the box of meteor-rocks, the effort hadn't been a complete failure.

Clark was also aware that the switch might have benefits he hadn't had time to explore, yet.

"Don't close the door!" Clark pleaded.

Sharon rolled her eyes and slammed the door behind her. The green lock indicator turned red.

Something had finally gone right, but Clark had only scored a minor victory. Darkness could be used to neutralize Max, but with the shadow-entity firmly wrapped around his legs, he couldn't use his gifts to find out how.

Lex got into the silver Porsche GT2, which was parked in front of the mansion. He placed his cell phone in the hands-free device on the dashboard and started the engine. He was waiting to hear back from his lawyers and Chloe Sullivan and needed to talk, steer, and shift simultaneously.

Lex had been in the final phases of setting up Great Games, Ltd. when the spunky young journalist called. Chloe wanted the lock code to access the primary personnel hatch at the Launch Control Facility, and he had given it to her.

The lease agreement with Lawrence Farley did not bind him to the secrecy clause if the doctor was engaged in illegal activities. While Lex supported stem cell research and therapeutic cloning for medical purposes, he didn't want to be accused of guilt by association with Farley. Protection against prosecution had been his motivation for the "illegal activity" provision. Fortuitously, by definition, kidnapping was covered.

Great Games, Ltd. was a tribute to Alexander the Great, the inspiration for Lex's own name. Given the financial triumph he anticipated, the reference was entirely fitting. It would be an annoying reminder to his father that the son was more than capable of building an empire of his own.

The new subsidiary of LexCorp would be dedicated to all computer entertainment projects, including the development of a virtual visor to provide players with a perceptual sense of actually being in, not just looking at, their make-believe worlds. Current technology was limited to three-dimensional glasses or virtual bodysuits that were too bulky, expensive, and primitive to catch on with individuals. The Lex-Connect visor would be inexpensive, easy to install and operate on any home computer, and programmable for person-to-person interaction and communications with selected players.

Kilya had come up with the idea when he had asked her to think outside the box of what was presently possible. Once his technical teams had a concept to work with, they had quickly ascertained the feasibility and projected costs. Since the Lex-Connect would only function with the fantasy worlds created by Great Games, Ltd., the three role-playing scenarios he had approved to launch the visor would quickly gain in popularity.

He had hired Kilya Warcrest to run the on-line PR and promotion department. Her husband, Trenal Bonecaster, had turned out to be a brilliant concept and graphic designer. The LexCorp board members still thought the enterprise and new hires were a joke. They'd be laughing for joy when millions were signing on to play virtual Macedonia, Rio Grande, and Centauri Station at twenty dollars a month per player.

Ancient warriors, Texas, and the wild side of space exploration, Lex thought with a profound sense of satisfaction. He might have to check into his cybercreations every once in a while, just to relax.

The phone rang, snapping Lex back to the second of his immediate concerns. Chloe's cell phone number appeared on the digital readout.

"Yes, Chloe." Anticipating a problem following Chloe and Pete's intrusion, Lex had decided to drive over to the missile silo to pacify Dr. Farley personally.

"The lock code doesn't work, Lex," Chloe said. "We can't get in."

"Are you certain you punched the correct sequence?" Lex asked. He frowned as Chloe read the lock code back to him. It was correct.

"We tried three times, Lex," Chloe said. "Access denied. They must have changed the code."

"Apparently." Lex struggled to maintain the unflustered Luthor timbre in his voice. "Wait there and keep your cell phone on, Chloe. I'll call back shortly."

Lex seethed as he stared out the windshield. Farley and Cutler had not been authorized to change the locks on the entry hatches. In fact, they had been expressly *forbidden* to do so. Secrecy and privacy from outsiders was one thing, but Lex had balked at not being able to access his own property.

Lex had employed one of the best security companies in the country to install a state-of-the-art system the tenants should not have been able to dismantle. However, in spite of their assurances, his expensive "experts" had underestimated Max Cutler's abilities and the extent of his CIA training. The ex-agent had not only overcome the obstacles intended to prevent him from changing the code, he had done it without anyone knowing the system's integrity had been breached.

Impressive, but annoying, Lex thought. There was, however, a positive aspect to the unexpected development. As soon as the immediate situation was settled, he'd have the security and surveillance systems in the mansion and the plant checked and modified by specialized "experts" with government agency training and expertise.

First, he had to help Chloe access the underground installation.

He could not call Dr. Farley to demand that he open the hatch. Cutler had not activated the phone lines for fear of being wire tapped. Cell phones didn't work so far underground. They used ordinary walkie-talkies to communicate within the facility itself.

Lex had thought Cutler and Farley's concessions to paranoia were extreme, even given the mostly financial penalties for conducting illegal medical research. However, he had never confirmed his assumption that they were working with stem cells. It was possible Farley had developed something legal and innovative that other interests might want to steal—or stop.

That might explain the situation, but it didn't solve the problem.

Whether Clark Kent and Lana Lang had been kidnapped or not, he *would* get into his missile silo.

Lex had estimated Farley's power consumption and collected in advance because the Kansas State Water and Power account for the missile installation was still billed to LexCorp.

Lex dialed the phone as he roared down the drive.

Clark's patience was running out. Although the pain wasn't as great now that the box of meteor-rocks was gone, an agonizing misery of one kind or another had seeped into every cell. Max being wrapped around his ankles, combined with the long exposure to meteor material, had drained his energies and depleted his visual powers. He couldn't see though paper or use his vision to even heat water. The frustration was compounded by Lana's muffled cries in her sedated delirium. At least she was starting to revive.

Clark didn't let himself get really angry very often. He didn't want to take the chance that he might destroy something it would take the rest of his life to pay off. The treacherous Dr. Farley might qualify for retribution, but the facility belonged to Lex.

So even if he could, breaking things was out. He had to make his move soon, though, before Sharon or her father came back. However, he hadn't finished tearing down Max's defenses.

"I can't believe you're letting Sharon play you like that, Max," Clark said. "She's a spoiled brat."

As Clark expected, the shadow flexed and tightened. The conversation during the past several minutes had not been one-sided. He talked, and Max reacted. He had learned that the agent despised Dr. Farley's daughter, was terrified of turning into Layton, and was becoming increasingly agitated whenever he said anything.

"What does Sharon know about anything?" Clark scoffed. "I can't even *imagine* what it would be like to have my mind separated from my body."

Max began to twine up Clark's legs. The pain intensified the closer the shadow got to his torso and vital organs, which was obviously the intention. Whether Max was moving to punish him or silence him, Clark knew the agent's confidence was on the verge of breaking.

"I've heard they experience the same fear"—Clark paused for effect—"of not being able to get back into their bodies. How far away do you think they go?"

Max slid back down to Clark's shins, perhaps hoping to convince him to shut up or change subjects.

"I'm tied up, Max," Clark said weakly with a despondent sigh. "I've been exposed to you and those rocks for so long, it'll take me a week to recover. You don't have to stay so far away from your body."

Clark closed his eyes and sighed again. He wasn't sure how shadow-Max did it, but he perceived everything. He wanted the agent to think he was surrendering to the futility of his circumstances.

Max became still.

Clark concentrated on breathing. The solitary lightbulb in the ceiling shone with an unrelenting glare. It blazed against his closed eyelids as he prepared to focus his depleted power on a single desperate act.

The shadow weighed almost nothing, yet Clark was aware of every tremor. Max moved another few inches, paused, then moved over his ankles and stopped on his shoes.

Clark waited, breathing.

When Max hit the floor and bolted for his body, Clark had two seconds at most. His eyes snapped open. The heat ray was weaker than normal, but already aimed at the bulb. Everything Clark had went into the burst of alien energy that shattered the fragile bulb and cast the room into total darkness.

He did not hear Max scream, but he sensed it.

Freed from direct contact with the meteor dust in Max's shadow, Clark began to recover. The pain receded quickly, but his full strength did not return. He strained and was able to break the ropes that bound his hands and untie the ropes around his feet. As he scrambled over to Lana, he wondered how long it would take to recharge.

"Lana?" Clark whispered, and gently shook her shoulder.

"Too early." Lana tried to brush him off, but her hands were still tied.

Clark's vision didn't adjust to the dark right away. Clasping Lana's hands to hold them still, he fumbled the knot untied, then moved on to the ropes binding her feet. When she was free, he stood up and stretched to get his own muscles working again. He wasn't sure how long it had been since Sharon had left with the box of meteor-rocks. Locked in a room with no one to talk to but a frantic shadow had distorted his sense of time.

But not my sense of urgency, Clark thought. *It's time to get out.*

A slight dizziness swam in Clark's head as he leaned over to pull Lana to her feet. She swayed unsteadily and leaned against him. Although she was standing, she was still heavily sedated, and he was too weak to carry her.

With an arm around Lana's shoulders, Clark urged her toward the storeroom door. Her feet moved, but she clung to him to stay upright. Since his eyes hadn't adjusted to the dark, he held his arm out so they wouldn't collide with a wall. They both stumbled over nothing, Lana in a stupor and he from the lingering exhaustion. The prolonged weakness puzzled him, until he saw the glowing green sheen on the floor ahead.

Meteor dust.

He had thought the shadow entity would be disabled in the darkness. Instead, the dark essence had been absorbed, and Max Cutler had died.

Clark did not have time for regrets. He hoped that once he was out of the cramped room and away from the residue, his recuperative powers would speed up.

"I'm tired." Lana slipped from his grasp and slumped to the floor behind him.

Since Lana was fine for the moment, Clark turned his attention to the door. The red light on the electronic lock was a beacon in the dark, guiding his hand. However, as he reached out to grab the handle, he realized that they wouldn't be getting out of the room soon.

Shadow-Max had expired by his body's feet, leaving his meteor-dust remains directly in front of the door.

Clark didn't have the strength to break the electronic lock.

CHAPTER 18

Cursing the slow, but steady pace of the tractor, Jonathan turned into Charley Haskin's cornfield. He cast a wary glance toward his neighbor's distant farmhouse when a dog barked an intruder alert. Charley was a levelheaded man, but he kept a loaded shotgun by the back door. Rather than risk being shot at, Jonathan turned off the headlights, hunched over the steering wheel, and kept going toward the fertilizer plant.

When Chloe had called a short time before, she had delivered her message in an anxious rush. She was waiting for Lex to call back and hurriedly explained that his renters in the old missile installation might have taken Clark and Lana hostage. She didn't say why before she hung up, only that a Dr. Farley was likely experimenting with meteor dust in ways that had probably killed Howard Stoner and Gary Mundy.

Jonathan had almost called her back, but leaving the line open so Lex could get through was more important. As much as he distrusted Lex Luthor, he couldn't deny that Lex cared about Clark. Since LexCorp owned the old military facility, Lex might have information that would help resolve the situation.

Provided Lex wasn't responsible for the crisis in the first place. Jonathan still suspected that Lex had had something to do with the hostage situation that had imperiled his father and Martha at LuthorCorp. He just couldn't prove it.

However, if Chloe's information was correct, Howard

Stoner and the CEP agent had not died because of chemical contamination from the fertilizer plant. Clark had been right to stop him from launching a premature lawsuit.

When Jonathan came to the end of Charley's field, he turned onto a dirt access road that skirted the fertilizer plant property. He couldn't risk having the old machine break down, nor did he want to waste time. Keeping the gears set in low for rough terrain, he pushed his speed to twenty on the rutted track.

Martha had taken the pickup to the grocery store for muffin supplies. The retirement center was having a visitors' reception tomorrow, and they had forgotten to call to double their regular order. While she always had the LuthorCorp cell phone with her during business hours, his wife had walked off leaving it on the kitchen counter, plugged in to recharge.

Jonathan had had no choice but to take the tractor cross-country. He just hoped he got to the old missile site in time to help his son.

Chloe paced, checking the digital readout on her watch to mark time and her cell phone screen to make sure she hadn't missed any calls. Jonathan Kent was on his way, but it would take him a while by tractor. Lex still hadn't called back.

Pete had taken the broken padlock and chain off the gate and stuffed them in his back pockets. They weren't ideal weapons, but he had to work with what they had.

Know the enemy had been on his mind as he walked the yard in a quick reconnoiter of the enclosure.

The automated lid over the shaft where the Minuteman II had stood rested on a metal frame of ten-inch-wide rails. Pete still didn't know the extent of Clark's abilities, but at three feet high and ten feet across, the concrete-and-steel silo cover might be too heavy for his alien friend to move.

The smaller hatch a few feet away appeared to be broken. The ground seal was out of line and the digital readout on the locking mechanism was dark. Pete tried, but he couldn't budge it. Clark probably could, which wasn't a good sign.

The only way anyone could hold Clark Kent hostage was by exposing him to meteor-rocks. Since Clark was nowhere to be found, that was exactly what Pete thought had happened.

"Did you find anything?" Chloe asked, as Pete walked toward her across a cement slab on the ground. The aluminum baseball bat still rested on his shoulder.

"Nothing that will help us get inside." Pete dropped the bat and knelt by the main hatch. "Although I'm not sure what we'd do if we could."

"Me, neither." Chloe's shoulders sagged. "I was sort of hoping we'd open the hatch, and Clark and Lana would rush out."

"That would be good, but probably too much to hope for." Pete began to punch random numbers into the lock panel. He didn't expect to hit on the right combination, but trying to open the hatch might alert someone inside to their presence. If anyone wanted to get out to get them, they'd have to open the hatch to do it.

"For all we know, there's more than one creepy killer." Chloe scanned the dark enclosure again.

"That's a possibility," Pete agreed. "So bring your trusty fly spray over here. Just in case something besides Clark or Lana pops out of this thing."

Chloe stepped over and assumed a gunslinger stance with the aerosol can ready. "This is nuts."

"It's the best we can do," Pete said. When Chloe's phone rang, he stopped playing with the lock to listen.

"You're on your way over here?" Chloe looked relieved. "So is Mr. Kent, Lex, but if we can't open—"

Pete grabbed the baseball bat and stood up. With Mr. Kent and Lex joining forces with them, the odds were better. The trouble was, they didn't know anything specific about the enemy. Sharon's father could have a creepy guy army.

"What?" Chloe spoke into the phone, but her gaze snapped to Pete. "Okay, but you'd better hurry."

"Problem?" Pete asked, his pulse quickening.

"We're about to find out." Chloe signed off and dropped the phone back in her pocket. "Lex called Kansas State Water and Power. This facility was on a separate generator when the military was here, and it still is. The power company is going to shut off the juice."

"Bingo!" Pete glanced at the hatch. Without power, the electronic lock would disengage. However, the heavy cover was motorized. "Except I don't think we can lift the hatch without power."

"Lex said that unless it's damaged, it was designed to be opened manually, too. Does balanced with counterweights mean anything to you?" Chloe raised the fly spray can and pressed the nozzle button. The spray was set to mist. She twisted the plastic button to narrow the stream.

"Makes perfect sense," Pete said. The other hatch had been dislodged, disrupting the manual apparatus. Clark had shown him several pictures of the interior, including the elevator platform just below the hatch. The counterweights had to be positioned in the wall behind the ladder.

"Get ready because we'll only have a few seconds." Chloe stepped to the other side of the circular door. She held the spray can in her right hand, leaving her left hand free to lift the hatch.

"Why only a few seconds?" Following Chloe's lead, Pete braced the bat on his shoulder with his left hand. He gripped the rim of the hatch with his right.

"The emergency generator will automatically kick in to take over." Chloe blew a strand of hair off her face, planted her feet wide for stability, and focused on the hatch.

Every muscle in Pete's body tensed. He stared at the digital readout on the lock panel and counted the passing seconds. At forty-two, the digital lock readout went dark.

"Pull!" Pete stumbled back a step as the hatch cover flipped up to rest against a brace. The dark interior below was dimly lit by the red glow from a battery-powered emergency light.

"That was too easy." Chloe stared down into the dark.

"Makes me nervous." Pete's whole body was on an adrenaline alert. He clamped his hands around the baseball bat and flexed his fingers as though getting ready for the pitch.

The emergency power came on suddenly.

Although they were expecting it, the flash of light was startling. They both rocked backward and took a moment to reorient. Neither one was prepared for the sight that met their astonished eyes when they looked back through the hatch.

"Oh, boy." Pete's mouth went dry.

Chloe gasped.

A spindly, naked man sprang out of the elevator and looked up. He opened his mouth as though to laugh, but the orifice stretched into a gaping maw.

Pete and Chloe watched, mesmerized, as the creature clutched the ladder with elastic arms. He pushed off the floor with flattened feet and shot upward toward Chloe. There was little doubt that he intended to engulf her in his enlarging mouth.

"Not!" Chloe aimed the spray can and shot the rubber man in the eye. "Take that, you—freak!"

Pete swung the bat and hit the hideous being in the back. The bat sank right into the thing's mushy, malleable flesh.

"No, no, no, no!" The man let go of the ladder with both hands to rub his burning eyes.

Pete pulled the bat back and swung again. This time he brought it down on the top of the man's misshapen head instead of swinging in from the side. The action drove the naked man farther down the ladder.

Chloe dropped the aerosol can and slammed the hatch closed. The electronic lock automatically engaged.

"Uh—" Pete stared at the red light on the lock panel as he fought to catch his breath.

Clark was still locked in.

"Clark!" Chloe came to the same conclusion. She hit

her forehead with the palm of her hand. "How could I have been so stupid?"

"Yeah, well, with Stretch getting ready to chow down on Chloe-to-go," Pete quipped, "we didn't have much choice."

When a loud, grating noise sounded behind him, Pete whirled with the bat ready.

The massive silo lid began sliding open.

CHAPTER 19

Clark stood in the farthest corner of the dark storeroom, staring at the red lock-light on the door. His strength was beginning to return, and the nausea had abated—as long as he stayed clear of the meteor dust.

He had tried shaking Lana awake, thinking she could use his shirt to sweep the potent green residue aside, but she couldn't help. Barely lucid and physically sickened by the sedative, she needed to sleep, and he had left her alone.

But he couldn't delay too long. Every second that passed brought him closer to a confrontation with Sharon or Dr. Farley. He did not think Sharon would risk carrying a meteor-rock, but her father might, and that would end their chances of escape.

Clark breathed deeply. Several minutes had passed since his last attempt to storm the door, and he had become stronger in the interim. His strategy involved speed and every ounce of brute force at his command.

"Dad!" Sharon's shout sounded close.

Clark reached down and pulled Lana to her feet, hoping he hadn't waited too long. If Sharon came through the door, he would run her down if necessary, whatever he needed to do to get out.

"Layton's missing!" Sharon screeched.

"He can't be. Layton never misses a meal." Dr. Farley's voice receded as he passed by. The metallic sound of boots on metal dimmed as father and daughter left the Launch Control Center area.

Clark held Lana close, but he was caught in a dilemma. Dr. Farley and Sharon were between him and the exits, and Layton was loose. Since the installation was a closed system, he didn't want to escape and hide. The scientist could use meteor dust to flush him out.

"But we're going to have to take our chances." With one arm around Lana's back, Clark tightened his grip on her arms. As he prepared to make his move, the red light on the lock blinked out.

Clark opened the door and pulled Lana through in a split second. He paused in the narrow corridor by the kitchen.

"My head." Lana moaned, and tried to double over.

Clark pushed the storeroom door closed, but it wasn't made of lead and did little to shield him from the dust on the floor. Half-dragging Lana, he stumbled toward the open doorway by the metal bridge attached to the wall.

Beyond the thick wall in the tunnel junction, Sharon screamed. "Get away! Don't touch me, you filthy beast!"

"Back inside, Edgar!" Dr. Farley shouted. "No cigarettes unless—Edgar!"

The power outage had sprung the locks on the cells, and now Layton wasn't the only mutant loose in the compound.

Clark sensed a rumble as the massive generator in the Equipment Building suddenly came on-line. Power was restored a moment later.

Clark's meteor-symptoms subsided as he moved farther away from the storeroom. His ability to speed began to build when he hit the bridge, but he reined himself in to clear the thick wall. A high-speed collision with Sharon, her dad, or one of the mutated men in the narrow opening wouldn't hurt Clark, but neither they nor Lana would survive.

Once he hit the wide tunnel hub, however, he could carry Lana up the elevator-shaft staircase and out the primary access hatch. With his gifts restored, there were no barriers to stop him.

Except the gnarled little man covered with porcupine hair blocking the junction doorway.

The nausea hit Clark's stomach like a runaway locomotive smashing into a mountain. He reeled backward, holding on to Lana and cushioning her fall with his own tormented body.

"Shhhmok!" Edgar took a step inside the opening. The barbed hairs that covered his body were more pliant than they appeared. He wore a pair of baggy shorts and actually looked more like a giant chimpanzee than a porcupine. His angry frown was evident through the brush of fine hair that covered his face. "Now, you."

"Okay, Edgar, okay." Clark held up a hand to keep the meteor-mutant back. He remembered that Dr. Farley refused to give the hairy man a cigarette earlier. "Just stay back, and you can have smoke."

"Yessssss." Edgar glared, his eyes bright with the glint of insanity. He took a step forward. "Shhhmok!"

The veins in Clark's hands throbbed. Muscle and tendons stretched and twisted in violent convulsions. As he tried to wave Edgar off, Clark realized he had a twofold meteor-related problem.

Dr. Farley had used meteor dust to alter the molecular structure in all his subjects. Max, obviously the last of the six, was a refined, functional mutation compared to his predecessors. Perhaps, as the scientist had learned more about the potent properties of meteor material, he had used less in subsequent subjects. Edgar, being one of his earlier attempts, contained more meteor dust than the shadow had. The effects on Clark were amplified in the narrow confines on the passageway.

Clark could edge backward out of the enclosed space. Once he was clear, Edgar could enter the lab area without causing a violent meteor-induced reaction. But Clark could not leave Lana to an uncertain fate in the passage. Layton had killed for fun. Edgar might kill for cigarettes.

Then Clark recalled Edgar's behavior in the cell. Angered because Dr. Farley wouldn't give him a smoke, the mutant had leaped to the ceiling and stuck there.

Clark gently rolled Lana to the side and positioned himself as a buffer between her and the annoyed mutant. Edgar would have to go through him to harm her.

But Edgar had only one thing on his mind.

Clark felt a guarded sympathy for the impatient addict. Farley had had some kind of leverage over the men who had submitted to his experiments. Homeless addicts and alcoholics were a source of volunteers that wouldn't arouse suspicion, but using their vices to manipulate them was an unconscionable cruelty.

Waving Edgar to go by, Clark braced for the waves of excruciating pain he expected to cascade through his body. "Look in the kitchen, Edgar."

"Good." Edgar hesitated instead of charging past. He smiled and hissed, showing rotten teeth. Then he leaped to the ceiling and scurried past Clark and Lana overhead. The distance didn't completely protect Clark, but the new agony in his savaged body was minimal.

"Lana. Can you hear me?"

Lana stirred slightly, but she didn't open her eyes. "In a minute, Mr. Sullivan."

"Right." Sighing, Clark glanced behind him. Edgar was sitting outside the storeroom door lighting up. *One down.* Rising, he pulled Lana up and hurried through the tunnel.

When Clark finally emerged in the junction, it was immediately obvious that escape was still an elusive prospect.

Screaming in short, shrill bursts, Layton dropped to the ground in front of the closed elevator doors. His hands were still clasped around a staircase railing fifteen feet high and his arms stretched like rubber. They snapped back into their original form when he let go. Still screeching, the elastic man rubbed his right eye with one fist and pounded on the floor with the other.

Because of the meteor dust in Layton's body, the elastic man was an impassable wall between Clark and the elevator.

Dr. Farley and Sharon were in the third cell along the back wall. The door was open, but they were barricaded in by the rudimentary shapeshifter with a limited ability to morph. Shaped like a lumpy rectangle, it had planted itself in front of the cell door. Every time Sharon or Dr. Farley made a move, it lashed out with an arm or leg and shoved them back inside.

"Clark!" Sharon called, her voice frantic. "You can draw Nathan off with chocolate. It's on the cart in the kitchen!"

Dr. Farley looked at his daughter as though she'd gone as mad as his mutant menagerie. Since they had held him prisoner and tortured him with meteor-rocks, it was ridiculous for Sharon to expect Clark to help. But she did, Clark realized. Chloe or Pete must have made a crack about his hyperactive sense of right and wrong.

He had to help. He just wasn't sure what to do. One thing was definite. He wasn't going back into the LCC to get chocolate for Nathan. He lowered Lana to the floor on the yellow swing line by the massive LCC door. She looked dazed, but she didn't fall over.

The chameleon man with kaleidoscopic skin ran back and forth between the cells and the elevator.

"Stop, Cooper!" Sharon yelled angrily. "You're making me crazy watching you."

Cooper continuously swatted at his arms and legs, trying to catch the colorful patterns that flitted over his skin. Clark hadn't realized that the man was literally skin and bones.

When Cooper got too close to the elevator, Layton suddenly shrieked. His head and arms extended outward like a three-dimensional elastic cartoon without the popping eyes.

Clark wasn't laughing. He couldn't get close to a mutant without suffering a meteor-sickness attack, and Layton was blocking the fastest exit out of the installation. If he couldn't remove Layton, he'd have to find another way out.

"Clark!" Sharon jumped back to avoid Nathan's foot. "We've got an emergency system to subdue these animals, but we've got to get out to activate it."

"Is that true, Dr. Farley?" Clark asked.

"Check the storage cabinet by the LFEB door," the scientist said. "There are gas masks there and at other key points throughout the station."

A quick look with his X-ray vision confirmed the doctor's claim. When he heard a faint whooshing sound, Clark glanced to the cell on his left. Hoover's vacant, drugged eyes were now empty and dead. "It looks like Hoover's gone."

"We'll all be gone if you don't do something, Clark!" Sharon tossed her head in indignation.

Clark ignored her as he surveyed the whole area again. Unless they had someone else stashed somewhere else, everyone was accounted for. When his gaze settled on the red-metal-framed glass box by the elevator, Dr. Farley interpreted his thoughts and corrected his assumption.

"That's not the gas release, son. That'll take out everything."

Clark's head snapped around. "A destruct mechanism?"

The doctor shrugged. "Three-minute countdown. Things could get out of control."

Could? The man's cavalier attitude about death and destruction was stunning. The monstrosities he had created would run amuck until they released a knockout gas or brought the whole place crashing down.

Sharon was no better, but the blame was her father's. As Lex had once told him, people were not born bad or good. They were molded by design or example, deliberately or accidentally in a cosmic game of character roulette.

Clark was stricken with a twinge of dizziness when

the chameleon man altered course and ran by him. He recovered quickly, and his decision was made without deliberation. Once Dr. Farley and Sharon were free, they could handle the mutants while he got Lana to safety.

He glanced back toward the door where he had left Lana. She was sitting cross-legged, rocking and holding her head in her hands.

Clark was not feeling one hundred percent himself. Between the infested mutated men and loose meteor dust that permeated the whole installation, he had not been completely out of contact with the vile element since Layton had dragged him into the hatch.

"Get ready to run for it, Sharon."

Clark didn't give the girl, her father, or Nathan time to react. He rushed forward, grabbed the blob-man, and tossed him into an empty cell. Sharon and her father were outside before he had the cell door closed and locked. From this point on, whatever happened was out of his control.

"Masks first, Dad." Sharon turned toward the cabinet by the Equipment Building and ripped the doors open. She tossed her father a gas mask and grabbed another for herself.

Clark ran to Lana as Dr. Farley and Sharon raced into the LCC tunnel. Drawing Lana up on her feet again, he slipped an arm around her back and lifted her.

"C'mon, c'mon. Hurry!" Sharon demanded shrilly.

As Clark sped back to the cabinet, he realized he was only moving at a fraction of his usual speed. He pulled the third and last mask from the cabinet and slipped it over Lana's face. He had no idea where additional gas masks were kept, and he couldn't take time to look. Speed was his only ally, and he had to get clear of the meteor dust.

"Got it!" Dr. Farley's voice was flooded with relief.

Clark held his breath. As he turned to run, the colorful chameleon man stopped suddenly and crumpled. Nathan fell over in his cell, and Clark zipped toward the elevator with Lana in his arms. He suddenly realized that he didn't know whether or not the gas was deadly.

Probably not, Clark thought, when he saw that Layton had not yet succumbed to the poison's effects.

The rubber man was pacing in front of the elevator doors with an odd, gorillalike gait. When he saw Clark, he slammed his fist into the floor, then hauled his arm back and let it fly like a lasso.

Still holding his breath, Clark ducked the elastic arm and jumped back. He glanced toward the connecting tunnel, which was the only alternate route out of the installation, then back at the elastic man.

Layton's malleable bone density was similar to Nathan's. His skeletal legs expanded and compressed as he jumped up and down in frenzied fury by the elevator. He stopped suddenly and resumed his normal form.

Was Layton resistant to the poison? Clark wondered, as Sharon and Dr. Farley raced out of the Launch Control Center. The scientist carried the lead box full of meteor rocks, and they both headed directly for the elevator. They stopped when they saw Layton.

Sharon turned her mask-covered face to stare at Clark with clear-plastic-covered eyes.

Still holding his breath, Clark motioned toward the connecting tunnel with his head. The girl and her father didn't have to worry about meteor dust, but the rampaging elastic man was still a threat.

Sharon shook her head and waved him to leave.

Clark hesitated. Although Layton hadn't harmed Farley in the past, the rubbery mutant was agitated and cornered. Since Clark couldn't force Sharon and Dr. Farley to follow him while he was carrying Lana, he darted to the tunnel entrance.

The hatch door was closed, but unlocked. He yanked it open and placed Lana on the floor inside. As he stepped out, Layton slid to the floor in front of the elevator doors.

The elastic mutant had finally succumbed to the gas.

Sharon stamped her foot and waved Clark back again.

Since the girl and her father had gas masks and Layton was no longer a threat, Clark had no reason to force them into the tunnel. However, the silo was the only way out for him and Lana.

Clark stepped inside the passageway and pulled the hatch door closed. His tormented body began to adjust to the meteor-dust-free atmosphere, but the healing was incomplete. He felt sluggish as he turned, but did not know if he was reacting to traces of the gas or the meteor dust that seemed to be everywhere.

A Klaxon blared, and the hatch automatically locked.

There was no dramatic countdown to doom uttered in a feminine voice, but Clark suspected that the destruct mechanism had been activated. Focusing his X-ray vision, he concentrated on the door into the junction.

Sharon and Dr. Farley were standing by the elevator. The scientist was near the glass case that contained the trigger. Apparently, he wanted to bury the evidence of his inhumane work and experiments.

The elevator would take Sharon and her father to safety on the surface before the countdown hit zero, but Clark had only one way out. He lifted Lana and sped into the tunnel.

CHAPTER 20

Sharon halted beside her father eight feet from the elevator when she saw Layton standing by the elevator. She was even more startled when she noticed Clark. He was still standing, too, with Lana in his arms as the installation filled with gas.

When Clark nodded toward the tunnel that connected the main sections of the facility with the silo, she shook her head no and waved him to leave. It wasn't that she cared what happened to Clark or Lana. She and her father needed to make a quick, clean getaway once they hit the surface. They'd be long gone by the time Clark found out the silo exit was filled with cement and doubled back to take the elevator.

Clark finally got the message when Layton slid to the floor. He fled into the tunnel and closed the hatch door.

Sharon sighed with relief and glanced at her father. He was frozen in place, with a tight grip on the meteor-rock box, his eyes wide and staring, his breathing labored under the gas mask. Frowning, she looked toward the elevator.

The childlike man sitting in front of the metal outer doors was staring at them.

Why wasn't Layton unconscious?

Sharon glanced back at Cooper, who had fallen outside Nathan's cell. Edgar had collapsed by the storeroom door.

Sharon grabbed her father's arm, but as soon as she

moved, Layton's rubbery arm snaked out to push her back.

He smiled.

And she remembered.

Her father had created Layton with immunity to poisons.

Before either Sharon or her father could react, the elastic man bounded upright and smashed the glass covering the destruct panel. He turned the key and pushed the button, activating the mechanism.

Sharon gasped as the Klaxon sounded the beginning of the three-minute countdown.

They had to get in the elevator now!

Sharon was right behind him when her father dropped the meteor box and sprang toward the elevator.

"Get out of the way, Layton!" Dr. Farley's voice was muffled by the cumbersome mask as he ordered Layton to move.

Layton grinned as his arms suddenly elongated.

Sharon's scream was choked off by gas when the mutant's nimble fingers ripped the mask off her face.

Clark quickly covered the hundred feet to the maintenance area that was attached to the silo shaft. The tunnel had been well lit, with not a single bulb missing. The same was true in the empty utility room. Cement from the sixty-foot access tube had overflowed and hardened on a third of the floor. He hadn't thought to ask, but the exit had probably been blocked to keep Layton in.

Although the effects of the sedative were finally wearing off, Lana was still groggy. She clung to him, unaware of her surroundings. The gas mask over her face further distorted her perceptions.

Counting the seconds in his head, Clark stepped up to the hatch that opened into the shaft. He had just over two minutes to make the sixty-foot climb to the silo lid before the old military installation became a pile of rubble.

As Clark had gotten older, his speed and strength had increased and new gifts had manifested. He suspected that as he continued to mature, moving one hundred tons of concrete and steel would be easy.

But he wasn't there yet, and he had just endured his longest exposure ever to meteor-rocks.

With a silent apology, Clark flipped Lana over his shoulder. He held on to her with one arm and opened the hatch. He'd need his other arm free to climb the ladder rungs recessed into the silo wall.

Although the silo shaft was dark, Clark did not look down. The drop to the floor was eighty feet. He was determined to conquer his fear of heights and had made progress, but committing himself to the hundred-forty-foot vertical climb still required an extra measure of resolve.

The seconds counted down.

Recalling the diagrams he had shown Pete, Clark tightened his grip on Lana and felt for the inset metal bars located beside the hatch. When his hand closed over one, he swung out and found capture with his feet on a lower rung. Having to hold Lana made the climb exceptionally perilous. He had to rely on balance to prevent a tragic fall backward.

However, he quickly developed a swift, rhythmic pattern of ascent. Once he was comfortable with the climb, he looked up—and saw stars. The silo lid was open.

Clark knew the cover had been securely in place earlier, which suggested the opening had been automatically triggered when the power failed. Perhaps, once the process was in motion, the full cycle of opening and closing had to run its course.

With less than a minute to go before an explosive firestorm rampaged through the facility, Clark looked up again.

The lid was closing faster than he could climb.

CHAPTER 21

Pete hovered near the moving lid, checking inside the silo every couple minutes, wishing Clark and Lana would appear. He wasn't sure how long he could keep Chloe away. Protecting Clark's secret by diverting the *Torch* editor's attention was a major part of his job description. There was a lot more to being a sidekick than most people realized.

For the moment, Chloe was standing watch over the primary access hatch. Her fly spray was primed to fire, and she was ready to run if the freaky rubber guy showed up instead of their friends. It was going to get crowded soon. Lex would be arriving any minute by car, and the headlights on Mr. Kent's tractor were visible across the LexCorp cornfield.

"See anything?" Chloe asked.

"Not yet." Pete glanced at the huge six-sided cover as it slowly slid back into the closed position. If Clark was going to exit through the silo, he'd better hurry.

They were both convinced that Lana and Clark were down there. Based on the mice and the locked car at the stable, Chloe had deduced that the killer had captured Lana, and Clark had gone to save her.

Except now Clark seemed to be in trouble, too.

Why else would Lana's rescue be taking so long? Pete couldn't help pondering the question, but he really didn't want to contemplate something that was able to give Clark Kent a hard time and get away with it.

Sighing, Pete shifted his handy aluminum head basher

onto his other shoulder and stole another peek into the silo. This time he was not disappointed. He could see a silhouette in the lighted hatch sixty feet down. With Lana slung over his shoulder, Clark swung onto the ladder rungs built into the silo wall and started climbing upward.

Slowly.

Pete cast a glance at Chloe.

"There's Lex!" Stepping back from the access hatch, Chloe turned. Lex stopped the silver sports car on the side of the dirt access road and turned out the headlights.

"Why don't you go see if he's got a flashlight, Chloe," Pete suggested. He had one in his car, but he need Chloe gone. "We could use one."

"Yeah, good idea." Chloe half turned back as she headed for the gate. "Either nobody cares that we're hanging around up here, or nobody knows."

Except elastic guy, Pete thought as he glanced down to check Clark's progress. He looked to the side to gauge his rate of ascent against the lid's rate of closure. If Clark didn't speed things up, the lid was going to win.

"Pssst! Clark." Pete kept his voice low so he wouldn't alert Chloe. The sound of concrete grinding along the rails was louder.

Jonathan Kent's tractor stopped out in the field.

Pete knew that if something didn't change in the Clark-silo equation, Clark and Lana Lang would be trapped in the silo before his father reached the enclosure.

On the off chance Clark *was* strong enough to move the concrete lid, his cover as an ordinary, small-town teenager would end if Lex Luthor saw him do it.

"This is how we separate the serious sidekicks from the comic relief," Pete muttered.

He had to do something, but there was no visible control panel he could break to stop the cover's steady advance. Except he didn't have to stop it, just slow it down. The length of chain he had taken off the gate might buy a few crucial seconds.

Pete dropped the chain on the metal rail under the corner of the lid. The steady grinding noise became a tortured squeal as the massive slab jammed.

"Hello?" Clark called out.

Pete leaned over so the shaft would muffle his shout. "Get a move on, Clark! I don't know how long this will hold!"

Clark moved faster when he realized the concrete lid had stopped moving.

Pete had apparently figured out that he needed a few extra seconds to clear the shaft before the lid closed. Somehow he had jammed the mechanism.

Pete *didn't* know that the silo cover had to be closed to minimize the aboveground effects of the imminent explosion.

As though shot from a cannon, Clark summoned a burst of alien speed. He scaled the remaining interior of the wall with surefooted quickness.

Jonathan Kent darted through the gate just as Clark appeared above the rim of the deep shaft. "Clark?"

"Take Lana!" Clark yelled to be heard over the whine of the heavy silo cover. He still held the limp girl over his shoulder.

Pete dropped the baseball bat and helped Clark's father

lift Lana out of the deep hole. As they set her on the ground, Jonathan eased the gas mask off her face.

"What's going on?" Lana's voice was choked, her throat still constricted by the waning sedative. She rubbed her temples, then looked up sharply. "That man! He was eating mice whole—"

"He was a victim of a genetic manipulation experiment Sharon's father was conducting." Clark pulled himself through the narrow space between the edge of the lid and the silo wall. Pete had acted without a second to spare. "Details at eleven. Right now we've got other problems."

"I'll pass on the details, thanks." Lana dragged herself upright. "As it is, I'll have nightmares for a month."

Clark quickly assessed the situation on the ground. The beam of a flashlight bobbed where the drive cut through the trees to the road. He could discern Lex and Chloe's dark outlines in spite of the lingering meteor effects. Particles of the dust still clung to his hair and clothes, exerting a miniscule but steady drain on his physical abilities.

"You have to run," Clark said, relying on the dead-seriousness of his tone to convince them in the dark. "There are explosive charges down there, set to go off in fifteen seconds."

"Go, Pete!" Jonathan barked, then took a softer tone with Lana. "Can you run?"

"From an explosion? Yes!" Lana took off after Pete, stumbling in the dark.

"Clark?" Jonathan hesitated.

"Get out of here, Dad! I'll be okay."

Jonathan ran, catching Lana and checking his pace to stay with her.

Clark had to close the silo lid before the shaft became

a giant rifle barrel loaded with a blazing inferno. If the explosion wasn't contained, his father and friends wouldn't be able to run far enough fast enough to avoid severe, and maybe even fatal, injuries from fire and debris.

If he was caught in a blast peppered with meteor-rock particles, his chances of survival weren't terribly good, either.

"Chloe! Lex!" Pete yelled. "Go back!

The flashlight beam stopped then swung as Chloe and Lex turned back toward the road.

A split-second scan revealed the chain that was caught between the edge of the silo lid and the ten-inch-wide rail. Pete's decision to use the lock chain from the gate was impressive, but it had worked too well. When Clark tried to pull the obstruction out, the chain broke.

Ten seconds and counting.

The motorized mechanism that moved the one-hundred-ton lid open and closed over the missile shaft shrieked with the strain of being stalled.

Clark sped to the far side of the cover. He had to get it moving before the mechanism froze. Leaning into the huge apparatus, he pushed. Every muscle tensed with the effort of trying to force concrete, steel, and lead past the links of chain on the rail.

Five seconds.

The bulky cover moved an inch, gears grinding, then three more inches. The remaining gap was less than a foot wide.

Digging in, Clark willed the strength to shove the cover closed.

Three, two—

The silo cover slid cleanly into place as the explosive charges began going off.

As Clark scrambled over the trembling ground to the gate, his gaze darted to the closed primary access hatch. The elevator took less than a minute to reach the surface after the doors were closed, but there was no sign of Sharon and her father. He would never had left them if he thought there was any chance they'd be trapped. Something he couldn't have anticipated must have gone terribly wrong.

And there was nothing he could do to save them now.

Clark ran with an eye on the flashlight beam ahead and his senses attuned to the changes below. He dared not speed with Lex in the vicinity taking mental notes. Sharon Farley had discovered his ability by cross-checking times. Eventually, Lex might make the same connections and arrive at the same conclusion.

But not tonight.

Clark heard and felt the series of explosions that ripped through the Missile Launch Facility. The ground shook, sinking and buckling as areas below imploded or exploded.

After clearing the gate into the woods, Clark allowed himself a small burst of speed. The blast he most feared was yet to come. When he hit the end of the drive, he slowed to calculate the danger in relation to the people on the road. Lex, his dad, and his friends kept running without hesitation or looking back.

Clark assured himself they were clear just as thousands of gallons of generator fuel ignited in the buried tank outside the Equipment Building sixty feet down.

Caught when an outgassing fissure opened under him,

Clark was blasted upward and hurled toward the woods. In the seconds he was airborne, he was able to take in the details of the entire scene.

The forces unleashed by the exploding fuel tank were funneled into paths of least resistance. The primary hatch cover rocketed skyward on a plume of fire, but the silo lid held, keeping most of the destructive blast underground.

Clark envisioned the massive destruction in the compound. Hatches were blown off as shock waves, fiery heat balls, and black smoke raced into every inch of the installation. Everyone and everything within the Equipment Building, tunnel junction, and Launch Control Center were instantly incinerated.

Not knowing they were safely outside the falling debris zone, Clark's father and friends dived for cover.

Clark arched into the woods on the far side of the access road. Branches broke beneath him as he fell, and he landed in a bed of brush and pine needles. Slightly winded because of the debilitating dust, he lay still for a minute, staring up at the stars in the night sky.

The same thought that crossed his mind every time he looked at the wonders of deep space through his telescope struck him again now. He might have been born on a planet orbiting one of those stars, but Earth was home.

"Clark!" Jonathan's frantic voice rose above the subterranean rumble of collapsing steel, cement, and rock.

Clark stood up and brushed himself off. Since no one else could have survived being blasted from one side of the dirt road to another, he hoped no one had seen his unscheduled flight.

"Clark!" Chloe sounded angry, hiding her fear for his

safety behind a façade of indignant fury. "Where are you?"

Clark moved quickly and silently, doubling back so his position wouldn't raise too many questions he didn't want to answer. He crept out of the woods by the dirt drive, close to where he had been.

"Over here!" Clark didn't realize his shirt was torn and charred until he waved. His face was probably covered with black soot like his hands and arms. Since the grime disguised the fact that he hadn't been cut or bruised, the smudges worked in his favor.

Jonathan ran ahead of the others, embracing him in a bear hug of relief. He looked knowingly into Clark's eyes as he stood back. "Are you all right?"

"Yeah." Clark nodded. "Tired, but that will pass after I get a shower and burn these clothes."

"Again?" Jonathan arched an eyebrow as the others drew closer.

Clark shrugged with an amused smile. He'd have plenty of time to tell his mom and dad everything later. His mother still had a few days of vacation left, and if his father was on schedule, the back pasture fence was finished. They could all use a day or two to veg.

"Don't ever scare me like that again!" Chloe's eyes flashed as she shook a can of fly spray. Catching his curious glance, she scowled. "Don't ask."

"Okay." Clark grinned. "Pete can fill me in."

"You're the one that needs to report, Clark," Pete said.

Clark glanced at Lana, wondering how much she remembered. "There's not a lot to tell."

Lana frowned and shook her head. "I'm afraid I won't

be much help. Except for that funny-looking man at the barn, it's all a blur."

"I'll have to tell my insurance agent something." Lex stepped forward, unruffled and calm.

Rather than let Lex speculate, Clark offered a simple explanation he would not be able to prove, disprove, or dispute.

"You were right, Lex," Clark said. "Dr. Farley was doing some kind of genetic research. His test subject was double-jointed and mentally deficient. Layton killed Howard Stoner, and Lana ran into him at the stable when he escaped. After talking to you, I got suspicious and came here looking for her when she disappeared. I guess Dr. Farley and Sharon were afraid we'd tell someone about their project."

Chloe exchanged a glance with Pete, but she didn't volunteer to fill in the blanks. She knew he'd debrief her in detail back at the *Torch*. She pulled her cell phone from her pocket.

"I'd better call my dad and let him know Lana is safe."

"He must be worried sick!" Lana looked stricken. "I left a note on the door that I was going to the stable, but I probably should have called."

"Don't worry. He'll be so relieved, he'll probably limit the responsibility lecture to five minutes." Chloe smiled as she dialed and turned away.

Lex looked toward the remains of the missile silo enclosure, his brow furrowed. "How did Farley manage to blow up an extensive underground military installation doing genetic research?"

"Dr. Farley's demented patient got loose again," Clark said truthfully. "Lana and I got away while Sharon and her father were looking for Layton. I suppose a lot of things could set off several thousand gallons of fuel stored in a tank."

"No doubt," Lex said. If he suspected there was more to the story, he didn't pursue it. He had what he needed to collect on the insurance policy and recoup the financial loss. "I just hope my car insurance covers flaming debris damage on the Porsche."

"I know my insurance doesn't!" Pete blinked, then gasped and ran to check the interior of the convertible.

Jonathan paled. "The tractor."

"Let's go check it out." Clark was anxious to get home where he could shed the only remaining evidence of Dr. Farley's work, the meteor dust on his skin and in his clothes.

A profound peace and quiet settled over the Kansas countryside as Lex roared off in the Porsche. The gleaming silver paint on the demonstration car was now pitted and scorched, but probably covered by insurance. Pete had offered to take Chloe and Lana home and followed in the blue convertible, which had miraculously survived falling cinders and ash unscathed.

Jonathan gripped Clark's shoulder as they walked toward the cornfield where he had left the tractor. "Looks like LexCorp had nothing to do with Howard's death."

"No," Clark said. "Lex rented the old missile silo site to Dr. Farley, but he didn't know what he was doing. Sharon told everyone that her father was writing a book."

Jonathan nodded as they skirted the field of smoldering brush and debris. "I'll call Lex tomorrow and apologize for almost suing him."

"He'll appreciate that, Dad. Thanks."

"Actually, I should be thanking you, Clark." Jonathan squeezed his shoulder then dropped his hand. "I have no doubt that Lex and Lionel are guilty of many things, but they weren't responsible for this. You stopped me from making a big mistake, one that might have cost us the farm."

Clark just nodded, overcome with affection for his father. "I'm just glad you trusted my judgment enough to listen."

They walked in silence for a few minutes. When Jonathan spoke again, it was a sign that life had already begun to return to normal.

"I'm not sure our insurance covers fire from the sky damage. Could you take a look, son? So I don't waste this walk wondering how I'm going to pay to fix it if it doesn't need to be fixed?"

"Sure." Clark focused his X-ray vision.

The tractor was parked in the field where his Dad had left it, and it appeared to be intact. Clark couldn't detect damaged paint or burn holes, but as long as the old machine ran, his father would be happy.

"We've been needing to get a new tractor for a long time, haven't we?" Clark asked, sounding serious.

"Oh, no." Jonathan stopped short. "It blew up?"

"Joking, Dad. Just joking." Ducking his father's playful punch, Clark laughed. There were far worse fates than being an alien teenager coping with a secret identity crisis.

ABOUT THE AUTHOR

DIANA G. GALLAGHER lives in Florida with her husband, Marty Burke, four dogs, seven cats, and a cranky parrot.

Although Diana had always wanted to be a writer, she spent several years teaching kids to ride horses and then spent a few more as a professional folk musician. When she discovered science fiction and *Star Trek* via *Star Wars*, she not only discovered what she wanted to write, but also an outlet for expression in music and art. While diligently pounding out a few million unsold words, she gained a certain notoriety among SF fans and space development advocates with her songs about humanity's future in space.

During the beginning stages of writing *The Alien Dark* (TSR 1990), her first published novel, Diana also tried her hand at whimsical fantasy art. What began as a means of paying convention expenses and having fun soon developed into a full-time artistic endeavor. Best known for her hand-colored prints depicting the doglike activities of *Woof: The House Dragon*, she won a Hugo for Best Fan Artist 1988.

However, when *The Alien Dark* finally sold, Diana decided she had to concentrate on writing. She has written more than forty novels for all ages in several series, including *Buffy the Vampire Slayer*, *Charmed*, *Sabrina the Teenage Witch*, and *Star Trek*.

READ MORE

SMALLVILLE

NOVELS!

STRANGE VISITORS
(0-446-61213-8)
By Roger Stern

◆

DRAGON
(0-446-61214-6)
By Alan Grant

◆

HAUNTINGS
(0-446-61215-4)
By Nancy Holder

◆

WHODUNNIT
(0-446-61216-2)
By Dean Wesley Smith

AVAILABLE AT BOOKSTORES EVERYWHERE FROM WARNER ASPECT

1212-D

VISIT WARNER ASPECT ON-LINE!

THE WARNER ASPECT HOMEPAGE
You'll find us at: www.twbookmark.com, then by clicking on Science Fiction and Fantasy.

NEW AND UPCOMING TITLES
Each month we feature our new titles and reader favorites.

AUTHOR INFO
Author bios, bibliographies, and links to personal Web sites.

CONTESTS AND OTHER FUN STUFF
Advance galley giveaways, autographed copies, and more.

THE ASPECT BUZZ
What's new, hot and upcoming from Warner Aspect: awards news, bestsellers, movie tie-in information . . .